Whirligigs

Whirligigs

O. Henry

MINT EDITIONS

Whirligigs was first published in 1923.

This edition published by Mint Editions 2020.

ISBN 9781513269917 | E-ISBN 9781513274911

Published by Mint Editions®

MINT
EDITIONS

minteditionbooks.com

Publishing Director: Jennifer Newens
Design & Production: Rachel Lopez Metzger
Project Manager: Micaela Clark
Typesetting: Westchester Publishing Services

Contents

I

The World and the Door

A favourite dodge to get your story read by the public is to assert that it is true, and then add that Truth is stranger than Fiction. I do not know if the yarn I am anxious for you to read is true; but the Spanish purser of the fruit steamer *El Carrero* swore to me by the shrine of Santa Guadalupe that he had the facts from the U. S. vice-consul at La Paz—a person who could not possibly have been cognizant of half of them.

As for the adage quoted above, I take pleasure in puncturing it by affirming that I read in a purely fictional story the other day the line: "'Be it so,' said the policeman." Nothing so strange has yet cropped out in Truth.

When H. Ferguson Hedges, millionaire promoter, investor and man-about-New-York, turned his thoughts upon matters convivial, and word of it went "down the line," bouncers took a precautionary turn at the Indian clubs, waiters put ironstone china on his favourite tables, cab drivers crowded close to the curbstone in front of all-night cafés, and careful cashiers in his regular haunts charged up a few bottles to his account by way of preface and introduction.

As a money power a one-millionaire is of small account in a city where the man who cuts your slice of beef behind the free-lunch counter rides to work in his own automobile. But Hedges spent his money as lavishly, loudly and showily as though he were only a clerk squandering a week's wages. And, after all, the bartender takes no interest in your reserve fund. He would rather look you up on his cash register than in Bradstreet.

On the evening that the material allegation of facts begins, Hedges was bidding dull care begone in the company of five or six good fellows—acquaintances and friends who had gathered in his wake.

Among them were two younger men—Ralph Merriam, a broker, and Wade, his friend.

Two deep-sea cabmen were chartered. At Columbus Circle they hove to long enough to revile the statue of the great navigator, unpatriotically rebuking him for having voyaged in search of land instead of liquids. Midnight overtook the party marooned in the rear of a cheap café far uptown.

Hedges was arrogant, overriding and quarrelsome. He was burly and tough, iron-gray but vigorous, "good" for the rest of the night. There was a dispute—about nothing that matters—and the five-fingered words were passed—the words that represent the glove cast into the lists. Merriam played the rôle of the verbal Hotspur.

Hedges rose quickly, seized his chair, swung it once and smashed wildly down at Merriam's head. Merriam dodged, drew a small revolver and shot Hedges in the chest. The leading roysterer stumbled, fell in a wry heap, and lay still.

Wade, a commuter, had formed that habit of promptness. He juggled Merriam out a side door, walked him to the corner, ran him a block and caught a hansom. They rode five minutes and then got out on a dark corner and dismissed the cab. Across the street the lights of a small saloon betrayed its hectic hospitality.

"Go in the back room of that saloon," said Wade, "and wait. I'll go find out what's doing and let you know. You may take two drinks while I am gone—no more."

At ten minutes to one o'clock Wade returned. "Brace up, old chap," he said. "The ambulance got there just as I did. The doctor says he's dead. You may have one more drink. You let me run this thing for you. You've got to skip. I don't believe a chair is legally a deadly weapon. You've got to make tracks, that's all there is to it."

Merriam complained of the cold querulously, and asked for another drink. "Did you notice what big veins he had on the back of his hands?" he said. "I never could stand—I never could—"

"Take one more," said Wade, "and then come on. I'll see you through."

Wade kept his promise so well that at eleven o'clock the next morning Merriam, with a new suit case full of new clothes and hair-brushes, stepped quietly on board a little 500-ton fruit steamer at an East River pier. The vessel had brought the season's first cargo of limes from Port Limon, and was homeward bound. Merriam had his bank balance of $2,800 in his pocket in large bills, and brief instructions to pile up as much water as he could between himself and New York. There was no time for anything more.

From Port Limon Merriam worked down the coast by schooner and sloop to Colon, thence across the isthmus to Panama, where he caught a tramp bound for Callao and such intermediate ports as might tempt the discursive skipper from his course.

It was at La Paz that Merriam decided to land—La Paz the Beautiful, a little harbourless town smothered in a living green ribbon that banded the foot of a cloud-piercing mountain. Here the little steamer stopped to tread water while the captain's dory took him ashore that he might feel the pulse of the cocoanut market. Merriam went too, with his suit case, and remained.

Kalb, the vice-consul, a Græco-Armenian citizen of the United States, born in Hessen-Darmstadt, and educated in Cincinnati ward primaries, considered all Americans his brothers and bankers. He attached himself to Merriam's elbow, introduced him to every one in La Paz who wore shoes, borrowed ten dollars and went back to his hammock.

There was a little wooden hotel in the edge of a banana grove, facing the sea, that catered to the tastes of the few foreigners that had dropped out of the world into the *triste* Peruvian town. At Kalb's introductory: "Shake hands with—," he had obediently exchanged manual salutations with a German doctor, one French and two Italian merchants, and three or four Americans who were spoken of as gold men, rubber men, mahogany men—anything but men of living tissue.

After dinner Merriam sat in a corner of the broad front *galeria* with Bibb, a Vermonter interested in hydraulic mining, and smoked and drank Scotch "smoke." The moonlit sea, spreading infinitely before him, seemed to separate him beyond all apprehension from his old life. The horrid tragedy in which he had played such a disastrous part now began, for the first time since he stole on board the fruiter, a wretched fugitive, to lose its sharper outlines. Distance lent assuagement to his view. Bibb had opened the flood-gates of a stream of long-dammed discourse, overjoyed to have captured an audience that had not suffered under a hundred repetitions of his views and theories.

"One year more," said Bibb, "and I'll go back to God's country. Oh, I know it's pretty here, and you get *dolce far niente* handed to you in chunks, but this country wasn't made for a white man to live in. You've got to have to plug through snow now and then, and see a game of baseball and wear a stiff collar and have a policeman cuss you. Still, La Paz is a good sort of a pipe-dreamy old hole. And Mrs. Conant is here. When any of us feels particularly like jumping into the sea we rush around to her house and propose. It's nicer to be rejected by

Mrs. Conant than it is to be drowned. And they say drowning is a delightful sensation."

"Many like her here?" asked Merriam.

"Not anywhere," said Bibb, with a comfortable sigh. "She's the only white woman in La Paz. The rest range from a dappled dun to the colour of a b-flat piano key. She's been here a year. Comes from—well, you know how a woman can talk—ask 'em to say 'string' and they'll say 'crow's foot' or 'cat's cradle.' Sometimes you'd think she was from Oshkosh, and again from Jacksonville, Florida, and the next day from Cape Cod."

"Mystery?" ventured Merriam.

"M—well, she looks it; but her talk's translucent enough. But that's a woman. I suppose if the Sphinx were to begin talking she'd merely say: 'Goodness me! more visitors coming for dinner, and nothing to eat but the sand which is here.' But you won't think about that when you meet her, Merriam. You'll propose to her too."

To make a hard story soft, Merriam did meet her and propose to her. He found her to be a woman in black with hair the colour of a bronze turkey's wings, and mysterious, *remembering* eyes that—well, that looked as if she might have been a trained nurse looking on when Eve was created. Her words and manner, though, were translucent, as Bibb had said. She spoke, vaguely, of friends in California and some of the lower parishes in Louisiana. The tropical climate and indolent life suited her; she had thought of buying an orange grove later on; La Paz, all in all, charmed her.

Merriam's courtship of the Sphinx lasted three months, although he did not know that he was courting her. He was using her as an antidote for remorse, until he found, too late, that he had acquired the habit. During that time he had received no news from home. Wade did not know where he was; and he was not sure of Wade's exact address, and was afraid to write. He thought he had better let matters rest as they were for a while.

One afternoon he and Mrs. Conant hired two ponies and rode out along the mountain trail as far as the little cold river that came tumbling down the foothills. There they stopped for a drink, and Merriam spoke his piece—he proposed, as Bibb had prophesied.

Mrs. Conant gave him one glance of brilliant tenderness, and then her face took on such a strange, haggard look that Merriam was shaken out of his intoxication and back to his senses.

"I beg your pardon, Florence," he said, releasing her hand; "but I'll have to hedge on part of what I said. I can't ask you to marry me, of course. I killed a man in New York—a man who was my friend—shot him down—in quite a cowardly manner, I understand. Of course, the drinking didn't excuse it. Well, I couldn't resist having my say; and I'll always mean it. I'm here as a fugitive from justice, and—I suppose that ends our acquaintance."

Mrs. Conant plucked little leaves assiduously from the low-hanging branch of a lime tree.

"I suppose so," she said, in low and oddly uneven tones; "but that depends upon you. I'll be as honest as you were. I poisoned my husband. I am a self-made widow. A man cannot love a murderess. So I suppose that ends our acquaintance."

She looked up at him slowly. His face turned a little pale, and he stared at her blankly, like a deaf-and-dumb man who was wondering what it was all about.

She took a swift step toward him, with stiffened arms and eyes blazing.

"Don't look at me like that!" she cried, as though she were in acute pain. "Curse me, or turn your back on me, but don't look that way. Am I a woman to be beaten? If I could show you—here on my arms, and on my back are scars—and it has been more than a year—scars that he made in his brutal rages. A holy nun would have risen and struck the fiend down. Yes, I killed him. The foul and horrible words that he hurled at me that last day are repeated in my ears every night when I sleep. And then came his blows, and the end of my endurance. I got the poison that afternoon. It was his custom to drink every night in the library before going to bed a hot punch made of rum and wine. Only from my fair hands would he receive it—because he knew the fumes of spirits always sickened me. That night when the maid brought it to me I sent her downstairs on an errand. Before taking him his drink I went to my little private cabinet and poured into it more than a tea-spoonful of tincture of aconite—enough to kill three men, so I had learned. I had drawn $6,000 that I had in bank, and with that and a few things in a satchel I left the house without any one seeing me. As I passed the library I heard him stagger up and fall heavily on a couch. I took a night train for New Orleans, and from there I sailed to the Bermudas. I finally cast anchor in La Paz. And now what have you to say? Can you open your mouth?"

Merriam came back to life.

"Florence," he said earnestly, "I want you. I don't care what you've done. If the world—"

"Ralph," she interrupted, almost with a scream, "be my world!"

Her eyes melted; she relaxed magnificently and swayed toward Merriam so suddenly that he had to jump to catch her.

Dear me! in such scenes how the talk runs into artificial prose. But it can't be helped. It's the subconscious smell of the footlights' smoke that's in all of us. Stir the depths of your cook's soul sufficiently and she will discourse in Bulwer-Lyttonese.

Merriam and Mrs. Conant were very happy. He announced their engagement at the Hotel Orilla del Mar. Eight foreigners and four native Astors pounded his back and shouted insincere congratulations at him. Pedrito, the Castilian-mannered barkeep, was goaded to extra duty until his agility would have turned a Boston cherry-phosphate clerk a pale lilac with envy.

They were both very happy. According to the strange mathematics of the god of mutual affinity, the shadows that clouded their pasts when united became only half as dense instead of darker. They shut the world out and bolted the doors. Each was the other's world. Mrs. Conant lived again. The remembering look left her eyes. Merriam was with her every moment that was possible. On a little plateau under a grove of palms and calabash trees they were going to build a fairy bungalow. They were to be married in two months. Many hours of the day they had their heads together over the house plans. Their joint capital would set up a business in fruit or woods that would yield a comfortable support. "Good night, my world," would say Mrs. Conant every evening when Merriam left her for his hotel. They were very happy. Their love had, circumstantially, that element of melancholy in it that it seems to require to attain its supremest elevation. And it seemed that their mutual great misfortune or sin was a bond that nothing could sever.

One day a steamer hove in the offing. Bare-legged and bare-shouldered La Paz scampered down to the beach, for the arrival of a steamer was their loop-the-loop, circus, Emancipation Day and four-o'clock tea.

When the steamer was near enough, wise ones proclaimed that she was the *Pajaro*, bound up-coast from Callao to Panama.

The *Pajaro* put on brakes a mile off shore. Soon a boat came bobbing shoreward. Merriam strolled down on the beach to look on. In the shallow water the Carib sailors sprang out and dragged the boat with a mighty rush to the firm shingle. Out climbed the purser, the captain and two passengers, ploughing their way through the deep sand toward the hotel. Merriam glanced toward them with the mild interest due to strangers. There was something familiar to him in the walk of one of the passengers. He looked again, and his blood seemed to turn to strawberry ice cream in his veins. Burly, arrogant, debonair as ever, H. Ferguson Hedges, the man he had killed, was coming toward him ten feet away.

When Hedges saw Merriam his face flushed a dark red. Then he shouted in his old, bluff way: "Hello, Merriam. Glad to see you. Didn't expect to find you out here. Quinby, this is my old friend Merriam, of New York—Merriam, Mr. Quinby."

Merriam gave Hedges and then Quinby an ice-cold hand. "Br-r-r!" said Hedges. "But you've got a frappéd flipper! Man, you're not well. You're as yellow as a Chinaman. Malarial here? Steer us to a bar if there is such a thing, and let's take a prophylactic."

Merriam, still half comatose, led them toward the Hotel Orilla del Mar.

"Quinby and I," explained Hedges, puffing through the slippery sand, "are looking out along the coast for some investments. We've just come up from Concepción and Valparaiso and Lima. The captain of this subsidized ferry boat told us there was some good picking around here in silver mines. So we got off. Now, where is that café, Merriam? Oh, in this portable soda water pavilion?"

Leaving Quinby at the bar, Hedges drew Merriam aside.

"Now, what does this mean?" he said, with gruff kindness. "Are you sulking about that fool row we had?"

"I thought," stammered Merriam—"I heard—they told me you were—that I had—"

"Well, you didn't, and I'm not," said Hedges. "That fool young ambulance surgeon told Wade I was a candidate for a coffin just because I'd got tired and quit breathing. I laid up in a private hospital for a month; but here I am, kicking as hard as ever. Wade and I tried to find you, but couldn't. Now, Merriam, shake hands and forget it all. I was as much to blame as you were; and the shot really did me good—I came out of the hospital as healthy and fit as a cab horse. Come on; that drink's waiting."

"Old man," said Merriam, brokenly, "I don't know how to thank you—I—well, you know—"

"Oh, forget it," boomed Hedges. "Quinby'll die of thirst if we don't join him."

Bibb was sitting on the shady side of the gallery waiting for the eleven-o'clock breakfast. Presently Merriam came out and joined him. His eye was strangely bright.

"Bibb, my boy," said he, slowly waving his hand, "do you see those mountains and that sea and sky and sunshine?—they're mine, Bibbsy—all mine."

"You go in," said Bibb, "and take eight grains of quinine, right away. It won't do in this climate for a man to get to thinking he's Rockefeller, or James O'Neill either."

Inside, the purser was untying a great roll of newspapers, many of them weeks old, gathered in the lower ports by the *Pajaro* to be distributed at casual stopping-places. Thus do the beneficent voyagers scatter news and entertainment among the prisoners of sea and mountains.

Tio Pancho, the hotel proprietor, set his great silver-rimmed *anteojos* upon his nose and divided the papers into a number of smaller rolls. A barefooted *muchacho* dashed in, desiring the post of messenger.

"*Bien venido*," said Tio Pancho. "This to Señora Conant; that to el Doctor S-S-Schlegel—*Dios*! what a name to say!—that to Señor Davis—one for Don Alberto. These two for the *Casa de Huespedes, Numero 6, en la calle de las Buenas Gracias*. And say to them all, *muchacho*, that the *Pajaro* sails for Panama at three this afternoon. If any have letters to send by the post, let them come quickly, that they may first pass through the *correo*."

Mrs. Conant received her roll of newspapers at four o'clock. The boy was late in delivering them, because he had been deflected from his duty by an iguana that crossed his path and to which he immediately gave chase. But it made no hardship, for she had no letters to send.

She was idling in a hammock in the patio of the house that she occupied, half awake, half happily dreaming of the paradise that she and Merriam had created out of the wrecks of their pasts. She was content now for the horizon of that shimmering sea to be the horizon of her life. They had shut out the world and closed the door.

Merriam was coming to her house at seven, after his dinner at the hotel. She would put on a white dress and an apricot-coloured lace mantilla, and they would walk an hour under the cocoanut palms by the lagoon. She smiled contentedly, and chose a paper at random from the roll the boy had brought.

At first the words of a certain headline of a Sunday newspaper meant nothing to her; they conveyed only a visualized sense of familiarity. The largest type ran thus: "Lloyd B. Conant secures divorce." And then the subheadings: "Well-known Saint Louis paint manufacturer wins suit, pleading one year's absence of wife." "Her mysterious disappearance recalled." "Nothing has been heard of her since."

Twisting herself quickly out of the hammock, Mrs. Conant's eye soon traversed the half-column of the "Recall." It ended thus: "It will be remembered that Mrs. Conant disappeared one evening in March of last year. It was freely rumoured that her marriage with Lloyd B. Conant resulted in much unhappiness. Stories were not wanting to the effect that his cruelty toward his wife had more than once taken the form of physical abuse. After her departure a full bottle of tincture of aconite, a deadly poison, was found in a small medicine cabinet in her bedroom. This might have been an indication that she meditated suicide. It is supposed that she abandoned such an intention if she possessed it, and left her home instead."

Mrs. Conant slowly dropped the paper, and sat on a chair, clasping her hands tightly.

"Let me think—O God!—let me think," she whispered. "I took the bottle with me. . . I threw it out of the window of the train. . . I—. . . there was another bottle in the cabinet. . . there were two, side by side— the aconite—and the valerian that I took when I could not sleep. . . If they found the aconite bottle full, why—but, he is alive, of course—I gave him only a harmless dose of valerian. . . I am not a murderess in fact. . . Ralph, I—O God, don't let this be a dream!"

She went into the part of the house that she rented from the old Peruvian man and his wife, shut the door, and walked up and down her room swiftly and feverishly for half an hour. Merriam's photograph stood in a frame on a table. She picked it up, looked at it with a smile of exquisite tenderness, and—dropped four tears on it. And Merriam only twenty rods away! Then she stood still for ten minutes, looking into space. She looked into space through a slowly opening door. On her side of the door was the building material for a castle of Romance— love, an Arcady of waving palms, a lullaby of waves on the shore of a haven of rest, respite, peace, a lotus land of dreamy ease and security—a life of poetry and heart's ease and refuge. Romanticist, will you tell me what Mrs. Conant saw on the other side of the door? You cannot?— that is, you will not? Very well; then listen.

She saw herself go into a department store and buy five spools of silk thread and three yards of gingham to make an apron for the cook. "Shall I charge it, ma'am?" asked the clerk. As she walked out a lady whom she met greeted her cordially. "Oh, where did you get the pattern for those sleeves, dear Mrs. Conant?" she said. At the corner a policeman helped her across the street and touched his helmet. "Any callers?" she asked the maid when she reached home. "Mrs. Waldron," answered the maid, "and the two Misses Jenkinson." "Very well," she said. "You may bring me a cup of tea, Maggie."

Mrs. Conant went to the door and called Angela, the old Peruvian woman. "If Mateo is there send him to me." Mateo, a half-breed, shuffling and old but efficient, came.

"Is there a steamer or a vessel of any kind leaving this coast to-night or to-morrow that I can get passage on?" she asked.

Mateo considered.

"At Punta Reina, thirty miles down the coast, señora," he answered, "there is a small steamer loading with cinchona and dyewoods. She sails for San Francisco to-morrow at sunrise. So says my brother, who arrived in his sloop to-day, passing by Punta Reina."

"You must take me in that sloop to that steamer to-night. Will you do that?"

"Perhaps—" Mateo shrugged a suggestive shoulder. Mrs. Conant took a handful of money from a drawer and gave it to him.

"Get the sloop ready behind the little point of land below the town," she ordered. "Get sailors, and be ready to sail at six o'clock. In half an hour bring a cart partly filled with straw into the patio here, and take my trunk to the sloop. There is more money yet. Now, hurry."

For one time Mateo walked away without shuffling his feet.

"Angela," cried Mrs. Conant, almost fiercely, "come and help me pack. I am going away. Out with this trunk. My clothes first. Stir yourself. Those dark dresses first. Hurry."

From the first she did not waver from her decision. Her view was clear and final. Her door had opened and let the world in. Her love for Merriam was not lessened; but it now appeared a hopeless and unrealizable thing. The visions of their future that had seemed so blissful and complete had vanished. She tried to assure herself that her renunciation was rather for his sake than for her own. Now that she was cleared of her burden—at least, technically—would not his own weigh too heavily upon him? If she should cling to him, would not the difference forever silently mar and corrode their happiness? Thus she reasoned; but there were a thousand little voices calling to her that she could feel rather than hear, like the hum of distant, powerful machinery—the little voices of the world, that, when raised in unison, can send their insistent call through the thickest door.

Once while packing, a brief shadow of the lotus dream came back to her. She held Merriam's picture to her heart with one hand, while she threw a pair of shoes into the trunk with her other.

At six o'clock Mateo returned and reported the sloop ready. He and his brother lifted the trunk into the cart, covered it with straw and conveyed it to the point of embarkation. From there they transferred it on board in the sloop's dory. Then Mateo returned for additional orders.

Mrs. Conant was ready. She had settled all business matters with Angela, and was impatiently waiting. She wore a long, loose black-silk duster that she often walked about in when the evenings were chilly. On her head was a small round hat, and over it the apricot-coloured lace mantilla.

Dusk had quickly followed the short twilight. Mateo led her by dark and grass-grown streets toward the point behind which the sloop was anchored. On turning a corner they beheld the Hotel Orilla del Mar three streets away, nebulously aglow with its array of kerosene lamps.

Mrs. Conant paused, with streaming eyes. "I must, I *must* see him once before I go," she murmured in anguish. But even then she did not falter in her decision. Quickly she invented a plan by which she might speak to him, and yet make her departure without his knowing. She would walk past the hotel, ask some one to call him out and talk a few moments on some trivial excuse, leaving him expecting to see her at her home at seven.

She unpinned her hat and gave it to Mateo. "Keep this, and wait here till I come," she ordered. Then she draped the mantilla over her head as she usually did when walking after sunset, and went straight to the Orilla del Mar.

She was glad to see the bulky, white-clad figure of Tio Pancho standing alone on the gallery.

"Tio Pancho," she said, with a charming smile, "may I trouble you to ask Mr. Merriam to come out for just a few moments that I may speak with him?"

Tio Pancho bowed as an elephant bows.

"Buenas tardes, Señora Conant," he said, as a cavalier talks. And then he went on, less at his ease:

"But does not the señora know that Señor Merriam sailed on the *Pajaro* for Panama at three o'clock of this afternoon?"

II

The Theory and the Hound

Not many days ago my old friend from the tropics, J. P. Bridger, United States consul on the island of Ratona, was in the city. We had wassail and jubilee and saw the Flatiron building, and missed seeing the Bronxless menagerie by about a couple of nights. And then, at the ebb tide, we were walking up a street that parallels and parodies Broadway.

A woman with a comely and mundane countenance passed us, holding in leash a wheezing, vicious, waddling, brute of a yellow pug. The dog entangled himself with Bridger's legs and mumbled his ankles in a snarling, peevish, sulky bite. Bridger, with a happy smile, kicked the breath out of the brute; the woman showered us with a quick rain of well-conceived adjectives that left us in no doubt as to our place in her opinion, and we passed on. Ten yards farther an old woman with disordered white hair and her bankbook tucked well hidden beneath her tattered shawl begged. Bridger stopped and disinterred for her a quarter from his holiday waistcoat.

On the next corner a quarter of a ton of well-clothed man with a rice-powdered, fat, white jowl, stood holding the chain of a devil-born bulldog whose forelegs were strangers by the length of a dachshund. A little woman in a last-season's hat confronted him and wept, which was plainly all she could do, while he cursed her in low sweet, practised tones.

Bridger smiled again—strictly to himself—and this time he took out a little memorandum book and made a note of it. This he had no right to do without due explanation, and I said so.

"It's a new theory," said Bridger, "that I picked up down in Ratona. I've been gathering support for it as I knock about. The world isn't ripe for it yet, but—well I'll tell you; and then you run your mind back along the people you've known and see what you make of it."

And so I cornered Bridger in a place where they have artificial palms and wine; and he told me the story which is here in my words and on his responsibility.

One afternoon at three o'clock, on the island of Ratona, a boy raced along the beach screaming, "*Pajaro*, ahoy!"

Thus he made known the keenness of his hearing and the justice of his discrimination in pitch.

He who first heard and made oral proclamation concerning the toot of an approaching steamer's whistle, and correctly named the steamer, was a small hero in Ratona—until the next steamer came. Wherefore, there was rivalry among the barefoot youth of Ratona, and many fell victims to the softly blown conch shells of sloops which, as they enter harbour, sound surprisingly like a distant steamer's signal. And some could name you the vessel when its call, in your duller ears, sounded no louder than the sigh of the wind through the branches of the cocoanut palms.

But to-day he who proclaimed the *Pajaro* gained his honours. Ratona bent its ear to listen; and soon the deep-tongued blast grew louder and nearer, and at length Ratona saw above the line of palms on the low "point" the two black funnels of the fruiter slowly creeping toward the mouth of the harbour.

You must know that Ratona is an island twenty miles off the south of a South American republic. It is a port of that republic; and it sleeps sweetly in a smiling sea, toiling not nor spinning; fed by the abundant tropics where all things "ripen, cease and fall toward the grave."

Eight hundred people dream life away in a green-embowered village that follows the horseshoe curve of its bijou harbour. They are mostly Spanish and Indian *mestizos*, with a shading of San Domingo Negroes, a lightening of pure-blood Spanish officials and a slight leavening of the froth of three or four pioneering white races. No steamers touch at Ratona save the fruit steamers which take on their banana inspectors there on their way to the coast. They leave Sunday newspapers, ice, quinine, bacon, watermelons and vaccine matter at the island and that is about all the touch Ratona gets with the world.

The *Pajaro* paused at the mouth of the harbour, rolling heavily in the swell that sent the whitecaps racing beyond the smooth water inside. Already two dories from the village—one conveying fruit inspectors, the other going for what it could get—were halfway out to the steamer.

The inspectors' dory was taken on board with them, and the *Pajaro* steamed away for the mainland for its load of fruit.

The other boat returned to Ratona bearing a contribution from the *Pajaro's* store of ice, the usual roll of newspapers and one passenger— Taylor Plunkett, sheriff of Chatham County, Kentucky.

Bridger, the United States consul at Ratona, was cleaning his rifle in the official shanty under a bread-fruit tree twenty yards from the water of the harbour. The consul occupied a place somewhat near the tail of his political party's procession. The music of the band wagon sounded very faintly to him in the distance. The plums of office went to others. Bridger's share of the spoils—the consulship at Ratona—was little more than a prune—a dried prune from the boarding-house department of the public crib. But $900 yearly was opulence in Ratona. Besides, Bridger had contracted a passion for shooting alligators in the lagoons near his consulate, and was not unhappy.

He looked up from a careful inspection of his rifle lock and saw a broad man filling his doorway. A broad, noiseless, slow-moving man, sunburned almost to the brown of Vandyke. A man of forty-five, neatly clothed in homespun, with scanty light hair, a close-clipped brown-and-gray beard and pale-blue eyes expressing mildness and simplicity.

"You are Mr. Bridger, the consul," said the broad man. "They directed me here. Can you tell me what those big bunches of things like gourds are in those trees that look like feather dusters along the edge of the water?"

"Take that chair," said the consul, reoiling his cleaning rag. "No, the other one—that bamboo thing won't hold you. Why, they're cocoanuts—green cocoanuts. The shell of 'em is always a light green before they're ripe."

"Much obliged," said the other man, sitting down carefully. "I didn't quite like to tell the folks at home they were olives unless I was sure about it. My name is Plunkett. I'm sheriff of Chatham County, Kentucky. I've got extradition papers in my pocket authorizing the arrest of a man on this island. They've been signed by the President of this country, and they're in correct shape. The man's name is Wade Williams. He's in the cocoanut raising business. What he's wanted for is the murder of his wife two years ago. Where can I find him?"

The consul squinted an eye and looked through his rifle barrel.

"There's nobody on the island who calls himself 'Williams,'" he remarked.

"Didn't suppose there was," said Plunkett mildly. "He'll do by any other name."

"Besides myself," said Bridger, "there are only two Americans on Ratona—Bob Reeves and Henry Morgan."

"The man I want sells cocoanuts," suggested Plunkett.

"You see that cocoanut walk extending up to the point?" said the consul, waving his hand toward the open door. "That belongs to Bob Reeves. Henry Morgan owns half the trees to loo'ard on the island."

"One, month ago," said the sheriff, "Wade Williams wrote a confidential letter to a man in Chatham county, telling him where he was and how he was getting along. The letter was lost; and the person that found it gave it away. They sent me after him, and I've got the papers. I reckon he's one of your cocoanut men for certain."

"You've got his picture, of course," said Bridger. "It might be Reeves or Morgan, but I'd hate to think it. They're both as fine fellows as you'd meet in an all-day auto ride."

"No," doubtfully answered Plunkett; "there wasn't any picture of Williams to be had. And I never saw him myself. I've been sheriff only a year. But I've got a pretty accurate description of him. About 5 feet 11; dark-hair and eyes; nose inclined to be Roman; heavy about the shoulders; strong, white teeth, with none missing; laughs a good deal, talkative; drinks considerably but never to intoxication; looks you square in the eye when talking; age thirty-five. Which one of your men does that description fit?"

The consul grinned broadly.

"I'll tell you what you do," he said, laying down his rifle and slipping on his dingy black alpaca coat. "You come along, Mr. Plunkett, and I'll take you up to see the boys. If you can tell which one of 'em your description fits better than it does the other you have the advantage of me."

Bridger conducted the sheriff out and along the hard beach close to which the tiny houses of the village were distributed. Immediately back of the town rose sudden, small, thickly wooded hills. Up one of these, by means of steps cut in the hard clay, the consul led Plunkett. On the very verge of an eminence was perched a two-room wooden cottage with a thatched roof. A Carib woman was washing clothes outside. The consul ushered the sheriff to the door of the room that overlooked the harbour.

Two men were in the room, about to sit down, in their shirt sleeves, to a table spread for dinner. They bore little resemblance one to the other in detail; but the general description given by Plunkett could have been justly applied to either. In height, colour of hair, shape of nose, build and manners each of them tallied with it. They were fair types of jovial, ready-witted, broad-gauged Americans who had gravitated together for companionship in an alien land.

"Hello, Bridger" they called in unison at sight Of the consul. "Come and have dinner with us!" And then they noticed Plunkett at his heels, and came forward with hospitable curiosity.

"Gentlemen," said the consul, his voice taking on unaccustomed formality, "this is Mr. Plunkett. Mr. Plunkett—Mr. Reeves and Mr. Morgan."

The cocoanut barons greeted the newcomer joyously. Reeves seemed about an inch taller than Morgan, but his laugh was not quite as loud. Morgan's eyes were deep brown; Reeves's were black. Reeves was the host and busied himself with fetching other chairs and calling to the Carib woman for supplemental table ware. It was explained that Morgan lived in a bamboo shack to "loo'ard," but that every day the two friends dined together. Plunkett stood still during the preparations, looking about mildly with his pale-blue eyes. Bridger looked apologetic and uneasy.

At length two other covers were laid and the company was assigned to places. Reeves and Morgan stood side by side across the table from the visitors. Reeves nodded genially as a signal for all to seat themselves. And then suddenly Plunkett raised his hand with a gesture of authority. He was looking straight between Reeves and Morgan.

"Wade Williams," he said quietly, "you are under arrest for murder."

Reeves and Morgan instantly exchanged a quick, bright glance, the quality of which was interrogation, with a seasoning of surprise. Then, simultaneously they turned to the speaker with a puzzled and frank deprecation in their gaze.

"Can't say that we understand you, Mr. Plunkett," said Morgan, cheerfully. "Did you say 'Williams'?"

"What's the joke, Bridgy?" asked Reeves, turning, to the consul with a smile.

Before Bridger could answer Plunkett spoke again.

"I'll explain," he said, quietly. "One of you don't need any explanation, but this is for the other one. One of you is Wade Williams of Chatham County, Kentucky. You murdered your wife on May 5, two years ago, after ill-treating and abusing her continually for five years. I have the proper papers in my pocket for taking you back with me, and you are going. We will return on the fruit steamer that comes back by this island to-morrow to leave its inspectors. I acknowledge, gentlemen, that I'm not quite sure which one of you is Williams. But Wade Williams goes back to Chatham County to-morrow. I want you to understand that."

A great sound of merry laughter from Morgan and Reeves went out over the still harbour. Two or three fishermen in the fleet of sloops anchored there looked up at the house of the diablos Americanos on the hill and wondered.

"My dear Mr. Plunkett," cried Morgan, conquering his mirth, "the dinner is getting cold. Let us sit down and eat. I am anxious to get my spoon into that shark-fin soup. Business afterward."

"Sit down, gentlemen, if you please," added Reeves, pleasantly. "I am sure Mr. Plunkett will not object. Perhaps a little time may be of advantage to him in identifying—the gentleman he wishes to arrest."

"No objections, I'm sure," said Plunkett, dropping into his chair heavily. "I'm hungry myself. I didn't want to accept the hospitality of you folks without giving you notice; that's all."

Reeves set bottles and glasses on the table.

"There's cognac," he said, "and anisada, and Scotch 'smoke,' and rye. Take your choice."

Bridger chose rye, Reeves poured three fingers of Scotch for himself, Morgan took the same. The sheriff, against much protestation, filled his glass from the water bottle.

"Here's to the appetite," said Reeves, raising his glass, "of Mr. Williams!" Morgan's laugh and his drink encountering sent him into a choking splutter. All began to pay attention to the dinner, which was well cooked and palatable.

"Williams!" called Plunkett, suddenly and sharply.

All looked up wonderingly. Reeves found the sheriff's mild eye resting upon him. He flushed a little.

"See here," he said, with some asperity, "my name's Reeves, and I don't want you to—" But the comedy of the thing came to his rescue, and he ended with a laugh.

"I suppose, Mr. Plunkett," said Morgan, carefully seasoning an alligator pear, "that you are aware of the fact that you will import a good deal of trouble for yourself into Kentucky if you take back the wrong man—that is, of course, if you take anybody back?"

"Thank you for the salt," said the sheriff. "Oh, I'll take somebody back. It'll be one of you two gentlemen. Yes, I know I'd get stuck for damages if I make a mistake. But I'm going to try to get the right man."

"I'll tell you what you do," said Morgan, leaning forward with a jolly twinkle in his eyes. "You take me. I'll go without any trouble. The cocoanut business hasn't panned out well this year, and I'd like to make some extra money out of your bondsmen."

"That's not fair," chimed in Reeves. "I got only $16 a thousand for my last shipment. Take me, Mr. Plunkett."

"I'll take Wade Williams," said the sheriff, patiently, "or I'll come pretty close to it."

"It's like dining with a ghost," remarked Morgan, with a pretended shiver. "The ghost of a murderer, too! Will somebody pass the toothpicks to the shade of the naughty Mr. Williams?"

Plunkett seemed as unconcerned as if he were dining at his own table in Chatham County. He was a gallant trencherman, and the strange tropic viands tickled his palate. Heavy, commonplace, almost slothful in his movements, he appeared to be devoid of all the cunning and watchfulness of the sleuth. He even ceased to observe, with any sharpness or attempted discrimination, the two men, one of whom he had undertaken with surprising self-confidence, to drag away upon the serious charge of wife-murder. Here, indeed, was a problem set before him that if wrongly solved would have amounted to his serious discomfiture, yet there he sat puzzling his soul (to all appearances) over the novel flavour of a broiled iguana cutlet.

The consul felt a decided discomfort. Reeves and Morgan were his friends and pals; yet the sheriff from Kentucky had a certain right to his official aid and moral support. So Bridger sat the silentest around the board and tried to estimate the peculiar situation. His conclusion was that both Reeves and Morgan, quickwitted, as he knew them to be, had conceived at the moment of Plunkett's disclosure of his mission—and in the brief space of a lightning flash—the idea that the other might be the guilty Williams; and that each of them had decided in that moment loyally to protect his comrade against the doom that threatened him. This was the consul's theory and if he had been a bookmaker at a race of wits for life and liberty he would have offered heavy odds against the plodding sheriff from Chatham County, Kentucky.

When the meal was concluded the Carib woman came and removed the dishes and cloth. Reeves strewed the table with excellent cigars, and Plunkett, with the others, lighted one of these with evident gratification.

"I may be dull," said Morgan, with a grin and a wink at Bridger; "but I want to know if I am. Now, I say this is all a joke of Mr. Plunkett's, concocted to frighten two babes-in-the-woods. Is this Williamson to be taken seriously or not?"

"'Williams,'" corrected Plunkett gravely. "I never got off any jokes in my life. I know I wouldn't travel 2,000 miles to get off a poor one as this would be if I didn't take Wade Williams back with me. Gentlemen!" continued the sheriff, now letting his mild eyes travel impartially from one of the company to another, "see if you can find any joke in this case. Wade Williams is listening to the words I utter now; but out of politeness, I will speak of him as a third person. For five years he made his wife lead the life of a dog—No; I'll take that back. No dog in Kentucky was ever treated as she was. He spent the money that she brought him—spent it at races, at the card table and on horses and hunting. He was a good fellow to his friends, but a cold, sullen demon at home. He wound up the five years of neglect by striking her with his closed hand—a hand as hard as a stone—when she was ill and weak from suffering. She died the next day; and he skipped. That's all there is to it. It's enough. I never saw Williams; but I knew his wife. I'm not a man to tell half. She and I were keeping company when she met him. She went to Louisville on a visit and saw him there. I'll admit that he spoilt my chances in no time. I lived then on the edge of the Cumberland mountains. I was elected sheriff of Chatham County a year after Wade Williams killed his wife. My official duty sends me out here after him; but I'll admit that there's personal feeling, too. And he's going back with me. Mr.—er—Reeves, will you pass me a match?

"Awfully imprudent of Williams," said Morgan, putting his feet up against the wall, "to strike a Kentucky lady. Seems to me I've heard they were scrappers."

"Bad, bad Williams," said Reeves, pouring out more Scotch.

The two men spoke lightly, but the consul saw and felt the tension and the carefulness in their actions and words. "Good old fellows," he said to himself; "they're both all right. Each of 'em is standing by the other like a little brick church."

And then a dog walked into the room where they sat—a black-and-tan hound, long-eared, lazy, confident of welcome.

Plunkett turned his head and looked at the animal, which halted, confidently, within a few feet of his chair.

Suddenly the sheriff, with a deep-mouthed oath, left his seat and, bestowed upon the dog a vicious and heavy kick, with his ponderous shoe.

The hound, heartbroken, astonished, with flapping ears and incurved tail, uttered a piercing yelp of pain and surprise.

Reeves and the consul remained in their chairs, saying nothing, but astonished at the unexpected show of intolerance from the easy-going man from Chatham county.

But Morgan, with a suddenly purpling face, leaped, to his feet and raised a threatening arm above the guest.

"You—brute!" he shouted, passionately; "why did you do that?"

Quickly the amenities returned, Plunkett muttered some indistinct apology and regained his seat. Morgan with a decided effort controlled his indignation and also returned to his chair.

And then Plunkett with the spring of a tiger, leaped around the corner of the table and snapped handcuffs on the paralyzed Morgan's wrists.

"Hound-lover and woman-killer!" he cried; "get ready to meet your God."

When Bridger had finished I asked him:

"Did he get the right man?"

"He did," said the Consul.

"And how did he know?" I inquired, being in a kind of bewilderment.

"When he put Morgan in the dory," answered Bridger, "the next day to take him aboard the *Pajaro*, this man Plunkett stopped to shake hands with me and I asked him the same question."

"'Mr. Bridger,' said he, 'I'm a Kentuckian, and I've seen a great deal of both men and animals. And I never yet saw a man that was overfond of horses and dogs but what was cruel to women.'"

III

THE HYPOTHESES OF FAILURE

Lawyer Gooch bestowed his undivided attention upon the engrossing arts of his profession. But one flight of fancy did he allow his mind to entertain. He was fond of likening his suite of office rooms to the bottom of a ship. The rooms were three in number, with a door opening from one to another. These doors could also be closed.

"Ships," Lawyer Gooch would say, "are constructed for safety, with separate, water-tight compartments in their bottoms. If one compartment springs a leak it fills with water; but the good ship goes on unhurt. Were it not for the separating bulkheads one leak would sink the vessel. Now it often happens that while I am occupied with clients, other clients with conflicting interests call. With the assistance of Archibald—an office boy with a future—I cause the dangerous influx to be diverted into separate compartments, while I sound with my legal plummet the depth of each. If necessary, they may be baled into the hallway and permitted to escape by way of the stairs, which we may term the lee scuppers. Thus the good ship of business is kept afloat; whereas if the element that supports her were allowed to mingle freely in her hold we might be swamped—ha, ha, ha!"

The law is dry. Good jokes are few. Surely it might be permitted Lawyer Gooch to mitigate the bore of briefs, the tedium of torts and the prosiness of processes with even so light a levy upon the good property of humour.

Lawyer Gooch's practice leaned largely to the settlement of marital infelicities. Did matrimony languish through complications, he mediated, soothed and arbitrated. Did it suffer from implications, he readjusted, defended and championed. Did it arrive at the extremity of duplications, he always got light sentences for his clients.

But not always was Lawyer Gooch the keen, armed, wily belligerent, ready with his two-edged sword to lop off the shackles of Hymen. He had been known to build up instead of demolishing, to reunite instead of severing, to lead erring and foolish ones back into the fold instead of scattering the flock. Often had he by his eloquent and moving appeals sent husband and wife, weeping, back into each other's arms. Frequently he had coached childhood so successfully that, at the psychological moment (and at a given signal) the plaintive pipe of "Papa, won't you tum home adain to me and muvver?" had won the day and upheld the pillars of a tottering home.

Unprejudiced persons admitted that Lawyer Gooch received as big fees from these reyoked clients as would have been paid him had the cases been contested in court. Prejudiced ones intimated that his fees were doubled, because the penitent couples always came back later for the divorce, anyhow.

There came a season in June when the legal ship of Lawyer Gooch (to borrow his own figure) was nearly becalmed. The divorce mill grinds slowly in June. It is the month of Cupid and Hymen.

Lawyer Gooch, then, sat idle in the middle room of his clientless suite. A small anteroom connected—or rather separated—this apartment from the hallway. Here was stationed Archibald, who wrested from visitors their cards or oral nomenclature which he bore to his master while they waited.

Suddenly, on this day, there came a great knocking at the outermost door.

Archibald, opening it, was thrust aside as superfluous by the visitor, who without due reverence at once penetrated to the office of Lawyer Gooch and threw himself with good-natured insolence into a comfortable chair facing that gentlemen.

"You are Phineas C. Gooch, attorney-at-law?" said the visitor, his tone of voice and inflection making his words at once a question, an assertion and an accusation.

Before committing himself by a reply, the lawyer estimated his possible client in one of his brief but shrewd and calculating glances.

The man was of the emphatic type—large-sized, active, bold and debonair in demeanour, vain beyond a doubt, slightly swaggering, ready and at ease. He was well-clothed, but with a shade too much ornateness. He was seeking a lawyer; but if that fact would seem to saddle him with troubles they were not patent in his beaming eye and courageous air.

"My name is Gooch," at length the lawyer admitted. Upon pressure he would also have confessed to the Phineas C. But he did not consider it good practice to volunteer information. "I did not receive your card," he continued, by way of rebuke, "so I—"

"I know you didn't," remarked the visitor, coolly; "And you won't just yet. Light up?" He threw a leg over an arm of his chair, and tossed a handful of rich-hued cigars upon the table. Lawyer Gooch knew the brand. He thawed just enough to accept the invitation to smoke.

"You are a divorce lawyer," said the cardless visitor. This time there was no interrogation in his voice. Nor did his words constitute a simple assertion. They formed a charge—a denunciation—as one would say to a dog: "You are a dog." Lawyer Gooch was silent under the imputation.

"You handle," continued the visitor, "all the various ramifications of busted-up connubiality. You are a surgeon, we might saw, who extracts Cupid's darts when he shoots 'em into the wrong parties. You furnish patent, incandescent lights for premises where the torch of Hymen has burned so low you can't light a cigar at it. Am I right, Mr. Gooch?"

"I have undertaken cases," said the lawyer, guardedly, "in the line to which your figurative speech seems to refer. Do you wish to consult me professionally, Mr. —" The lawyer paused, with significance.

"Not yet," said the other, with an arch wave of his cigar, "not just yet. Let us approach the subject with the caution that should have been used in the original act that makes this pow-wow necessary. There exists a matrimonial jumble to be straightened out. But before I give you names I want your honest—well, anyhow, your professional opinion on the merits of the mix-up. I want you to size up the catastrophe—abstractly—you understand? I'm Mr. Nobody; and I've got a story to tell you. Then you say what's what. Do you get my wireless?"

"You want to state a hypothetical case?" suggested Lawyer Gooch.

"That's the word I was after. 'Apothecary' was the best shot I could make at it in my mind. The hypothetical goes. I'll state the case. Suppose there's a woman—a deuced fine-looking woman—who has run away from her husband and home? She's badly mashed on another man who went to her town to work up some real estate business. Now, we may as well call this woman's husband Thomas R. Billings, for that's his name. I'm giving you straight tips on the cognomens. The Lothario chap is Henry K. Jessup. The Billingses lived in a little town called Susanville—a good many miles from here. Now, Jessup leaves Susanville two weeks ago. The next day Mrs. Billings follows him. She's dead gone on this man Jessup; you can bet your law library on that."

Lawyer Gooch's client said this with such unctuous satisfaction that even the callous lawyer experienced a slight ripple of repulsion. He now saw clearly in his fatuous visitor the conceit of the lady-killer, the egoistic complacency of the successful trifler.

"Now," continued the visitor, "suppose this Mrs. Billings wasn't happy at home? We'll say she and her husband didn't gee worth a cent. They've got incompatibility to burn. The things she likes, Billings wouldn't have as a gift with trading-stamps. It's Tabby and Rover with them all the time. She's an educated woman in science and culture, and she reads things out loud at meetings. Billings is not on. He don't appreciate progress and obelisks and ethics, and things of that sort. Old Billings is simply a blink when it comes to such things. The lady is out and out above his class. Now, lawyer, don't it look like a fair equalization of rights and wrongs that a woman like that should be allowed to throw down Billings and take the man that can appreciate her?"

"Incompatibility," said Lawyer Gooch, "is undoubtedly the source of much marital discord and unhappiness. Where it is positively proved, divorce would seem to be the equitable remedy. Are you—excuse me— is this man Jessup one to whom the lady may safely trust her future?"

"Oh, you can bet on Jessup," said the client, with a confident wag of his head. "Jessup's all right. He'll do the square thing. Why, he left Susanville just to keep people from talking about Mrs. Billings. But she followed him up, and now, of course, he'll stick to her. When she gets a divorce, all legal and proper, Jessup will do the proper thing."

"And now," said Lawyer Gooch, "continuing the hypothesis, if you prefer, and supposing that my services should be desired in the case, what—"

The client rose impulsively to his feet.

"Oh, dang the hypothetical business," he exclaimed, impatiently. "Let's let her drop, and get down to straight talk. You ought to know who I am by this time. I want that woman to have her divorce. I'll pay for it. The day you set Mrs. Billings free I'll pay you five hundred dollars."

Lawyer Gooch's client banged his fist upon the table to punctuate his generosity.

"If that is the case—" began the lawyer.

"Lady to see you, sir," bawled Archibald, bouncing in from his anteroom. He had orders to always announce immediately any client that might come. There was no sense in turning business away.

Lawyer Gooch took client number one by the arm and led him suavely into one of the adjoining rooms. "Favour me by remaining here a few minutes, sir," said he. "I will return and resume our consultation with the least possible delay. I am rather expecting a visit from a very wealthy old lady in connection with a will. I will not keep you waiting long."

The breezy gentleman seated himself with obliging acquiescence, and took up a magazine. The lawyer returned to the middle office, carefully closing behind him the connecting door.

"Show the lady in, Archibald," he said to the office boy, who was awaiting the order.

A tall lady, of commanding presence and sternly handsome, entered the room. She wore robes—robes; not clothes—ample and fluent. In her eye could be perceived the lambent flame of genius and soul. In her hand was a green bag of the capacity of a bushel, and an umbrella that also seemed to wear a robe, ample and fluent. She accepted a chair.

"Are you Mr. Phineas C. Gooch, the lawyer?" she asked, in formal and unconciliatory tones.

"I am," answered Lawyer Gooch, without circumlocution. He never circumlocuted when dealing with a woman. Women circumlocute. Time is wasted when both sides in debate employ the same tactics.

"As a lawyer, sir," began the lady, "you may have acquired some knowledge of the human heart. Do you believe that the pusillanimous and petty conventions of our artificial social life should stand as an obstacle in the way of a noble and affectionate heart when it finds its true mate among the miserable and worthless wretches in the world that are called men?"

"Madam," said Lawyer Gooch, in the tone that he used in curbing his female clients, "this is an office for conducting the practice of law. I am a lawyer, not a philosopher, nor the editor of an 'Answers to the Lovelorn' column of a newspaper. I have other clients waiting. I will ask you kindly to come to the point."

"Well, you needn't get so stiff around the gills about it," said the lady, with a snap of her luminous eyes and a startling gyration of her umbrella. "Business is what I've come for. I want your opinion in the matter of a suit for divorce, as the vulgar would call it, but which is really only the readjustment of the false and ignoble conditions that the short-sighted laws of man have interposed between a loving—"

"I beg your pardon, madam," interrupted Lawyer Gooch, with some impatience, "for reminding you again that this is a law office. Perhaps Mrs. Wilcox—"

"Mrs. Wilcox is all right," cut in the lady, with a hint of asperity. "And so are Tolstoi, and Mrs. Gertrude Atherton, and Omar Khayyam, and Mr. Edward Bok. I've read 'em all. I would like to discuss with you the divine right of the soul as opposed to the freedom-destroying restrictions of a bigoted and narrow-minded society. But I will proceed to business. I would prefer to lay the matter before you in an impersonal way until you pass upon its merits. That is to describe it as a supposable instance, without—"

"You wish to state a hypothetical case?" said Lawyer Gooch.

"I was going to say that," said the lady, sharply. "Now, suppose there is a woman who is all soul and heart and aspirations for a complete existence. This woman has a husband who is far below her in intellect, in taste—in everything. Bah! he is a brute. He despises literature. He sneers at the lofty thoughts of the world's great thinkers. He thinks only of real estate and such sordid things. He is no mate for a woman with soul. We will say that this unfortunate wife one day meets with her ideal—a man with brain and heart and force. She loves him. Although this man feels the thrill of a new-found affinity he is too noble, too honourable to declare himself. He flies from the presence of his beloved. She flies after him, trampling, with superb indifference, upon the fetters with which an unenlightened social system would bind her. Now, what will a divorce cost? Eliza Ann Timmins, the poetess of Sycamore Gap, got one for three hundred and forty dollars. Can I—I mean can this lady I speak of get one that cheap?"

"Madam," said Lawyer Gooch, "your last two or three sentences delight me with their intelligence and clearness. Can we not now abandon the hypothetical and come down to names and business?"

"I should say so," exclaimed the lady, adopting the practical with admirable readiness. "Thomas R. Billings is the name of the low brute who stands between the happiness of his legal—his legal, but not his spiritual—wife and Henry K. Jessup, the noble man whom nature intended for her mate. I," concluded the client, with an air of dramatic revelation, "am Mrs. Billings!"

"Gentlemen to see you, sir," shouted Archibald, invading the room almost at a handspring. Lawyer Gooch arose from his chair.

"Mrs. Billings," he said courteously, "allow me to conduct you into the adjoining office apartment for a few minutes. I am expecting a very wealthy old gentleman on business connected with a will. In a very short while I will join you, and continue our consultation."

With his accustomed chivalrous manner, Lawyer Gooch ushered his soulful client into the remaining unoccupied room, and came out, closing the door with circumspection.

The next visitor introduced by Archibald was a thin, nervous, irritable-looking man of middle age, with a worried and apprehensive expression of countenance. He carried in one hand a small satchel, which he set down upon the floor beside the chair which the lawyer placed for him. His clothing was of good quality, but it was worn without regard to neatness or style, and appeared to be covered with the dust of travel.

"You make a specialty of divorce cases," he said, in, an agitated but business-like tone.

"I may say," began Lawyer Gooch, "that my practice has not altogether avoided—"

"I know you do," interrupted client number three. "You needn't tell me. I've heard all about you. I have a case to lay before you without necessarily disclosing any connection that I might have with it—that is—"

"You wish," said Lawyer Gooch, "to state a hypothetical case."

"You may call it that. I am a plain man of business. I will be as brief as possible. We will first take up hypothetical woman. We will say she is married uncongenially. In many ways she is a superior woman. Physically she is considered to be handsome. She is devoted to what she calls literature—poetry and prose, and such stuff. Her husband is a plain man in the business walks of life. Their home has not been happy, although the husband has tried to make it so. Some time ago a man—a stranger—came to the peaceful town in which they lived and engaged in some real estate operations. This woman met him, and became unaccountably infatuated with him. Her attentions became so open that the man felt the community to be no safe place for him, so he left it. She abandoned husband and home, and followed him. She forsook her home, where she was provided with every comfort, to follow this man who had inspired her with such a strange affection. Is there anything more to be deplored," concluded the client, in a trembling voice, "than the wrecking of a home by a woman's uncalculating folly?"

Lawyer Gooch delivered the cautious opinion that there was not.

"This man she has gone to join," resumed the visitor, "is not the man to make her happy. It is a wild and foolish self-deception that makes her think he will. Her husband, in spite of their many disagreements, is the only one capable of dealing with her sensitive and peculiar nature. But this she does not realize now."

"Would you consider a divorce the logical cure in the case you present?" asked Lawyer Gooch, who felt that the conversation was wandering too far from the field of business.

"A divorce!" exclaimed the client, feelingly—almost tearfully. "No, no—not that. I have read, Mr. Gooch, of many instances where your sympathy and kindly interest led you to act as a mediator between estranged husband and wife, and brought them together again. Let us drop the hypothetical case—I need conceal no longer that it is I who am the sufferer in this sad affair—the names you shall have—Thomas R. Billings and wife—and Henry K. Jessup, the man with whom she is infatuated."

Client number three laid his hand upon Mr. Gooch's arm. Deep emotion was written upon his careworn face. "For Heaven's sake", he said fervently, "help me in this hour of trouble. Seek out Mrs. Billings, and persuade her to abandon this distressing pursuit of her lamentable folly. Tell her, Mr. Gooch, that her husband is willing to receive her back to his heart and home—promise her anything that will induce her to return. I have heard of your success in these matters. Mrs. Billings cannot be very far away. I am worn out with travel and weariness. Twice during the pursuit I saw her, but various circumstances prevented our having an interview. Will you undertake this mission for me, Mr. Gooch, and earn my everlasting gratitude?"

"It is true," said Lawyer Gooch, frowning slightly at the other's last words, but immediately calling up an expression of virtuous benevolence, "that on a number of occasions I have been successful in persuading couples who sought the severing of their matrimonial bonds to think better of their rash intentions and return to their homes reconciled. But I assure you that the work is often exceedingly difficult. The amount of argument, perseverance, and, if I may be allowed to say it, eloquence that it requires would astonish you. But this is a case in which my sympathies would be wholly enlisted. I feel deeply for you sir, and I would be most happy to see husband and wife reunited. But my time," concluded the lawyer, looking at his watch as if suddenly reminded of the fact, "is valuable."

"I am aware of that," said the client, "and if you will take the case and persuade Mrs. Billings to return home and leave the man alone that she is following—on that day I will pay you the sum of one thousand dollars. I have made a little money in real estate during the recent boom in Susanville, and I will not begrudge that amount."

"Retain your seat for a few moments, please," said Lawyer Gooch, arising, and again consulting his watch. "I have another client waiting in an adjoining room whom I had very nearly forgotten. I will return in the briefest possible space."

The situation was now one that fully satisfied Lawyer Gooch's love of intricacy and complication. He revelled in cases that presented such subtle problems and possibilities. It pleased him to think that he was master of the happiness and fate of the three individuals who sat, unconscious of one another's presence, within his reach. His old figure of the ship glided into his mind. But now the figure failed, for to have filled every compartment of an actual vessel would have been to endanger her safety; with his compartments full, his ship of affairs could but sail on to the advantageous port of a fine, fat fee. The thing for him to do, of course, was to wring the best bargain he could from some one of his anxious cargo.

First he called to the office boy: "Lock the outer door, Archibald, and admit no one." Then he moved, with long, silent strides into the room in which client number one waited. That gentleman sat, patiently scanning the pictures in the magazine, with a cigar in his mouth and his feet upon a table.

"Well," he remarked, cheerfully, as the lawyer entered, "have you made up your mind? Does five hundred dollars go for getting the fair lady a divorce?"

"You mean that as a retainer?" asked Lawyer Gooch, softly interrogative.

"Hey? No; for the whole job. It's enough, ain't it?"

"My fee," said Lawyer Gooch, "would be one thousand five hundred dollars. Five hundred dollars down, and the remainder upon issuance of the divorce."

A loud whistle came from client number one. His feet descended to the floor.

"Guess we can't close the deal," he said, arising, "I cleaned up five hundred dollars in a little real estate dicker down in Susanville. I'd do anything I could to free the lady, but it out-sizes my pile."

"Could you stand one thousand two hundred dollars?" asked the lawyer, insinuatingly.

"Five hundred is my limit, I tell you. Guess I'll have to hunt up a cheaper lawyer." The client put on his hat.

"Out this way, please," said Lawyer Gooch, opening the door that led into the hallway.

As the gentleman flowed out of the compartment and down the stairs, Lawyer Gooch smiled to himself. "Exit Mr. Jessup," he murmured, as he fingered the Henry Clay tuft of hair at his ear. "And now for the forsaken husband." He returned to the middle office, and assumed a businesslike manner.

"I understand," he said to client number three, "that you agree to pay one thousand dollars if I bring about, or am instrumental in bringing about, the return of Mrs. Billings to her home, and her abandonment of her infatuated pursuit of the man for whom she has conceived such a violent fancy. Also that the case is now unreservedly in my hands on that basis. Is that correct?"

"Entirely", said the other, eagerly. "And I can produce the cash any time at two hours' notice."

Lawyer Gooch stood up at his full height. His thin figure seemed to expand. His thumbs sought the arm-holes of his vest. Upon his face was a look of sympathetic benignity that he always wore during such undertakings.

"Then, sir," he said, in kindly tones, "I think I can promise you an early relief from your troubles. I have that much confidence in my powers of argument and persuasion, in the natural impulses of the human heart toward good, and in the strong influence of a husband's unfaltering love. Mrs. Billings, sir, is here—in that room—" the lawyer's long arm pointed to the door. "I will call her in at once; and our united pleadings—"

Lawyer Gooch paused, for client number three had leaped from his chair as if propelled by steel springs, and clutched his satchel.

"What the devil," he exclaimed, harshly, "do you mean? That woman in there! I thought I shook her off forty miles back."

He ran to the open window, looked out below, and threw one leg over the sill.

"Stop!" cried Lawyer Gooch, in amazement. "What would you do? Come, Mr. Billings, and face your erring but innocent wife. Our combined entreaties cannot fail to—"

"Billings!" shouted the now thoroughly moved client. "I'll Billings you, you old idiot!"

Turning, he hurled his satchel with fury at the lawyer's head. It struck that astounded peacemaker between the eyes, causing him to stagger backward a pace or two. When Lawyer Gooch recovered his wits he saw that his client had disappeared. Rushing to the window, he leaned out, and saw the recreant gathering himself up from the top of a shed upon which he had dropped from the second-story window. Without stopping to collect his hat he then plunged downward the remaining ten feet to the alley, up which he flew with prodigious celerity until the surrounding building swallowed him up from view.

Lawyer Gooch passed his hand tremblingly across his brow. It was a habitual act with him, serving to clear his thoughts. Perhaps also it now seemed to soothe the spot where a very hard alligator-hide satchel had struck.

The satchel lay upon the floor, wide open, with its contents spilled about. Mechanically, Lawyer Gooch stooped to gather up the articles. The first was a collar; and the omniscient eye of the man of law perceived, wonderingly, the initials H. K. J. marked upon it. Then came a comb, a brush, a folded map, and a piece of soap. Lastly, a handful of old business letters, addressed—every one of them—to "Henry K. Jessup, Esq."

Lawyer Gooch closed the satchel, and set it upon the table. He hesitated for a moment, and then put on his hat and walked into the office boy's anteroom.

"Archibald," he said mildly, as he opened the hall door, "I am going around to the Supreme Court rooms. In five minutes you may step into the inner office, and inform the lady who is waiting there that"— here Lawyer Gooch made use of the vernacular—"that there's nothing doing."

IV

CALLOWAY'S CODE

The New York *Enterprise* sent H. B. Calloway as special correspondent to the Russo-Japanese-Portsmouth war.

For two months Calloway hung about Yokohama and Tokio, shaking dice with the other correspondents for drinks of 'rickshaws—oh, no, that's something to ride in; anyhow, he wasn't earning the salary that his paper was paying him. But that was not Calloway's fault. The little brown men who held the strings of Fate between their fingers were not ready for the readers of the *Enterprise* to season their breakfast bacon and eggs with the battles of the descendants of the gods.

But soon the column of correspondents that were to go out with the First Army tightened their field-glass belts and went down to the Yalu with Kuroki. Calloway was one of these.

Now, this is no history of the battle of the Yalu River. That has been told in detail by the correspondents who gazed at the shrapnel smoke rings from a distance of three miles. But, for justice's sake, let it be understood that the Japanese commander prohibited a nearer view.

Calloway's feat was accomplished before the battle. What he did was to furnish the *Enterprise* with the biggest beat of the war. That paper published exclusively and in detail the news of the attack on the lines of the Russian General on the same day that it was made. No other paper printed a word about it for two days afterward, except a London paper, whose account was absolutely incorrect and untrue.

Calloway did this in face of the fact that General Kuroki was making his moves and laying his plans with the profoundest secrecy as far as the world outside his camps was concerned. The correspondents were forbidden to send out any news whatever of his plans; and every message that was allowed on the wires was censored with rigid severity.

The correspondent for the London paper handed in a cablegram describing Kuroki's plans; but as it was wrong from beginning to end the censor grinned and let it go through.

So, there they were—Kuroki on one side of the Yalu with forty-two thousand infantry, five thousand cavalry, and one hundred and twenty-four guns. On the other side, Zassulitch waited for him with only twenty-three thousand men, and with a long stretch of river to guard. And Calloway had got hold of some important inside information that he knew would bring the *Enterprise* staff around a cablegram as thick as flies around a Park Row lemonade stand. If he could only get that message past the censor—the new censor who had arrived and taken his post that day!

Calloway did the obviously proper thing. He lit his pipe and sat down on a gun carriage to think it over. And there we must leave him; for the rest of the story belongs to Vesey, a sixteen-dollar-a-week reporter on the *Enterprise*.

CALLOWAY'S CABLEGRAM WAS HANDED TO the managing editor at four o'clock in the afternoon. He read it three times; and then drew a pocket mirror from a pigeon-hole in his desk, and looked at his reflection carefully. Then he went over to the desk of Boyd, his assistant (he usually called Boyd when he wanted him), and laid the cablegram before him.

"It's from Calloway," he said. "See what you make of it."

The message was dated at Wi-ju, and these were the words of it:

Foregone preconcerted rash witching goes muffled rumour mine dark silent unfortunate richmond existing great hotly brute select mooted parlous beggars ye angel incontrovertible.

Boyd read it twice.

"It's either a cipher or a sunstroke," said he.

"Ever hear of anything like a code in the office—a secret code?" asked the m. e., who had held his desk for only two years. Managing editors come and go.

"None except the vernacular that the lady specials write in," said Boyd. "Couldn't be an acrostic, could it?"

"I thought of that," said the m. e., "but the beginning letters contain only four vowels. It must be a code of some sort."

"Try em in groups," suggested Boyd. "Let's see—'Rash witching goes'—not with me it doesn't. 'Muffled rumour mine'—must have an underground wire. 'Dark silent unfortunate richmond'—no reason why he should knock that town so hard. 'Existing great hotly'—no it doesn't pan out. I'll call Scott."

The city editor came in a hurry, and tried his luck. A city editor must know something about everything; so Scott knew a little about cipher-writing.

"It may be what is called an inverted alphabet cipher," said he. "I'll try that. 'R' seems to be the oftenest used initial letter, with the exception of 'm.' Assuming 'r' to mean 'e', the most frequently used vowel, we transpose the letters—so."

Scott worked rapidly with his pencil for two minutes; and then showed the first word according to his reading—the word "Scejtzez."

"Great!" cried Boyd. "It's a charade. My first is a Russian general. Go on, Scott."

"No, that won't work," said the city editor. "It's undoubtedly a code. It's impossible to read it without the key. Has the office ever used a cipher code?"

"Just what I was asking," said the m.e. "Hustle everybody up that ought to know. We must get at it some way. Calloway has evidently got hold of something big, and the censor has put the screws on, or he wouldn't have cabled in a lot of chop suey like this."

Throughout the office of the *Enterprise* a dragnet was sent, hauling in such members of the staff as would be likely to know of a code, past or present, by reason of their wisdom, information, natural intelligence, or length of servitude. They got together in a group in the city room, with the m. e. in the centre. No one had heard of a code. All began to explain to the head investigator that newspapers never use a code, anyhow—that is, a cipher code. Of course the Associated Press stuff is a sort of code—an abbreviation, rather—but—

The m. e. knew all that, and said so. He asked each man how long he had worked on the paper. Not one of them had drawn pay from an *Enterprise* envelope for longer than six years. Calloway had been on the paper twelve years.

"Try old Heffelbauer," said the m. e. "He was here when Park Row was a potato patch."

Heffelbauer was an institution. He was half janitor, half handyman about the office, and half watchman—thus becoming the peer of thirteen and one-half tailors. Sent for, he came, radiating his nationality.

"Heffelbauer," said the m. e., "did you ever hear of a code belonging to the office a long time ago—a private code? You know what a code is, don't you?"

"Yah," said Heffelbauer. "Sure I know vat a code is. Yah, apout dwelf or fifteen year ago der office had a code. Der reborters in der city-room haf it here."

"Ah!" said the m. e. "We're getting on the trail now. Where was it kept, Heffelbauer? What do you know about it?"

"Somedimes," said the retainer, "dey keep it in der little room behind der library room."

"Can you find it?" asked the m. e. eagerly. "Do you know where it is?"

"Mein Gott!" said Heffelbauer. "How long you dink a code live? Der reborters call him a maskeet. But von day he butt mit his head der editor, und—"

"Oh, he's talking about a goat," said Boyd. "Get out, Heffelbauer."

Again discomfited, the concerted wit and resource of the *Enterprise* huddled around Calloway's puzzle, considering its mysterious words in vain.

Then Vesey came in.

Vesey was the youngest reporter. He had a thirty-two-inch chest and wore a number fourteen collar; but his bright Scotch plaid suit gave him presence and conferred no obscurity upon his whereabouts. He wore his hat in such a position that people followed him about to see him take it off, convinced that it must be hung upon a peg driven into the back of his head. He was never without an immense, knotted, hard-wood cane with a German-silver tip on its crooked handle. Vesey was the best photograph hustler in the office. Scott said it was because no living human being could resist the personal triumph it was to hand his picture over to Vesey. Vesey always wrote his own news stories, except the big ones, which were sent to the rewrite men. Add to this fact that among all the inhabitants, temples, and groves of the earth nothing existed that could abash Vesey, and his dim sketch is concluded.

Vesey butted into the circle of cipher readers very much as Heffelbauer's "code" would have done, and asked what was up. Some one explained, with the touch of half-familiar condescension that they always used toward him. Vesey reached out and took the cablegram from the m. e. 's hand. Under the protection of some special Providence, he was always doing appalling things like that, and coming, off unscathed.

"It's a code," said Vesey. "Anybody got the key?"

"The office has no code," said Boyd, reaching for the message. Vesey held to it.

"Then old Calloway expects us to read it, anyhow," said he. "He's up a tree, or something, and he's made this up so as to get it by the censor. It's up to us. Gee! I wish they had sent me, too. Say—we can't afford to fall down on our end of it. 'Foregone, preconcerted rash, witching'—h'm."

Vesey sat down on a table corner and began to whistle softly, frowning at the cablegram.

"Let's have it, please," said the m. e. "We've got to get to work on it."

"I believe I've got a line on it," said Vesey. "Give me ten minutes."

He walked to his desk, threw his hat into a waste-basket, spread out flat on his chest like a gorgeous lizard, and started his pencil going. The wit and wisdom of the *Enterprise* remained in a loose group, and smiled at one another, nodding their heads toward Vesey. Then they began to exchange their theories about the cipher.

It took Vesey exactly fifteen minutes. He brought to the m. e. a pad with the code-key written on it.

"I felt the swing of it as soon as I saw it," said Vesey. "Hurrah for old Calloway! He's done the Japs and every paper in town that prints literature instead of news. Take a look at that."

Thus had Vesey set forth the reading of the code:

Foregone – conclusion
Preconcerted – arrangement
Rash – act
Witching – hour of midnight
Goes – without saying
Muffled – report
Rumour – hath it
Mine – host
Dark – horse
Silent – majority
Unfortunate – pedestrians*
Richmond – in the field
Existing – conditions
Great – White Way
Hotly – contested
Brute – force
Select – few
Mooted – question
Parlous – times

---

* Mr. Vesey afterward explained that the logical journalistic complement of the word "unfortunate" was once the word "victim." But, since the automobile became so popular, the correct following word is now "pedestrians." Of course, in Calloway's code it meant infantry.

Beggars – description
Ye – correspondent
Angel – unawares
Incontrovertible – fact

"It's simply newspaper English," explained Vesey. "I've been reporting on the *Enterprise* long enough to know it by heart. Old Calloway gives us the cue word, and we use the word that naturally follows it just as we use 'em in the paper. Read it over, and you'll see how pat they drop into their places. Now, here's the message he intended us to get."

Vesey handed out another sheet of paper.

Concluded arrangement to act at hour of midnight without saying. Report hath it that a large body of cavalry and an overwhelming force of infantry will be thrown into the field. Conditions white. Way contested by only a small force. Question the Times description. Its correspondent is unaware of the facts.

"Great stuff!" cried Boyd excitedly. "Kuroki crosses the Yalu to-night and attacks. Oh, we won't do a thing to the sheets that make up with Addison's essays, real estate transfers, and bowling scores!"

"Mr. Vesey," said the m. e., with his jollying-which-you-should-regard-as-a-favour manner, "you have cast a serious reflection upon the literary standards of the paper that employs you. You have also assisted materially in giving us the biggest 'beat' of the year. I will let you know in a day or two whether you are to be discharged or retained at a larger salary. Somebody send Ames to me."

Ames was the king-pin, the snowy-petalled Marguerite, the star-bright looloo of the rewrite men. He saw attempted murder in the pains of green-apple colic, cyclones in the summer zephyr, lost children in every top-spinning urchin, an uprising of the down-trodden masses in every hurling of a derelict potato at a passing automobile. When not rewriting, Ames sat on the porch of his Brooklyn villa playing checkers with his ten-year-old son.

Ames and the "war editor" shut themselves in a room. There was a map in there stuck full of little pins that represented armies and divisions. Their fingers had been itching for days to move those pins along the crooked line of the Yalu. They did so now; and in words of fire Ames translated Calloway's brief message into a front page masterpiece that set the world talking. He told of the secret councils of the Japanese officers; gave Kuroki's flaming speeches in full; counted the cavalry and infantry to a man and a horse; described the quick and silent building, of the bridge at Suikauchen, across which the Mikado's legions were hurled upon the surprised Zassulitch, whose troops were widely scattered along the river. And the battle!—well, you know what Ames can do with a battle if you give him just one smell of smoke for a foundation. And in the same story, with seemingly supernatural knowledge, he gleefully scored the most profound and ponderous paper in England for the false and misleading account of the intended movements of the Japanese First Army printed in its issue of *the same date*.

Only one error was made; and that was the fault of the cable operator at Wi-ju. Calloway pointed it out after he came back. The word "great" in his code should have been "gage," and its complemental words "of battle." But it went to Ames "conditions white," and of course he took that to mean snow. His description of the Japanese army struggling through the snowstorm, blinded by the whirling flakes, was thrillingly vivid. The artists turned out some effective illustrations that made a hit as pictures of the artillery dragging their guns through the drifts. But, as the attack was made on the first day of May, "conditions white" excited some amusement. But it in made no difference to the *Enterprise*, anyway.

It was wonderful. And Calloway was wonderful in having made the new censor believe that his jargon of words meant no more than a complaint of the dearth of news and a petition for more expense money. And Vesey was wonderful. And most wonderful of all are words, and how they make friends one with another, being oft associated, until not even obituary notices them do part.

On the second day following, the city editor halted at Vesey's desk where the reporter was writing the story of a man who had broken his leg by falling into a coal-hole—Ames having failed to find a murder motive in it.

"The old man says your salary is to be raised to twenty a week," said Scott.

"All right," said Vesey. "Every little helps. Say—Mr. Scott, which would you say—'We can state without fear of successful contradiction,' or, 'On the whole it can be safely asserted'?"

V

A Matter of Mean Elevation

One winter the Alcazar Opera Company of New Orleans made a speculative trip along the Mexican, Central American and South American coasts. The venture proved a most successful one. The music-loving, impressionable Spanish-Americans deluged the company with dollars and "vivas." The manager waxed plump and amiable. But for the prohibitive climate he would have put forth the distinctive flower of his prosperity—the overcoat of fur, braided, frogged and opulent. Almost was he persuaded to raise the salaries of his company. But with a mighty effort he conquered the impulse toward such an unprofitable effervescence of joy.

At Macuto, on the coast of Venezuela, the company scored its greatest success. Imagine Coney Island translated into Spanish and you will comprehend Macuto. The fashionable season is from November to March. Down from La Guayra and Caracas and Valencia and other interior towns flock the people for their holiday season. There are bathing and fiestas and bull fights and scandal. And then the people have a passion for music that the bands in the plaza and on the sea beach stir but do not satisfy. The coming of the Alcazar Opera Company aroused the utmost ardour and zeal among the pleasure seekers.

The illustrious Guzman Blanco, President and Dictator of Venezuela, sojourned in Macuto with his court for the season. That potent ruler—who himself paid a subsidy of 40,000 pesos each year to grand opera in Caracas—ordered one of the Government warehouses to be cleared for a temporary theatre. A stage was quickly constructed and rough wooden benches made for the audience. Private boxes were added for the use of the President and the notables of the army and Government.

The company remained in Macuto for two weeks. Each performance filled the house as closely as it could be packed. Then the music-mad people fought for room in the open doors and windows, and crowded about, hundreds deep, on the outside. Those audiences formed a brilliantly diversified patch of colour. The hue of their faces ranged from the clear olive of the pure-blood Spaniards down through the yellow and brown shades of the Mestizos to the coal-black Carib and the Jamaica Negro. Scattered among them were little groups of Indians with faces like stone idols, wrapped in gaudy fibre-woven blankets—Indians down from the mountain states of Zamora and Los Andes and Miranda to trade their gold dust in the coast towns.

The spell cast upon these denizens of the interior fastnesses was remarkable. They sat in petrified ecstasy, conspicuous among the excitable Macutians, who wildly strove with tongue and hand to give evidence of their delight. Only once did the sombre rapture of these aboriginals find expression. During the rendition of "Faust," Guzman Blanco, extravagantly pleased by the "Jewel Song," cast upon the stage a purse of gold pieces. Other distinguished citizens followed his lead to the extent of whatever loose coin they had convenient, while some of the fair and fashionable señoras were moved, in imitation, to fling a jewel or a ring or two at the feet of the Marguerite—who was, according to the bills, Mlle. Nina Giraud. Then, from different parts of the house rose sundry of the stolid hillmen and cast upon the stage little brown and dun bags that fell with soft "thumps" and did not rebound. It was, no doubt, pleasure at the tribute to her art that caused Mlle. Giraud's eyes to shine so brightly when she opened these little deerskin bags in her dressing room and found them to contain pure gold dust. If so, the pleasure was rightly hers, for her voice in song, pure, strong and thrilling with the feeling of the emotional artist, deserved the tribute that it earned.

But the triumph of the Alcazar Opera Company is not the theme—it but leans upon and colours it. There happened in Macuto a tragic thing, an unsolvable mystery, that sobered for a time the gaiety of the happy season.

One evening between the short twilight and the time when she should have whirled upon the stage in the red and black of the ardent Carmen, Mlle. Nina Giraud disappeared from the sight and ken of 6,000 pairs of eyes and as many minds in Macuto. There was the usual turmoil and hurrying to seek her. Messengers flew to the little French-kept hotel where she stayed; others of the company hastened here or there where she might be lingering in some tienda or unduly prolonging her bath upon the beach. All search was fruitless. Mademoiselle had vanished.

Half an hour passed and she did not appear. The dictator, unused to the caprices of prime donne, became impatient. He sent an aide from his box to say to the manager that if the curtain did not at once rise he would immediately hale the entire company to the calabosa, though it would desolate his heart, indeed, to be compelled to such an act. Birds in Macuto could be made to sing.

The manager abandoned hope for the time of Mlle. Giraud. A member of the chorus, who had dreamed hopelessly for years of the blessed opportunity, quickly Carmenized herself and the opera went on.

Afterward, when the lost cantatrice appeared not, the aid of the authorities was invoked. The President at once set the army, the police and all citizens to the search. Not one clue to Mlle. Giraud's disappearance was found. The Alcazar left to fill engagements farther down the coast.

On the way back the steamer stopped at Macuto and the manager made anxious inquiry. Not a trace of the lady had been discovered. The Alcazar could do no more. The personal belongings of the missing lady were stored in the hotel against her possible later reappearance and the opera company continued upon its homeward voyage to New Orleans.

ON THE CAMINO REAL ALONG the beach the two saddle mules and the four pack mules of Don Señor Johnny Armstrong stood, patiently awaiting the crack of the whip of the *arriero*, Luis. That would be the signal for the start on another long journey into the mountains. The pack mules were loaded with a varied assortment of hardware and cutlery. These articles Don Johnny traded to the interior Indians for the gold dust that they washed from the Andean streams and stored in quills and bags against his coming. It was a profitable business, and Señor Armstrong expected soon to be able to purchase the coffee plantation that he coveted.

Armstrong stood on the narrow sidewalk, exchanging garbled Spanish with old Peralto, the rich native merchant who had just charged him four prices for half a gross of pot-metal hatchets, and abridged English with Rucker, the little German who was Consul for the United States.

"Take with you, señor," said Peralto, "the blessings of the saints upon your journey."

"Better try quinine," growled Rucker through his pipe. "Take two grains every night. And don't make your trip too long, Johnny, because we haf needs of you. It is ein villainous game dot Melville play of whist, and dere is no oder substitute. *Auf wiedersehen*, und keep your eyes dot mule's ears between when you on der edge of der brecipices ride."

The bells of Luis's mule jingled and the pack train filed after the warning note. Armstrong, waved a good-bye and took his place at the tail of the procession. Up the narrow street they turned, and passed the two-story wooden Hotel Ingles, where Ives and Dawson and Richards and the rest of the chaps were dawdling on the broad piazza, reading week-old newspapers. They crowded to the railing and shouted many friendly and wise and foolish farewells after him. Across the plaza they trotted slowly past the bronze statue of Guzman Blanco, within its fence of bayoneted rifles captured from revolutionists, and out of the town between the rows of thatched huts swarming with the unclothed youth of Macuto. They plunged into the damp coolness of banana groves at length to emerge upon a bright stream, where brown women in scant raiment laundered clothes destructively upon the rocks. Then the pack train, fording the stream, attacked the sudden ascent, and bade adieu to such civilization as the coast afforded.

For weeks Armstrong, guided by Luis, followed his regular route among the mountains. After he had collected an arroba of the precious metal, winning a profit of nearly $5,000, the heads of the lightened mules were turned down-trail again. Where the head of the Guarico River springs from a great gash in the mountain-side, Luis halted the train.

"Half a day's journey from here, Señor," said he, "is the village of Tacuzama, which we have never visited. I think many ounces of gold may be procured there. It is worth the trial."

Armstrong concurred, and they turned again upward toward Tacuzama. The trail was abrupt and precipitous, mounting through a dense forest. As night fell, dark and gloomy, Luis once more halted. Before them was a black chasm, bisecting the path as far as they could see.

Luis dismounted. "There should be a bridge," he called, and ran along the cleft a distance. "It is here," he cried, and remounting, led the way. In a few moments Armstrong, heard a sound as though a thunderous drum were beating somewhere in the dark. It was the falling of the mules' hoofs upon the bridge made of strong hides lashed to poles and stretched across the chasm. Half a mile further was Tacuzama. The village was a congregation of rock and mud huts set in the profundity of an obscure wood. As they rode in a sound inconsistent with that brooding solitude met their ears. From a long, low mud hut that they were nearing rose the glorious voice of a woman in song. The words were English, the air familiar to Armstrong's memory, but not to his musical knowledge.

He slipped from his mule and stole to a narrow window in one end of the house. Peering cautiously inside, he saw, within three feet of him, a woman of marvellous, imposing beauty, clothed in a splendid loose robe of leopard skins. The hut was packed close to the small space in which she stood with the squatting figures of Indians.

The woman finished her song and seated herself close to the little window, as if grateful for the unpolluted air that entered it. When she had ceased several of the audience rose and cast little softly-falling bags at her feet. A harsh murmur—no doubt a barbarous kind of applause and comment—went through the grim assembly.

Armstrong, was used to seizing opportunities promptly. Taking advantage of the noise he called to the woman in a low but distinct voice: "Do not turn your head this way, but listen. I am an American. If you need assistance tell me how I can render it. Answer as briefly as you can."

The woman was worthy of his boldness. Only by a sudden flush of her pale cheek did she acknowledge understanding of his words. Then she spoke, scarcely moving her lips.

"I am held a prisoner by these Indians. God knows I need help. In two hours come to the little hut twenty yards toward the Mountainside. There will be a light and a red curtain in the window. There is always a guard at the door, whom you will have to overcome. For the love of heaven, do not fail to come."

The story seems to shrink from adventure and rescue and mystery. The theme is one too gentle for those brave and quickening tones. And yet it reaches as far back as time itself. It has been named "environment," which is as weak a word as any to express the unnameable kinship of man to nature, that queer fraternity that causes stones and trees and salt water and clouds to play upon our emotions. Why are we made serious and solemn and sublime by mountain heights, grave and contemplative by an abundance of overhanging trees, reduced to inconstancy and monkey capers by the ripples on a sandy beach? Did the protoplasm—but enough. The chemists are looking into the matter, and before long they will have all life in the table of the symbols.

Briefly, then, in order to confine the story within scientific bounds, John Armstrong, went to the hut, choked the Indian guard and carried away Mlle. Giraud. With her was also conveyed a number of pounds of gold dust she had collected during her six months' forced engagement in Tacuzama. The Carabobo Indians are easily the most enthusiastic lovers of music between the equator and the French Opera House in New Orleans. They are also strong believers that the advice of Emerson was good when he said: "The thing thou wantest, O discontented man—take it, and pay the price." A number of them had attended the performance of the Alcazar Opera Company in Macuto, and found Mlle. Giraud's style and technique satisfactory. They wanted her, so they took her one evening suddenly and without any fuss. They treated her with much consideration, exacting only one song recital each day. She was quite pleased at being rescued by Mr. Armstrong. So much for mystery and adventure. Now to resume the theory of the protoplasm.

John Armstrong and Mlle. Giraud rode among the Andean peaks, enveloped in their greatness and sublimity. The mightiest cousins, furthest removed, in nature's great family become conscious of the tie. Among those huge piles of primordial upheaval, amid those gigantic silences and elongated fields of distance the littlenesses of men are precipitated as one chemical throws down a sediment from another. They moved reverently, as in a temple. Their souls were uplifted in unison with the stately heights. They travelled in a zone of majesty and peace.

To Armstrong the woman seemed almost a holy thing. Yet bathed in the white, still dignity of her martyrdom that purified her earthly beauty and gave out, it seemed, an aura of transcendent loveliness, in those first hours of companionship she drew from him an adoration that was half human love, half the worship of a descended goddess.

Never yet since her rescue had she smiled. Over her dress she still wore the robe of leopard skins, for the mountain air was cold. She looked to be some splendid princess belonging to those wild and awesome altitudes. The spirit of the region chimed with hers. Her eyes were always turned upon the sombre cliffs, the blue gorges and the snow-clad turrets, looking a sublime melancholy equal to their own. At times on the journey she sang thrilling te deums and misereres that struck the true note of the hills, and made their route seem like a solemn march down a cathedral aisle. The rescued one spoke but seldom, her mood partaking of the hush of nature that surrounded them. Armstrong looked upon her as an angel. He could not bring himself to the sacrilege of attempting to woo her as other women may be wooed.

On the third day they had descended as far as the *tierra templada*, the zona of the table lands and foot hills. The mountains were receding in their rear, but still towered, exhibiting yet impressively their formidable heads. Here they met signs of man. They saw the white houses of coffee plantations gleam across the clearings. They struck into a road where they met travellers and pack-mules. Cattle were grazing on the slopes. They passed a little village where the round-eyed *niños* shrieked and called at sight of them.

Mlle. Giraud laid aside her leopard-skin robe. It seemed to be a trifle incongruous now. In the mountains it had appeared fitting and natural. And if Armstrong was not mistaken she laid aside with it something of the high dignity of her demeanour. As the country became more populous and significant of comfortable life he saw, with a feeling of joy, that the exalted princess and priestess of the Andean peaks was changing to a woman—an earth woman, but no less enticing. A little colour crept to the surface of her marble cheek. She arranged the conventional dress that the removal of the robe now disclosed with the solicitous touch of one who is conscious of the eyes of others. She smoothed the careless sweep of her hair. A mundane interest, long latent in the chilling atmosphere of the ascetic peaks, showed in her eyes.

This thaw in his divinity sent Armstrong's heart going faster. So might an Arctic explorer thrill at his first ken of green fields and liquescent waters. They were on a lower plane of earth and life and were succumbing to its peculiar, subtle influence. The austerity of the hills no longer thinned the air they breathed. About them was the breath of fruit and corn and builded homes, the comfortable smell of smoke and warm earth and the consolations man has placed between himself and the dust of his brother earth from which he sprung. While traversing those awful mountains, Mile. Giraud had seemed to be wrapped in their spirit of reverent reserve. Was this that same woman—now palpitating, warm, eager, throbbing with conscious life and charm, feminine to her finger-tips? Pondering over this, Armstrong felt certain misgivings intrude upon his thoughts. He wished he could stop there with this changing creature, descending no farther. Here was the elevation and environment to which her nature seemed to respond with its best. He feared to go down upon the man-dominated levels. Would her spirit not yield still further in that artificial zone to which they were descending?

Now from a little plateau they saw the sea flash at the edge of the green lowlands. Mile. Giraud gave a little, catching sigh.

"Oh! look, Mr. Armstrong, there is the sea! Isn't it lovely? I'm so tired of mountains." She heaved a pretty shoulder in a gesture of repugnance. "Those horrid Indians! Just think of what I suffered! Although I suppose

I attained my ambition of becoming a stellar attraction, I wouldn't care to repeat the engagement. It was very nice of you to bring me away. Tell me, Mr. Armstrong—honestly, now—do I look such an awful, awful fright? I haven't looked into a mirror, you know, for months."

Armstrong made answer according to his changed moods. Also he laid his hand upon hers as it rested upon the horn of her saddle. Luis was at the head of the pack train and could not see. She allowed it to remain there, and her eyes smiled frankly into his.

Then at sundown they dropped upon the coast level under the palms and lemons among the vivid greens and scarlets and ochres of the *tierra caliente*. They rode into Macuto, and saw the line of volatile bathers frolicking in the surf. The mountains were very far away.

Mlle. Giraud's eyes were shining with a joy that could not have existed under the chaperonage of the mountain-tops. There were other spirits calling to her—nymphs of the orange groves, pixies from the chattering surf, imps, born of the music, the perfumes, colours and the insinuating presence of humanity. She laughed aloud, musically, at a sudden thought.

"Won't there be a sensation?" she called to Armstrong. "Don't I wish I had an engagement just now, though! What a picnic the press agent would have! 'Held a prisoner by a band of savage Indians subdued by the spell of her wonderful voice'—wouldn't that make great stuff? But I guess I quit the game winner, anyhow—there ought to be a couple of thousand dollars in that sack of gold dust I collected as encores, don't you think?"

He left her at the door of the little Hotel de Buen Descansar, where she had stopped before. Two hours later he returned to the hotel. He glanced in at the open door of the little combined reception room and cafe.

Half a dozen of Macuto's representative social and official *caballeros* were distributed about the room. Señor Villablanca, the wealthy rubber concessionist, reposed his fat figure on two chairs, with an emollient smile beaming upon his chocolate-coloured face. Guilbert, the French mining engineer, leered through his polished nose-glasses. Colonel Mendez, of the regular army, in gold-laced uniform and fatuous grin, was busily extracting corks from champagne bottles. Other patterns of Macutian gallantry and fashion pranced and posed. The air was hazy with cigarette smoke. Wine dripped upon the floor.

Perched upon a table in the centre of the room in an attitude of easy preëminence was Mlle. Giraud. A chic costume of white lawn and cherry ribbons supplanted her travelling garb. There was a suggestion of lace, and a frill or two, with a discreet, small implication of hand-embroidered pink hosiery. Upon her lap rested a guitar. In her face was the light of resurrection, the peace of elysium attained through fire and suffering. She was singing to a lively accompaniment a little song:

> *"When you see de big round moon*
> *Comin' up like a balloon,*
> *Dis nigger skips fur to kiss de lips*
> *Ob his stylish, black-faced coon."*

The singer caught sight of Armstrong.

"Hi! there, Johnny," she called; "I've been expecting you for an hour. What kept you? Gee! but these smoked guys are the slowest you ever saw. They ain't on, at all. Come along in, and I'll make this coffee-coloured old sport with the gold epaulettes open one for you right off the ice."

"Thank you," said Armstrong; "not just now, I believe. I've several things to attend to."

He walked out and down the street, and met Rucker coming up from the Consulate.

"Play you a game of billiards," said Armstrong. "I want something to take the taste of the sea level out of my mouth."

VI

"GIRL"

In gilt letters on the ground glass of the door of room No. 962 were the words: "Robbins & Hartley, Brokers." The clerks had gone. It was past five, and with the solid tramp of a drove of prize Percherons, scrub-women were invading the cloud-capped twenty-story office building. A puff of red-hot air flavoured with lemon peelings, soft-coal smoke and train oil came in through the half-open windows.

Robbins, fifty, something of an overweight beau, and addicted to first nights and hotel palm-rooms, pretended to be envious of his partner's commuter's joys.

"Going to be something doing in the humidity line to-night," he said. "You out-of-town chaps will be the people, with your katydids and moonlight and long drinks and things out on the front porch."

Hartley, twenty-nine, serious, thin, good-looking, nervous, sighed and frowned a little.

"Yes," said he, "we always have cool nights in Floralhurst, especially in the winter."

A man with an air of mystery came in the door and went up to Hartley.

"I've found where she lives," he announced in the portentous half-whisper that makes the detective at work a marked being to his fellow men.

Hartley scowled him into a state of dramatic silence and quietude. But by that time Robbins had got his cane and set his tie pin to his liking, and with a debonair nod went out to his metropolitan amusements.

"Here is the address," said the detective in a natural tone, being deprived of an audience to foil.

Hartley took the leaf torn out of the sleuth's dingy memorandum book. On it were pencilled the words "Vivienne Arlington, No. 341 East ——th Street, care of Mrs. McComus."

"Moved there a week ago," said the detective. "Now, if you want any shadowing done, Mr. Hartley, I can do you as fine a job in that line as anybody in the city. It will be only $7 a day and expenses. Can send in a daily typewritten report, covering—"

"You needn't go on," interrupted the broker. "It isn't a case of that kind. I merely wanted the address. How much shall I pay you?"

"One day's work," said the sleuth. "A tenner will cover it."

Hartley paid the man and dismissed him. Then he left the office and boarded a Broadway car. At the first large crosstown artery of travel he took an eastbound car that deposited him in a decaying avenue, whose ancient structures once sheltered the pride and glory of the town.

Walking a few squares, he came to the building that he sought. It was a new flathouse, bearing carved upon its cheap stone portal its sonorous name, "The Vallambrosa." Fire-escapes zigzagged down its front—these laden with household goods, drying clothes, and squalling children evicted by the midsummer heat. Here and there a pale rubber plant peeped from the miscellaneous mass, as if wondering to what kingdom it belonged—vegetable, animal or artificial.

Hartley pressed the "McComus" button. The door latch clicked spasmodically—now hospitably, now doubtfully, as though in anxiety whether it might be admitting friends or duns. Hartley entered and began to climb the stairs after the manner of those who seek their friends in city flat-houses—which is the manner of a boy who climbs an apple-tree, stopping when he comes upon what he wants.

On the fourth floor he saw Vivienne standing in an open door. She invited him inside, with a nod and a bright, genuine smile. She placed a chair for him near a window, and poised herself gracefully upon the edge of one those Jekyll-and-Hyde pieces of furniture that are masked and mysteriously hooded, unguessable bulks by day and inquisitorial racks of torture by night.

Hartley cast a quick, critical, appreciative glance at her before speaking, and told himself that his taste in choosing had been flawless.

Vivienne was about twenty-one. She was of the purest Saxon type. Her hair was a ruddy golden, each filament of the neatly gathered mass shining with its own lustre and delicate graduation of colour. In perfect harmony were her ivory-clear complexion and deep sea-blue eyes that looked upon the world with the ingenuous calmness of a mermaid or the pixie of an undiscovered mountain stream. Her frame was strong and yet possessed the grace of absolute naturalness. And yet with all her Northern clearness and frankness of line and colouring, there seemed to be something of the tropics in her—something of languor in the droop of her pose, of love of ease in her ingenious complacency of satisfaction and comfort in the mere act of breathing—something that seemed to claim for her a right as a perfect work of nature to exist and be admired equally with a rare flower or some beautiful, milk-white dove among its sober-hued companions.

She was dressed in a white waist and dark skirt—that discreet masquerade of goose-girl and duchess.

"Vivienne," said Hartley, looking at her pleadingly, "you did not answer my last letter. It was only by nearly a week's search that I found where you had moved to. Why have you kept me in suspense when you knew how anxiously I was waiting to see you and hear from you?"

The girl looked out the window dreamily.

"Mr. Hartley," she said hesitatingly, "I hardly know what to say to you. I realize all the advantages of your offer, and sometimes I feel sure that I could be contented with you. But, again, I am doubtful. I was born a city girl, and I am afraid to bind myself to a quiet suburban life."

"My dear girl," said Hartley, ardently, "have I not told you that you shall have everything that your heart can desire that is in my power to give you? You shall come to the city for the theatres, for shopping and to visit your friends as often as you care to. You can trust me, can you not?"

"To the fullest," she said, turning her frank eyes upon him with a smile. "I know you are the kindest of men, and that the girl you get will be a lucky one. I learned all about you when I was at the Montgomerys'."

"Ah!" exclaimed Hartley, with a tender, reminiscent light in his eye; "I remember well the evening I first saw you at the Montgomerys'. Mrs. Montgomery was sounding your praises to me all the evening. And she hardly did you justice. I shall never forget that supper. Come, Vivienne, promise me. I want you. You'll never regret coming with me. No one else will ever give you as pleasant a home."

The girl sighed and looked down at her folded hands.

A sudden jealous suspicion seized Hartley.

"Tell me, Vivienne," he asked, regarding her keenly, "is there another—is there some one else?"

A rosy flush crept slowly over her fair cheeks and neck.

"You shouldn't ask that, Mr. Hartley," she said, in some confusion. "But I will tell you. There is one other—but he has no right—I have promised him nothing."

"His name?" demanded Hartley, sternly.

"Townsend."

"Rafford Townsend!" exclaimed Hartley, with a grim tightening of his jaw. "How did that man come to know you? After all I've done for him—"

"His auto has just stopped below," said Vivienne, bending over the window-sill. "He's coming for his answer. Oh I don't know what to do!"

The bell in the flat kitchen whirred. Vivienne hurried to press the latch button.

"Stay here," said Hartley. "I will meet him in the hall."

Townsend, looking like a Spanish grandee in his light tweeds, Panama hat and curling black mustache, came up the stairs three at a time. He stopped at sight of Hartley and looked foolish.

"Go back," said Hartley, firmly, pointing downstairs with his forefinger.

"Hullo!" said Townsend, feigning surprise. "What's up? What are you doing here, old man?"

"Go back," repeated Hartley, inflexibly. "The Law of the Jungle. Do you want the Pack to tear you in pieces? The kill is mine."

"I came here to see a plumber about the bathroom connections," said Townsend, bravely.

"All right," said Hartley. "You shall have that lying plaster to stick upon your traitorous soul. But, go back." Townsend went downstairs, leaving a bitter word to be wafted up the draught of the staircase. Hartley went back to his wooing.

"Vivienne," said he, masterfully. "I have got to have you. I will take no more refusals or dilly-dallying."

"When do you want me?" she asked.

"Now. As soon as you can get ready."

She stood calmly before him and looked him in the eye.

"Do you think for one moment," she said, "that I would enter your home while Héloise is there?"

Hartley cringed as if from an unexpected blow. He folded his arms and paced the carpet once or twice.

"She shall go," he declared grimly. Drops stood upon his brow. "Why should I let that woman make my life miserable? Never have I seen one day of freedom from trouble since I have known her. You are right, Vivienne. Héloise must be sent away before I can take you home. But she shall go. I have decided. I will turn her from my doors."

"When will you do this?" asked the girl.

Hartley clinched his teeth and bent his brows together.

"To-night," he said, resolutely. "I will send her away to-night."

"Then," said Vivienne, "my answer is 'yes.' Come for me when you will."

She looked into his eyes with a sweet, sincere light in her own. Hartley could scarcely believe that her surrender was true, it was so swift and complete.

"Promise me," he said feelingly, "on your word and honour."

"On my word and honour," repeated Vivienne, softly.

At the door he turned and gazed at her happily, but yet as one who scarcely trusts the foundations of his joy.

"To-morrow," he said, with a forefinger of reminder uplifted.

"To-morrow," she repeated with a smile of truth and candour.

In an hour and forty minutes Hartley stepped off the train at Floralhurst. A brisk walk of ten minutes brought him to the gate of a handsome two-story cottage set upon a wide and well-tended lawn. Halfway to the house he was met by a woman with jet-black braided hair and flowing white summer gown, who half strangled him without apparent cause.

When they stepped into the hall she said:

"Mamma's here. The auto is coming for her in half an hour. She came to dinner, but there's no dinner."

"I've something to tell you," said Hartley. "I thought to break it to you gently, but since your mother is here we may as well out with it."

He stooped and whispered something at her ear.

His wife screamed. Her mother came running into the hall. The dark-haired woman screamed again—the joyful scream of a well-beloved and petted woman.

"Oh, mamma!" she cried ecstatically, "what do you think? Vivienne is coming to cook for us! She is the one that stayed with the Montgomerys a whole year. And now, Billy, dear," she concluded, "you must go right down into the kitchen and discharge Héloise. She has been drunk again the whole day long."

VII

SOCIOLOGY IN SERGE AND STRAW

The season of irresponsibility is at hand. Come, let us twine round our brows wreaths of poison ivy (that is for idiocy), and wander hand in hand with sociology in the summer fields.

Likely as not the world is flat. The wise men have tried to prove that it is round, with indifferent success. They pointed out to us a ship going to sea, and bade us observe that, at length, the convexity of the earth hid from our view all but the vessel's topmast. But we picked up a telescope and looked, and saw the decks and hull again. Then the wise men said: "Oh, pshaw! anyhow, the variation of the intersection of the equator and the ecliptic proves it." We could not see this through our telescope, so we remained silent. But it stands to reason that, if the world were round, the queues of Chinamen would stand straight up from their heads instead of hanging down their backs, as travellers assure us they do.

Another hot-weather corroboration of the flat theory is the fact that all of life, as we know it, moves in little, unavailing circles. More justly than to anything else, it can be likened to the game of baseball. Crack! we hit the ball, and away we go. If we earn a run (in life we call it success) we get back to the home plate and sit upon a bench. If we are thrown out, we walk back to the home plate—and sit upon a bench.

The circumnavigators of the alleged globe may have sailed the rim of a watery circle back to the same port again. The truly great return at the high tide of their attainments to the simplicity of a child. The billionaire sits down at his mahogany to his bowl of bread and milk. When you reach the end of your career, just take down the sign "Goal" and look at the other side of it. You will find "Beginning Point" there. It has been reversed while you were going around the track.

But this is humour, and must be stopped. Let us get back to the serious questions that arise whenever Sociology turns summer boarder. You are invited to consider the scene of the story—wild, Atlantic waves, thundering against a wooded and rock-bound shore—in the Greater City of New York.

The town of Fishampton, on the south shore of Long Island, is noted for its clam fritters and the summer residence of the Van Plushvelts.

The Van Plushvelts have a hundred million dollars, and their name is a household word with tradesmen and photographers.

On the fifteenth of June the Van Plushvelts boarded up the front door of their city house, carefully deposited their cat on the sidewalk, instructed the caretaker not to allow it to eat any of the ivy on the walls, and whizzed away in a 40-horse-power to Fishampton to stray alone in the shade—Amaryllis not being in their class. If you are a subscriber to the *Toadies' Magazine*, you have often—You say you are not? Well, you buy it at a news-stand, thinking that the newsdealer is not wise to you. But he knows about it all. HE knows—HE knows! I say that you have often seen in the *Toadies' Magazine* pictures of the Van Plushvelts' summer home; so it will not be described here. Our business is with young Haywood Van Plushvelt, sixteen years old, heir to the century of millions, darling of the financial gods and great grandson of Peter Van Plushvelt, former owner of a particularly fine cabbage patch that has been ruined by an intrusive lot of downtown skyscrapers.

One afternoon young Haywood Van Plushvelt strolled out between the granite gate posts of "Dolce far Niente"—that's what they called the place; and it was an improvement on dolce Far Rockaway, I can tell you.

Haywood walked down into the village. He was human, after all, and his prospective millions weighed upon him. Wealth had wreaked upon him its direfullest. He was the product of private tutors. Even under his first hobby-horse had tan bark been strewn. He had been born with a gold spoon, lobster fork and fish-set in his mouth. For which I hope, later, to submit justification, I must ask your consideration of his haberdashery and tailoring.

Young Fortunatus was dressed in a neat suit of dark blue serge, a neat, white straw hat, neat low-cut tan shoes, of the well-known "immaculate" trade mark, a neat, narrow four-in-hand tie, and carried a slender, neat, bamboo cane.

Down Persimmon Street (there's never tree north of Hagerstown, Md.) came from the village "Smoky" Dodson, fifteen and a half, worst boy in Fishampton. "Smoky" was dressed in a ragged red sweater, wrecked and weather-worn golf cap, run-over shoes, and trousers of the "serviceable" brand. Dust, clinging to the moisture induced by free exercise, darkened wide areas of his face. "Smoky" carried a baseball bat, and a league ball that advertised itself in the rotundity of his trousers pocket. Haywood stopped and passed the time of day.

"Going to play ball?" he asked.

"Smoky's" eyes and countenance confronted him with a frank blue-and-freckled scrutiny.

"Me?" he said, with deadly mildness; "sure not. Can't you see I've got a divin' suit on? I'm goin' up in a submarine balloon to catch butterflies with a two-inch auger.

"Excuse me," said Haywood, with the insulting politeness of his caste, "for mistaking you for a gentleman. I might have known better."

"How might you have known better if you thought I was one?" said "Smoky," unconsciously a logician.

"By your appearance," said Haywood. "No gentleman is dirty, ragged and a liar."

"Smoky" hooted once like a ferry-boat, spat on his hand, got a firm grip on his baseball bat and then dropped it against the fence.

"Say," said he, "I knows you. You're the pup that belongs in that swell private summer sanitarium for city-guys over there. I seen you come out of the gate. You can't bluff nobody because you're rich. And because you got on swell clothes. Arabella! Yah!"

"Ragamuffin!" said Haywood.

"Smoky" picked up a fence-rail splinter and laid it on his shoulder.

"Dare you to knock it off," he challenged.

"I wouldn't soil my hands with you," said the aristocrat.

"'Fraid," said "Smoky" concisely. "Youse city-ducks ain't got the sand. I kin lick you with one-hand."

"I don't wish to have any trouble with you," said Haywood. "I asked you a civil question; and you replied, like a—like a—a cad."

"Wot's a cad?" asked "Smoky."

"A cad is a disagreeable person," answered Haywood, "who lacks manners and doesn't know his place. They sometimes play baseball."

"I can tell you what a mollycoddle is," said "Smoky." "It's a monkey dressed up by its mother and sent out to pick daisies on the lawn."

"When you have the honour to refer to the members of my family," said Haywood, with some dim ideas of a code in his mind, "you'd better leave the ladies out of your remarks."

"Ho! ladies!" mocked the rude one. "I say ladies! I know what them rich women in the city does. They, drink cocktails and swear and give parties to gorillas. The papers say so."

Then Haywood knew that it must be. He took off his coat, folded it neatly and laid it on the roadside grass, placed his hat upon it and began to unknot his blue silk tie.

"Hadn't yer better ring fer yer maid, Arabella?" taunted "Smoky." "Wot yer going to do—go to bed?"

"I'm going to give you a good trouncing," said the hero. He did not hesitate, although the enemy was far beneath him socially. He remembered that his father once thrashed a cabman, and the papers gave it two columns, first page. And the *Toadies' Magazine* had a special article on Upper Cuts by the Upper Classes, and ran new pictures of the Van Plushvelt country seat, at Fishampton.

"Wot's trouncing?" asked "Smoky," suspiciously. "I don't want your old clothes. I'm no—oh, you mean to scrap! My, my! I won't do a thing to mamma's pet. Criminy! I'd hate to be a hand-laundered thing like you.

"Smoky" waited with some awkwardness for his adversary to prepare for battle. His own decks were always clear for action. When he should spit upon the palm of his terrible right it was equivalent to "You may fire now, Gridley."

The hated patrician advanced, with his shirt sleeves neatly rolled up. "Smoky" waited, in an attitude of ease, expecting the affair to be conducted according to Fishampton's rules of war. These allowed combat to be prefaced by stigma, recrimination, epithet, abuse and insult gradually increasing in emphasis and degree. After a round of these "you're anothers" would come the chip knocked from the shoulder, or the advance across the "dare" line drawn with a toe on the ground. Next light taps given and taken, these also increasing in force until finally the blood was up and fists going at their best.

But Haywood did not know Fishampton's rules. Noblesse oblige kept a faint smile on his face as he walked slowly up to "Smoky" and said:

"Going to play ball?"

"Smoky" quickly understood this to be a putting of the previous question, giving him the chance to make practical apology by answering it with civility and relevance.

"Listen this time," said he. "I'm goin' skatin' on the river. Don't you see me automobile with Chinese lanterns on it standin' and waitin' for me?"

Haywood knocked him down.

"Smoky" felt wronged. To thus deprive him of preliminary wrangle and objurgation was to send an armoured knight full tilt against a crashing lance without permitting him first to caracole around the list to the flourish of trumpets. But he scrambled up and fell upon his foe, head, feet and fists.

The fight lasted one round of an hour and ten minutes. It was lengthened until it was more like a war or a family feud than a fight. Haywood had learned some of the science of boxing and wrestling from his tutors, but these he discarded for the more instinctive methods of battle handed down by the cave-dwelling Van Plushvelts.

So, when he found himself, during the mêlée, seated upon the kicking and roaring "Smoky's" chest, he improved the opportunity by vigorously kneading handfuls of sand and soil into his adversary's ears, eyes and mouth, and when "Smoky" got the proper leg hold and "turned" him, he fastened both hands in the Plushvelt hair and pounded the Plushvelt head against the lap of mother earth. Of course, the strife was not incessantly active. There were seasons when one sat upon the other, holding him down, while each blew like a grampus, spat out the more inconveniently large sections of gravel and earth and strove to subdue the spirit of his opponent with a frightful and soul-paralyzing glare.

At last, it seemed that in the language of the ring, their efforts lacked steam. They broke away, and each disappeared in a cloud as he brushed away the dust of the conflict. As soon as his breath permitted, Haywood walked close to "Smoky" and said:

"Going to play ball?"

"Smoky" looked pensively at the sky, at his bat lying on the ground, and at the "leaguer" rounding his pocket.

"Sure," he said, offhandedly. "The 'Yellowjackets' plays the 'Long Islands.' I'm cap'n of the 'Long Islands.'"

"I guess I didn't mean to say you were ragged," said Haywood. "But you are dirty, you know."

"Sure," said "Smoky." "Yer get that way knockin' around. Say, I don't believe them New York papers about ladies drinkin' and havin' monkeys dinin' at the table with 'em. I guess they're lies, like they print about people eatin' out of silver plates, and ownin' dogs that cost $100."

"Certainly," said Haywood. "What do you play on your team?"

"Ketcher. Ever play any?"

"Never in my life," said Haywood. "I've never known any fellows except one or two of my cousins."

"Jer like to learn? We're goin' to have a practice-game before the match. Wanter come along? I'll put yer in left-field, and yer won't be long ketchin' on."

"I'd like it bully," said Haywood. "I've always wanted to play baseball."

The ladies' maids of New York and the families of Western mine owners with social ambitions will remember well the sensation that was created by the report that the young multi-millionaire, Haywood Van Plushvelt, was playing ball with the village youths of Fishampton. It was conceded that the millennium of democracy had come. Reporters and photographers swarmed to the island. The papers printed half-page pictures of him as short-stop stopping a hot grounder. The *Toadies' Magazine* got out a Bat and Ball number that covered the subject historically, beginning with the vampire bat and ending with the Patriarchs' ball—illustrated with interior views of the Van Plushvelt country seat. Ministers, educators and sociologists everywhere hailed the event as the tocsin call that proclaimed the universal brotherhood of man.

One afternoon I was reclining under the trees near the shore at Fishampton in the esteemed company of an eminent, bald-headed young sociologist. By way of note it may be inserted that all sociologists are more or less bald, and exactly thirty-two. Look 'em over.

The sociologist was citing the Van Plushvelt case as the most important "uplift" symptom of a generation, and as an excuse for his own existence.

Immediately before us were the village baseball grounds. And now came the sportive youth of Fishampton and distributed themselves, shouting, about the diamond.

"There," said the sociologist, pointing, "there is young Van Plushvelt."

I raised myself (so far a cosycophant with Mary Ann) and gazed.

Young Van Plushvelt sat upon the ground. He was dressed in a ragged red sweater, wrecked and weather-worn golf cap, run-over shoes, and trousers of the "serviceable" brand. Dust clinging to the moisture induced by free exercise, darkened wide areas of his face.

"That is he," repeated the sociologist. If he had said "him" I could have been less vindictive.

On a bench, with an air, sat the young millionaire's chum.

He was dressed in a neat suit of dark blue serge, a neat white straw hat, neat low-cut tan shoes, linen of the well-known "immaculate" trade mark, a neat, narrow four-in-hand tie, and carried a slender, neat bamboo cane.

I laughed loudly and vulgarly.

"What you want to do," said I to the sociologist, "is to establish a reformatory for the Logical Vicious Circle. Or else I've got wheels. It looks to me as if things are running round and round in circles instead of getting anywhere."

"What do you mean?" asked the man of progress.

"Why, look what he has done to 'Smoky'," I replied.

"You will always be a fool," said my friend, the sociologist, getting up and walking away.

VIII

The Ransom of Red Chief

It looked like a good thing: but wait till I tell you. We were down South, in Alabama—Bill Driscoll and myself—when this kidnapping idea struck us. It was, as Bill afterward expressed it, "during a moment of temporary mental apparition"; but we didn't find that out till later.

There was a town down there, as flat as a flannel-cake, and called Summit, of course. It contained inhabitants of as undeleterious and self-satisfied a class of peasantry as ever clustered around a Maypole.

Bill and me had a joint capital of about six hundred dollars, and we needed just two thousand dollars more to pull off a fraudulent town-lot scheme in Western Illinois with. We talked it over on the front steps of the hotel. Philoprogenitiveness, says we, is strong in semi-rural communities; therefore and for other reasons, a kidnapping project ought to do better there than in the radius of newspapers that send reporters out in plain clothes to stir up talk about such things. We knew that Summit couldn't get after us with anything stronger than constables and maybe some lackadaisical bloodhounds and a diatribe or two in the *Weekly Farmers' Budget*. So, it looked good.

We selected for our victim the only child of a prominent citizen named Ebenezer Dorset. The father was respectable and tight, a mortgage fancier and a stern, upright collection-plate passer and forecloser. The kid was a boy of ten, with bas-relief freckles, and hair the colour of the cover of the magazine you buy at the news-stand when you want to catch a train. Bill and me figured that Ebenezer would melt down for a ransom of two thousand dollars to a cent. But wait till I tell you.

About two miles from Summit was a little mountain, covered with a dense cedar brake. On the rear elevation of this mountain was a cave. There we stored provisions. One evening after sundown, we drove in a buggy past old Dorset's house. The kid was in the street, throwing rocks at a kitten on the opposite fence.

"Hey, little boy!" says Bill, "would you like to have a bag of candy and a nice ride?"

The boy catches Bill neatly in the eye with a piece of brick.

"That will cost the old man an extra five hundred dollars," says Bill, climbing over the wheel.

That boy put up a fight like a welter-weight cinnamon bear; but, at last, we got him down in the bottom of the buggy and drove away. We took him up to the cave and I hitched the horse in the cedar brake. After dark I drove the buggy to the little village, three miles away, where we had hired it, and walked back to the mountain.

Bill was pasting court-plaster over the scratches and bruises on his features. There was a fire burning behind the big rock at the entrance of the cave, and the boy was watching a pot of boiling coffee, with two buzzard tail-feathers stuck in his red hair. He points a stick at me when I come up, and says:

"Ha! cursed paleface, do you dare to enter the camp of Red Chief, the terror of the plains?

"He's all right now," says Bill, rolling up his trousers and examining some bruises on his shins. "We're playing Indian. We're making Buffalo Bill's show look like magic-lantern views of Palestine in the town hall. I'm Old Hank, the Trapper, Red Chief's captive, and I'm to be scalped at daybreak. By Geronimo! that kid can kick hard."

Yes, sir, that boy seemed to be having the time of his life. The fun of camping out in a cave had made him forget that he was a captive himself. He immediately christened me Snake-eye, the Spy, and announced that, when his braves returned from the warpath, I was to be broiled at the stake at the rising of the sun.

Then we had supper; and he filled his mouth full of bacon and bread and gravy, and began to talk. He made a during-dinner speech something like this:

"I like this fine. I never camped out before; but I had a pet 'possum once, and I was nine last birthday. I hate to go to school. Rats ate up sixteen of Jimmy Talbot's aunt's speckled hen's eggs. Are there any real Indians in these woods? I want some more gravy. Does the trees moving make the wind blow? We had five puppies. What makes your nose so red, Hank? My father has lots of money. Are the stars hot? I whipped Ed Walker twice, Saturday. I don't like girls. You dassent catch toads unless with a string. Do oxen make any noise? Why are oranges round? Have you got beds to sleep on in this cave? Amos Murray has got six toes. A parrot can talk, but a monkey or a fish can't. How many does it take to make twelve?"

Every few minutes he would remember that he was a pesky redskin, and pick up his stick rifle and tiptoe to the mouth of the cave to rubber for the scouts of the hated paleface. Now and then he would let out a war-whoop that made Old Hank the Trapper shiver. That boy had Bill terrorized from the start.

"Red Chief," says I to the kid, "would you like to go home?"

"Aw, what for?" says he. "I don't have any fun at home. I hate to go to school. I like to camp out. You won't take me back home again, Snake-eye, will you?"

"Not right away," says I. "We'll stay here in the cave a while."

"All right!" says he. "That'll be fine. I never had such fun in all my life."

We went to bed about eleven o'clock. We spread down some wide blankets and quilts and put Red Chief between us. We weren't afraid he'd run away. He kept us awake for three hours, jumping up and reaching for his rifle and screeching: "Hist! pard," in mine and Bill's ears, as the fancied crackle of a twig or the rustle of a leaf revealed to his young imagination the stealthy approach of the outlaw band. At last, I fell into a troubled sleep, and dreamed that I had been kidnapped and chained to a tree by a ferocious pirate with red hair.

Just at daybreak, I was awakened by a series of awful screams from Bill. They weren't yells, or howls, or shouts, or whoops, or yawps, such as you'd expect from a manly set of vocal organs—they were simply indecent, terrifying, humiliating screams, such as women emit when they see ghosts or caterpillars. It's an awful thing to hear a strong, desperate, fat man scream incontinently in a cave at daybreak.

I jumped up to see what the matter was. Red Chief was sitting on Bill's chest, with one hand twined in Bill's hair. In the other he had the sharp case-knife we used for slicing bacon; and he was industriously and realistically trying to take Bill's scalp, according to the sentence that had been pronounced upon him the evening before.

I got the knife away from the kid and made him lie down again. But, from that moment, Bill's spirit was broken. He laid down on his side of the bed, but he never closed an eye again in sleep as long as that boy was with us. I dozed off for a while, but along toward sun-up I remembered that Red Chief had said I was to be burned at the stake at the rising of the sun. I wasn't nervous or afraid; but I sat up and lit my pipe and leaned against a rock.

"What you getting up so soon for, Sam?" asked Bill.

"Me?" says I. "Oh, I got a kind of a pain in my shoulder. I thought sitting up would rest it."

"You're a liar!" says Bill. "You're afraid. You was to be burned at sunrise, and you was afraid he'd do it. And he would, too, if he could find a match. Ain't it awful, Sam? Do you think anybody will pay out money to get a little imp like that back home?"

"Sure," said I. "A rowdy kid like that is just the kind that parents dote on. Now, you and the Chief get up and cook breakfast, while I go up on the top of this mountain and reconnoitre."

I went up on the peak of the little mountain and ran my eye over the contiguous vicinity. Over toward Summit I expected to see the sturdy yeomanry of the village armed with scythes and pitchforks beating the countryside for the dastardly kidnappers. But what I saw was a peaceful landscape dotted with one man ploughing with a dun mule. Nobody was dragging the creek; no couriers dashed hither and yon, bringing tidings of no news to the distracted parents. There was a sylvan attitude of somnolent sleepiness pervading that section of the external outward surface of Alabama that lay exposed to my view. "Perhaps," says I to myself, "it has not yet been discovered that the wolves have borne away the tender lambkin from the fold. Heaven help the wolves!" says I, and I went down the mountain to breakfast.

When I got to the cave I found Bill backed up against the side of it, breathing hard, and the boy threatening to smash him with a rock half as big as a cocoanut.

"He put a red-hot boiled potato down my back," explained Bill, "and then mashed it with his foot; and I boxed his ears. Have you got a gun about you, Sam?"

I took the rock away from the boy and kind of patched up the argument. "I'll fix you," says the kid to Bill. "No man ever yet struck the Red Chief but what he got paid for it. You better beware!"

After breakfast the kid takes a piece of leather with strings wrapped around it out of his pocket and goes outside the cave unwinding it.

"What's he up to now?" says Bill, anxiously. "You don't think he'll run away, do you, Sam?"

"No fear of it," says I. "He don't seem to be much of a home body. But we've got to fix up some plan about the ransom. There don't seem to be much excitement around Summit on account of his disappearance; but maybe they haven't realized yet that he's gone. His folks may think he's spending the night with Aunt Jane or one of the neighbours. Anyhow, he'll be missed to-day. To-night we must get a message to his father demanding the two thousand dollars for his return."

Just then we heard a kind Of war-whoop, such as David might have emitted when he knocked out the champion Goliath. It was a sling that Red Chief had pulled out of his pocket, and he was whirling it around his head.

I dodged, and heard a heavy thud and a kind of a sigh from Bill, like a horse gives out when you take his saddle off. A niggerhead rock the size of an egg had caught Bill just behind his left ear. He loosened himself all over and fell in the fire across the frying pan of hot water for washing the dishes. I dragged him out and poured cold water on his head for half an hour.

By and by, Bill sits up and feels behind his ear and says: "Sam, do you know who my favourite Biblical character is?"

"Take it easy," says I. "You'll come to your senses presently."

"King Herod," says he. "You won't go away and leave me here alone, will you, Sam?"

I went out and caught that boy and shook him until his freckles rattled.

"If you don't behave," says I, "I'll take you straight home. Now, are you going to be good, or not?"

"I was only funning," says he sullenly. "I didn't mean to hurt Old Hank. But what did he hit me for? I'll behave, Snake-eye, if you won't send me home, and if you'll let me play the Black Scout to-day."

"I don't know the game," says I. "That's for you and Mr. Bill to decide. He's your playmate for the day. I'm going away for a while, on business. Now, you come in and make friends with him and say you are sorry for hurting him, or home you go, at once."

I made him and Bill shake hands, and then I took Bill aside and told him I was going to Poplar Cove, a little village three miles from the cave, and find out what I could about how the kidnapping had been regarded in Summit. Also, I thought it best to send a peremptory letter to old man Dorset that day, demanding the ransom and dictating how it should be paid.

"You know, Sam," says Bill, "I've stood by you without batting an eye in earthquakes, fire and flood—in poker games, dynamite outrages, police raids, train robberies and cyclones. I never lost my nerve yet till we kidnapped that two-legged skyrocket of a kid. He's got me going. You won't leave me long with him, will you, Sam?"

"I'll be back some time this afternoon," says I. "You must keep the boy amused and quiet till I return. And now we'll write the letter to old Dorset."

Bill and I got paper and pencil and worked on the letter while Red Chief, with a blanket wrapped around him, strutted up and down, guarding the mouth of the cave. Bill begged me tearfully to make the ransom fifteen hundred dollars instead of two thousand. "I ain't attempting," says he, "to decry the celebrated moral aspect of parental affection, but we're dealing with humans, and it ain't human for anybody to give up two thousand dollars for that forty-pound chunk of freckled wildcat. I'm willing to take a chance at fifteen hundred dollars. You can charge the difference up to me."

So, to relieve Bill, I acceded, and we collaborated a letter that ran this way:

> *Ebenezer Dorset, Esq:*
> We have your boy concealed in a place far from Summit. It is useless for you or the most skilful detectives to attempt to find him. Absolutely, the only terms on which you can have him restored to you are these: We demand fifteen hundred dollars in large bills for his return; the money to be left at midnight to-night at the same spot and in the same box as your reply—as hereinafter described. If you agree to these terms, send your answer in writing by a solitary messenger to-night at half-past eight o'clock. After crossing Owl Creek, on the road to Poplar Cove, there are three large trees about a hundred yards apart, close to the fence of the wheat field on the right-hand side. At the bottom of the fence-post, opposite the third tree, will be found a small pasteboard box.
> The messenger will place the answer in this box and return immediately to Summit.
> If you attempt any treachery or fail to comply with our demand as stated, you will never see your boy again.
> If you pay the money as demanded, he will be returned to you safe and well within three hours. These terms are final, and if you do not accede to them no further communication will be attempted.
>
> TWO DESPERATE MEN

I addressed this letter to Dorset, and put it in my pocket. As I was about to start, the kid comes up to me and says:

"Aw, Snake-eye, you said I could play the Black Scout while you was gone."

"Play it, of course," says I. "Mr. Bill will play with you. What kind of a game is it?"

"I'm the Black Scout," says Red Chief, "and I have to ride to the stockade to warn the settlers that the Indians are coming. I'm tired of playing Indian myself. I want to be the Black Scout."

"All right," says I. "It sounds harmless to me. I guess Mr. Bill will help you foil the pesky savages."

"What am I to do?" asks Bill, looking at the kid suspiciously.

"You are the hoss," says Black Scout. "Get down on your hands and knees. How can I ride to the stockade without a hoss?"

"You'd better keep him interested," said I, "till we get the scheme going. Loosen up."

Bill gets down on his all fours, and a look comes in his eye like a rabbit's when you catch it in a trap.

"How far is it to the stockade, kid?" he asks, in a husky manner of voice.

"Ninety miles," says the Black Scout. "And you have to hump yourself to get there on time. Whoa, now!"

The Black Scout jumps on Bill's back and digs his heels in his side.

"For Heaven's sake," says Bill, "hurry back, Sam, as soon as you can. I wish we hadn't made the ransom more than a thousand. Say, you quit kicking me or I'll get up and warm you good."

I walked over to Poplar Cove and sat around the postoffice and store, talking with the chawbacons that came in to trade. One whiskerando says that he hears Summit is all upset on account of Elder Ebenezer Dorset's boy having been lost or stolen. That was all I wanted to know. I bought some smoking tobacco, referred casually to the price of black-eyed peas, posted my letter surreptitiously and came away. The postmaster said the mail-carrier would come by in an hour to take the mail on to Summit.

When I got back to the cave Bill and the boy were not to be found. I explored the vicinity of the cave, and risked a yodel or two, but there was no response.

So I lighted my pipe and sat down on a mossy bank to await developments.

In about half an hour I heard the bushes rustle, and Bill wabbled out into the little glade in front of the cave. Behind him was the kid, stepping softly like a scout, with a broad grin on his face. Bill stopped, took off his hat and wiped his face with a red handkerchief. The kid stopped about eight feet behind him.

"Sam," says Bill, "I suppose you'll think I'm a renegade, but I couldn't help it. I'm a grown person with masculine proclivities and habits of self-defense, but there is a time when all systems of egotism and predominance fail. The boy is gone. I have sent him home. All is off. There was martyrs in old times," goes on Bill, "that suffered death rather than give up the particular graft they enjoyed. None of 'em ever was subjugated to such supernatural tortures as I have been. I tried to be faithful to our articles of depredation; but there came a limit."

"What's the trouble, Bill?" I asks him.

"I was rode," says Bill, "the ninety miles to the stockade, not barring an inch. Then, when the settlers was rescued, I was given oats. Sand ain't a palatable substitute. And then, for an hour I had to try to explain to him why there was nothin' in holes, how a road can run both ways and what makes the grass green. I tell you, Sam, a human can only stand so much. I takes him by the neck of his clothes and drags him down the mountain. On the way he kicks my legs black-and-blue from the knees down; and I've got to have two or three bites on my thumb and hand cauterized.

"But he's gone"—continues Bill—"gone home. I showed him the road to Summit and kicked him about eight feet nearer there at one kick. I'm sorry we lose the ransom; but it was either that or Bill Driscoll to the madhouse."

Bill is puffing and blowing, but there is a look of ineffable peace and growing content on his rose-pink features.

"Bill," says I, "there isn't any heart disease in your family, is there?"

"No," says Bill, "nothing chronic except malaria and accidents. Why?"

"Then you might turn around," says I, "and have a took behind you."

Bill turns and sees the boy, and loses his complexion and sits down plump on the round and begins to pluck aimlessly at grass and little sticks. For an hour I was afraid for his mind. And then I told him that my scheme was to put the whole job through immediately and that we would get the ransom and be off with it by midnight if old Dorset fell in with our proposition. So Bill braced up enough to give the kid a weak sort of a smile and a promise to play the Russian in a Japanese war with him is soon as he felt a little better.

I had a scheme for collecting that ransom without danger of being caught by counterplots that ought to commend itself to professional kidnappers. The tree under which the answer was to be left—and the money later on—was close to the road fence with big, bare fields on all sides. If a gang of constables should be watching for any one to come for the note they could see him a long way off crossing the fields or in the road. But no, sirree! At half-past eight I was up in that tree as well hidden as a tree toad, waiting for the messenger to arrive.

Exactly on time, a half-grown boy rides up the road on a bicycle, locates the pasteboard box at the foot of the fence-post, slips a folded piece of paper into it and pedals away again back toward Summit.

I waited an hour and then concluded the thing was square. I slid down the tree, got the note, slipped along the fence till I struck the woods, and was back at the cave in another half an hour. I opened the note, got near the lantern and read it to Bill. It was written with a pen in a crabbed hand, and the sum and substance of it was this:

Two Desperate Men. Gentlemen:
I received your letter to-day by post, in regard to the ransom you ask for the return of my son. I think you are a little high in your demands, and I hereby make you a counter-proposition, which I am inclined to believe you will accept. You bring Johnny home and pay me two hundred and fifty dollars in cash, and I agree to take him off your hands. You had better come at night, for the neighbours believe he is lost, and I couldn't be responsible for what they would do to anybody they saw bringing him back.

Very respectfully,
Ebenezer Dorset

"Great pirates of Penzance!" says I; "of all the impudent—"

But I glanced at Bill, and hesitated. He had the most appealing look in his eyes I ever saw on the face of a dumb or a talking brute.

"Sam," says he, "what's two hundred and fifty dollars, after all? We've got the money. One more night of this kid will send me to a bed in Bedlam. Besides being a thorough gentleman, I think Mr. Dorset is a spendthrift for making us such a liberal offer. You ain't going to let the chance go, are you?"

"Tell you the truth, Bill," says I, "this little he ewe lamb has somewhat got on my nerves too. We'll take him home, pay the ransom and make our get-away."

We took him home that night. We got him to go by telling him that his father had bought a silver-mounted rifle and a pair of moccasins for him, and we were going to hunt bears the next day.

It was just twelve o'clock when we knocked at Ebenezer's front door. Just at the moment when I should have been abstracting the fifteen hundred dollars from the box under the tree, according to the original proposition, Bill was counting out two hundred and fifty dollars into Dorset's hand.

When the kid found out we were going to leave him at home he started up a howl like a calliope and fastened himself as tight as a leech to Bill's leg. His father peeled him away gradually, like a porous plaster.

"How long can you hold him?" asks Bill.

"I'm not as strong as I used to be," says old Dorset, "but I think I can promise you ten minutes."

"Enough," says Bill. "In ten minutes I shall cross the Central, Southern and Middle Western States, and be legging it trippingly for the Canadian border."

And, as dark as it was, and as fat as Bill was, and as good a runner as I am, he was a good mile and a half out of Summit before I could catch up with him.

IX

The Marry Month of May

Prithee, smite the poet in the eye when he would sing to you praises of the month of May. It is a month presided over by the spirits of mischief and madness. Pixies and flibbertigibbets haunt the budding woods: Puck and his train of midgets are busy in town and country.

In May nature holds up at us a chiding finger, bidding us remember that we are not gods, but overconceited members of her own great family. She reminds us that we are brothers to the chowder-doomed clam and the donkey; lineal scions of the pansy and the chimpanzee, and but cousins-german to the cooing doves, the quacking ducks and the housemaids and policemen in the parks.

In May Cupid shoots blindfolded—millionaires marry stenographers; wise professors woo white-aproned gum-chewers behind quick-lunch counters; schoolma'ams make big bad boys remain after school; lads with ladders steal lightly over lawns where Juliet waits in her trellissed window with her telescope packed; young couples out for a walk come home married; old chaps put on white spats and promenade near the Normal School; even married men, grown unwontedly tender and sentimental, whack their spouses on the back and growl: "How goes it, old girl?"

This May, who is no goddess, but Circe, masquerading at the dance given in honour of the fair débutante, Summer, puts the kibosh on us all.

Old Mr. Coulson groaned a little, and then sat up straight in his invalid's chair. He had the gout very bad in one foot, a house near Gramercy Park, half a million dollars and a daughter. And he had a housekeeper, Mrs. Widdup. The fact and the name deserve a sentence each. They have it.

When May poked Mr. Coulson he became elder brother to the turtle-dove. In the window near which he sat were boxes of jonquils, of hyacinths, geraniums and pansies. The breeze brought their odour into the room. Immediately there was a well-contested round between the breath of the flowers and the able and active effluvium from gout liniment. The liniment won easily; but not before the flowers got an uppercut to old Mr. Coulson's nose. The deadly work of the implacable, false enchantress May was done.

Across the park to the olfactories of Mr. Coulson came other unmistakable, characteristic, copyrighted smells of spring that belong to the-big-city-above-the-Subway, alone. The smells of hot asphalt, underground caverns, gasoline, patchouli, orange peel, sewer gas, Albany grabs, Egyptian cigarettes, mortar and the undried ink on newspapers. The inblowing air was sweet and mild. Sparrows wrangled happily everywhere outdoors. Never trust May.

Mr. Coulson twisted the ends of his white mustache, cursed his foot, and pounded a bell on the table by his side.

In came Mrs. Widdup. She was comely to the eye, fair, flustered, forty and foxy.

"Higgins is out, sir," she said, with a smile suggestive of vibratory massage. "He went to post a letter. Can I do anything for you, sir?"

"It's time for my aconite," said old Mr. Coulson. "Drop it for me. The bottle's there. Three drops. In water. D—— that is, confound Higgins! There's nobody in this house cares if I die here in this chair for want of attention."

Mrs. Widdup sighed deeply.

"Don't be saying that, sir," she said. "There's them that would care more than any one knows. Thirteen drops, you said, sir?"

"Three," said old man Coulson.

He took his dose and then Mrs. Widdup's hand. She blushed. Oh, yes, it can be done. Just hold your breath and compress the diaphragm.

"Mrs. Widdup," said Mr. Coulson, "the springtime's full upon us."

"Ain't that right?" said Mrs. Widdup. "The air's real warm. And there's bock-beer signs on every corner. And the park's all yaller and pink and blue with flowers; and I have such shooting pains up my legs and body."

"'In the spring,'" quoted Mr. Coulson, curling his mustache, "'a y—— that is, a man's—fancy lightly turns to thoughts of love.'"

"Lawsy, now!" exclaimed Mrs. Widdup; "ain't that right? Seems like it's in the air."

"'In the spring,'" continued old Mr. Coulson, "'a livelier iris shines upon the burnished dove.'"

"They do be lively, the Irish," sighed Mrs. Widdup pensively.

"Mrs. Widdup," said Mr. Coulson, making a face at a twinge of his gouty foot, "this would be a lonesome house without you. I'm an—that is, I'm an elderly man—but I'm worth a comfortable lot of money. If half a million dollars' worth of Government bonds and the true affection of a heart that, though no longer beating with the first ardour of youth, can still throb with genuine—"

The loud noise of an overturned chair near the portières of the adjoining room interrupted the venerable and scarcely suspecting victim of May.

In stalked Miss Van Meeker Constantia Coulson, bony, durable, tall, high-nosed, frigid, well-bred, thirty-five, in-the-neighbourhood-of-Gramercy-Parkish. She put up a lorgnette. Mrs. Widdup hastily stooped and arranged the bandages on Mr. Coulson's gouty foot.

"I thought Higgins was with you," said Miss Van Meeker Constantia.

"Higgins went out," explained her father, "and Mrs. Widdup answered the bell. That is better now, Mrs. Widdup, thank you. No; there is nothing else I require."

The housekeeper retired, pink under the cool, inquiring stare of Miss Coulson.

"This spring weather is lovely, isn't it, daughter?" said the old man, consciously conscious.

"That's just it," replied Miss Van Meeker Constantia Coulson, somewhat obscurely. "When does Mrs. Widdup start on her vacation, papa?"

"I believe she said a week from to-day," said Mr. Coulson.

Miss Van Meeker Constantia stood for a minute at the window gazing, toward the little park, flooded with the mellow afternoon sunlight. With the eye of a botanist she viewed the flowers—most potent weapons of insidious May. With the cool pulses of a virgin of Cologne she withstood the attack of the ethereal mildness. The arrows of the pleasant sunshine fell back, frostbitten, from the cold panoply of her unthrilled bosom. The odour of the flowers waked no soft sentiments in the unexplored recesses of her dormant heart. The chirp of the sparrows gave her a pain. She mocked at May.

But although Miss Coulson was proof against the season, she was keen enough to estimate its power. She knew that elderly men and thick-waisted women jumped as educated fleas in the ridiculous train of May, the merry mocker of the months. She had heard of foolish old gentlemen marrying their housekeepers before. What a humiliating thing, after all, was this feeling called love!

The next morning at 8 o'clock, when the iceman called, the cook told him that Miss Coulson wanted to see him in the basement.

"Well, ain't I the Olcott and Depew; not mentioning the first name at all?" said the iceman, admiringly, of himself.

As a concession he rolled his sleeves down, dropped his icehooks on a syringa and went back. When Miss Van Meeker Constantia Coulson addressed him he took off his hat.

"There is a rear entrance to this basement," said Miss Coulson, "which can be reached by driving into the vacant lot next door, where they are excavating for a building. I want you to bring in that way within two hours 1,000 pounds of ice. You may have to bring another man or two to help you. I will show you where I want it placed. I also want 1,000 pounds a day delivered the same way for the next four days. Your company may charge the ice on our regular bill. This is for your extra trouble."

Miss Coulson tendered a ten-dollar bill. The iceman bowed, and held his hat in his two hands behind him.

"Not if you'll excuse me, lady. It'll be a pleasure to fix things up for you any way you please."

Alas for May!

About noon Mr. Coulson knocked two glasses off his table, broke the spring of his bell and yelled for Higgins at the same time.

"Bring an axe," commanded Mr. Coulson, sardonically, "or send out for a quart of prussic acid, or have a policeman come in and shoot me. I'd rather that than be frozen to death."

"It does seem to be getting cool, Sir," said Higgins. "I hadn't noticed it before. I'll close the window, Sir."

"Do," said Mr. Coulson. "They call this spring, do they? If it keeps up long I'll go back to Palm Beach. House feels like a morgue."

Later Miss Coulson dutifully came in to inquire how the gout was progressing.

"'Stantia," said the old man, "how is the weather outdoors?"

"Bright," answered Miss Coulson, "but chilly."

"Feels like the dead of winter to me," said Mr. Coulson.

"An instance," said Constantia, gazing abstractedly out the window, "of 'winter lingering in the lap of spring,' though the metaphor is not in the most refined taste."

A little later she walked down by the side of the little park and on westward to Broadway to accomplish a little shopping.

A little later than that Mrs. Widdup entered the invalid's room.

"Did you ring, Sir?" she asked, dimpling in many places. "I asked Higgins to go to the drug store, and I thought I heard your bell."

"I did not," said Mr. Coulson.

"I'm afraid," said Mrs. Widdup, "I interrupted you sir, yesterday when you were about to say something."

"How comes it, Mrs. Widdup," said old man Coulson sternly, "that I find it so cold in this house?"

"Cold, Sir?" said the housekeeper, "why, now, since you speak of it it do seem cold in this room. But, outdoors it's as warm and fine as June, sir. And how this weather do seem to make one's heart jump out of one's shirt waist, sir. And the ivy all leaved out on the side of the house, and the hand-organs playing, and the children dancing on the sidewalk—'tis a great time for speaking out what's in the heart. You were saying yesterday, sir—"

"Woman!" roared Mr. Coulson; "you are a fool. I pay you to take care of this house. I am freezing to death in my own room, and you come in and drivel to me about ivy and hand-organs. Get me an overcoat at once. See that all doors and windows are closed below. An old, fat, irresponsible, one-sided object like you prating about springtime and flowers in the middle of winter! When Higgins comes back, tell him to bring me a hot rum punch. And now get out!"

But who shall shame the bright face of May? Rogue though she be and disturber of sane men's peace, no wise virgins cunning nor cold storage shall make her bow her head in the bright galaxy of months.

Oh, yes, the story was not quite finished.

A night passed, and Higgins helped old man Coulson in the morning to his chair by the window. The cold of the room was gone. Heavenly odours and fragrant mildness entered.

In hurried Mrs. Widdup, and stood by his chair. Mr. Coulson reached his bony hand and grasped her plump one.

"Mrs. Widdup," he said, "this house would be no home without you. I have half a million dollars. If that and the true affection of a heart no longer in its youthful prime, but still not cold, could—"

"I found out what made it cold," said Mrs. Widdup, leanin' against his chair. "'Twas ice—tons of it—in the basement and in the furnace room, everywhere. I shut off the registers that it was coming through into your room, Mr. Coulson, poor soul! And now it's Maytime again."

"A true heart," went on old man Coulson, a little wanderingly, "that the springtime has brought to life again, and—but what will my daughter say, Mrs. Widdup?"

"Never fear, sir," said Mrs. Widdup, cheerfully. "Miss Coulson, she ran away with the iceman last night, sir!"

X

A Technical Error

I never cared especially for feuds, believing them to be even more overrated products of our country than grapefruit, scrapple, or honeymoons. Nevertheless, if I may be allowed, I will tell you of an Indian Territory feud of which I was press-agent, camp-follower, and inaccessory during the fact.

I was on a visit to Sam Durkee's ranch, where I had a great time falling off unmanicured ponies and waving my bare hand at the lower jaws of wolves about two miles away. Sam was a hardened person of about twenty-five, with a reputation for going home in the dark with perfect equanimity, though often with reluctance.

Over in the Creek Nation was a family bearing the name of Tatum. I was told that the Durkees and Tatums had been feuding for years. Several of each family had bitten the grass, and it was expected that more Nebuchadnezzars would follow. A younger generation of each family was growing up, and the grass was keeping pace with them. But I gathered that they had fought fairly; that they had not lain in cornfields and aimed at the division of their enemies' suspenders in the back—partly, perhaps, because there were no cornfields, and nobody wore more than one suspender. Nor had any woman or child of either house ever been harmed. In those days—and you will find it so yet—their women were safe.

Sam Durkee had a girl. (If it were an all-fiction magazine that I expect to sell this story to, I should say, "Mr. Durkee rejoiced in a fiancée.") Her name was Ella Baynes. They appeared to be devoted to each other, and to have perfect confidence in each other, as all couples do who are and have or aren't and haven't. She was tolerably pretty, with a heavy mass of brown hair that helped her along. He introduced me to her, which seemed not to lessen her preference for him; so I reasoned that they were surely soul-mates.

Miss Baynes lived in Kingfisher, twenty miles from the ranch. Sam lived on a gallop between the two places.

One day there came to Kingfisher a courageous young man, rather small, with smooth face and regular features. He made many inquiries about the business of the town, and especially of the inhabitants cognominally. He said he was from Muscogee, and he looked it, with his yellow shoes and crocheted four-in-hand. I met him once when I rode in for the mail. He said his name was Beverly Travers, which seemed rather improbable.

There were active times on the ranch, just then, and Sam was too busy to go to town often. As an incompetent and generally worthless guest, it devolved upon me to ride in for little things such as post cards, barrels of flour, baking-powder, smoking-tobacco, and—letters from Ella.

One day, when I was messenger for half a gross of cigarette papers and a couple of wagon tires, I saw the alleged Beverly Travers in a yellow-wheeled buggy with Ella Baynes, driving about town as ostentatiously as the black, waxy mud would permit. I knew that this information would bring no balm of Gilead to Sam's soul, so I refrained from including it in the news of the city that I retailed on my return. But on the next afternoon an elongated ex-cowboy of the name of Simmons, an old-time pal of Sam's, who kept a feed store in Kingfisher, rode out to the ranch and rolled and burned many cigarettes before he would talk. When he did make oration, his words were these:

"Say, Sam, there's been a description of a galoot miscallin' himself Bevel-edged Travels impairing the atmospheric air of Kingfisher for the past two weeks. You know who he was? He was not otherwise than Ben Tatum, from the Creek Nation, son of old Gopher Tatum that your Uncle Newt shot last February. You know what he done this morning? He killed your brother Lester—shot him in the co't-house yard."

I wondered if Sam had heard. He pulled a twig from a mesquite bush, chewed it gravely, and said:

"He did, did he? He killed Lester?"

"The same," said Simmons. "And he did more. He run away with your girl, the same as to say Miss Ella Baynes. I thought you might like to know, so I rode out to impart the information."

"I am much obliged, Jim," said Sam, taking the chewed twig from his mouth. "Yes, I'm glad you rode Out. Yes, I'm right glad."

"Well, I'll be ridin' back, I reckon. That boy I left in the feed store don't know hay from oats. He shot Lester in the back."

"Shot him in the back?"

"Yes, while he was hitchin' his hoss."

"I'm much obliged, Jim."

"I kind of thought you'd like to know as soon as you could."

"Come in and have some coffee before you ride back, Jim?"

"Why, no, I reckon not; I must get back to the store."

"And you say—"

"Yes, Sam. Everybody seen 'em drive away together in a buckboard, with a big bundle, like clothes, tied up in the back of it. He was drivin' the team he brought over with him from Muscogee. They'll be hard to overtake right away."

"And which—"

"I was goin' on to tell you. They left on the Guthrie road; but there's no tellin' which forks they'll take—you know that."

"All right, Jim; much obliged."

"You're welcome, Sam."

Simmons rolled a cigarette and stabbed his pony with both heels. Twenty yards away he reined up and called back:

"You don't want no—assistance, as you might say?"

"Not any, thanks."

"I didn't think you would. Well, so long!"

Sam took out and opened a bone-handled pocket-knife and scraped a dried piece of mud from his left boot. I thought at first he was going to swear a vendetta on the blade of it, or recite "The Gipsy's Curse." The few feuds I had ever seen or read about usually opened that way. This one seemed to be presented with a new treatment. Thus offered on the stage, it would have been hissed off, and one of Belasco's thrilling melodramas demanded instead.

"I wonder," said Sam, with a profoundly thoughtful expression, "if the cook has any cold beans left over!"

He called Wash, the Negro cook, and finding that he had some, ordered him to heat up the pot and make some strong coffee. Then we went into Sam's private room, where he slept, and kept his armoury, dogs, and the saddles of his favourite mounts. He took three or four six-shooters out of a bookcase and began to look them over, whistling "The Cowboy's Lament" abstractedly. Afterward he ordered the two best horses on the ranch saddled and tied to the hitching-post.

Now, in the feud business, in all sections of the country, I have observed that in one particular there is a delicate but strict etiquette belonging. You must not mention the word or refer to the subject in the presence of a feudist. It would be more reprehensible than commenting upon the mole on the chin of your rich aunt. I found, later on, that there is another unwritten rule, but I think that belongs solely to the West.

It yet lacked two hours to supper-time; but in twenty minutes Sam and I were plunging deep into the reheated beans, hot coffee, and cold beef.

"Nothing like a good meal before a long ride," said Sam. "Eat hearty."

I had a sudden suspicion.

"Why did you have two horses saddled?" I asked.

"One, two—one, two," said Sam. "You can count, can't you?"

His mathematics carried with it a momentary qualm and a lesson. The thought had not occurred to him that the thought could possibly occur to me not to ride at his side on that red road to revenge and justice. It was the higher calculus. I was booked for the trail. I began to eat more beans.

In an hour we set forth at a steady gallop eastward. Our horses were Kentucky-bred, strengthened by the mesquite grass of the west. Ben Tatum's steeds may have been swifter, and he had a good lead; but if he had heard the punctual thuds of the hoofs of those trailers of ours, born in the heart of feudland, he might have felt that retribution was creeping up on the hoof-prints of his dapper nags.

I knew that Ben Tatum's card to play was flight—flight until he came within the safer territory of his own henchmen and supporters. He knew that the man pursuing him would follow the trail to any end where it might lead.

During the ride Sam talked of the prospect for rain, of the price of beef, and of the musical glasses. You would have thought he had never had a brother or a sweetheart or an enemy on earth. There are some subjects too big even for the words in the "Unabridged." Knowing this phase of the feud code, but not having practised it sufficiently, I overdid the thing by telling some slightly funny anecdotes. Sam laughed at exactly the right place—laughed with his mouth. When I caught sight of his mouth, I wished I had been blessed with enough sense of humour to have suppressed those anecdotes.

Our first sight of them we had in Guthrie. Tired and hungry, we stumbled, unwashed, into a little yellow-pine hotel and sat at a table. In the opposite corner we saw the fugitives. They were bent upon their meal, but looked around at times uneasily.

The girl was dressed in brown—one of these smooth, half-shiny, silky-looking affairs with lace collar and cuffs, and what I believe they call an accordion-plaited skirt. She wore a thick brown veil down to her nose, and a broad-brimmed straw hat with some kind of feathers adorning it. The man wore plain, dark clothes, and his hair was trimmed very short. He was such a man as you might see anywhere.

There they were—the murderer and the woman he had stolen. There we were—the rightful avenger, according to the code, and the supernumerary who writes these words.

For one time, at least, in the heart of the supernumerary there rose the killing instinct. For one moment he joined the force of combatants—orally.

"What are you waiting for, Sam?" I said in a whisper. "Let him have it now!"

Sam gave a melancholy sigh.

"You don't understand; but *he* does," he said. "*He* knows. Mr. Tenderfoot, there's a rule out here among white men in the Nation that you can't shoot a man when he's with a woman. I never knew it to be broke yet. You *can't* do it. You've got to get him in a gang of men or by himself. That's why. He knows it, too. We all know. So, that's Mr. Ben Tatum! One of the 'pretty men'! I'll cut him out of the herd before they leave the hotel, and regulate his account!"

After supper the flying pair disappeared quickly. Although Sam haunted lobby and stairway and halls half the night, in some mysterious way the fugitives eluded him; and in the morning the veiled lady in the brown dress with the accordion-plaited skirt and the dapper young man with the close-clipped hair, and the buckboard with the prancing nags, were gone.

It is a monotonous story, that of the ride; so it shall be curtailed. Once again we overtook them on a road. We were about fifty yards behind. They turned in the buckboard and looked at us; then drove on without whipping up their horses. Their safety no longer lay in speed. Ben Tatum knew. He knew that the only rock of safety left to him was the code. There is no doubt that, had he been alone, the matter would have been settled quickly with Sam Durkee in the usual way; but he had something at his side that kept still the trigger-finger of both. It seemed likely that he was no coward.

So, you may perceive that woman, on occasions, may postpone instead of precipitating conflict between man and man. But not willingly or consciously. She is oblivious of codes.

Five miles farther, we came upon the future great Western city of Chandler. The horses of pursuers and pursued were starved and weary.

There was one hotel that offered danger to man and entertainment to beast; so the four of us met again in the dining room at the ringing of a bell so resonant and large that it had cracked the welkin long ago. The dining room was not as large as the one at Guthrie.

Just as we were eating apple pie—how Ben Davises and tragedy impinge upon each other!—I noticed Sam looking with keen intentness at our quarry where they were seated at a table across the room. The girl still wore the brown dress with lace collar and cuffs, and the veil drawn down to her nose. The man bent over his plate, with his close cropped head held low.

"There's a code," I heard Sam say, either to me or to himself, "that won't let you shoot a man in the company of a woman; but, by thunder, there ain't one to keep you from killing a woman in the company of a man!"

And, quicker than my mind could follow his argument, he whipped a Colt's automatic from under his left arm and pumped six bullets into the body that the brown dress covered—the brown dress with the lace collar and cuffs and the accordion-plaited skirt.

The young person in the dark sack suit, from whose head and from whose life a woman's glory had been clipped, laid her head on her arms stretched upon the table; while people came running to raise Ben Tatum from the floor in his feminine masquerade that had given Sam the opportunity to set aside, technically, the obligations of the code.

XI

Suite Homes and Their Romance

Few young couples in the Big-City-of-Bluff began their married existence with greater promise of happiness than did Mr. and Mrs. Claude Turpin. They felt no especial animosity toward each other; they were comfortably established in a handsome apartment house that had a name and accommodations like those of a sleeping-car; they were living as expensively as the couple on the next floor above who had twice their income; and their marriage had occurred on a wager, a ferry-boat and first acquaintance, thus securing a sensational newspaper notice with their names attached to pictures of the Queen of Roumania and M. Santos-Dumont.

Turpin's income was $200 per month. On pay day, after calculating the amounts due for rent, instalments on furniture and piano, gas, and bills owed to the florist, confectioner, milliner, tailor, wine merchant and cab company, the Turpins would find that they still had $200 left to spend. How to do this is one of the secrets of metropolitan life.

The domestic life of the Turpins was a beautiful picture to see. But you couldn't gaze upon it as you could at an oleograph of "Don't Wake Grandma," or "Brooklyn by Moonlight."

You had to blink when looked at it; and you heard a fizzing sound just like the machine with a "scope" at the end of it. Yes; there wasn't much repose about the picture of the Turpins' domestic life. It was something like "Spearing Salmon in the Columbia River," or "Japanese Artillery in Action."

Every day was just like another; as the days are in New York. In the morning Turpin would take bromo-seltzer, his pocket change from under the clock, his hat, no breakfast and his departure for the office. At noon Mrs. Turpin would get out of bed and humour, put on a kimono, airs, and the water to boil for coffee.

Turpin lunched downtown. He came home at 6 to dress for dinner. They always dined out. They strayed from the chop-house to chop-sueydom, from terrace to table d'hôte, from rathskeller to roadhouse, from café to casino, from Maria's to the Martha Washington. Such is domestic life in the great city. Your vine is the mistletoe; your fig tree bears dates. Your household gods are Mercury and John Howard Payne. For the wedding march you now hear only "Come with the Gypsy Bride." You rarely dine at the same place twice in succession. You tire of the food; and, besides, you want to give them time for the question of that souvenir silver sugar bowl to blow over.

The Turpins were therefore happy. They made many warm and delightful friends, some of whom they remembered the next day. Their home life was an ideal one, according to the rules and regulations of the Book of Bluff.

There came a time when it dawned upon Turpin that his wife was getting away with too much money. If you belong to the near-swell class in the Big City, and your income is $200 per month, and you find at the end of the month, after looking over the bills for current expenses, that you, yourself, have spent $150, you very naturally wonder what has become of the other $50. So you suspect your wife. And perhaps you give her a hint that something needs explanation.

"I say, Vivien," said Turpin, one afternoon when they were enjoying in rapt silence the peace and quiet of their cozy apartment, "you've been creating a hiatus big enough for a dog to crawl through in this month's honorarium. You haven't been paying your dressmaker anything on account, have you?"

There was a moment's silence. No sounds could be heard except the breathing of the fox terrier, and the subdued, monotonous sizzling of Vivien's fulvous locks against the insensate curling irons. Claude Turpin, sitting upon a pillow that he had thoughtfully placed upon the convolutions of the apartment sofa, narrowly watched the riante, lovely face of his wife.

"Claudie, dear," said she, touching her finger to her ruby tongue and testing the unresponsive curling irons, "you do me an injustice. Mme. Toinette has not seen a cent of mine since the day you paid your tailor ten dollars on account."

Turpin's suspicions were allayed for the time. But one day soon there came an anonymous letter to him that read:

> Watch your wife. She is blowing in your money secretly.
> I was a sufferer just as you are. The place is No. 345 Blank
> Street. A word to the wise, etc.
>
> A MAN WHO KNOWS

Turpin took this letter to the captain of police of the precinct that he lived in.

"My precinct is as clean as a hound's tooth," said the captain. "The lid's shut down as close there as it is over the eye of a Williamsburg girl when she's kissed at a party. But if you think there's anything queer at the address, I'll go there with ye."

On the next afternoon at 3, Turpin and the captain crept softly up the stairs of No. 345 Blank Street. A dozen plain-clothes men, dressed in full police uniforms, so as to allay suspicion, waited in the hall below.

At the top of the stairs was a door, which was found to be locked. The captain took a key from his pocket and unlocked it. The two men entered.

They found themselves in a large room, occupied by twenty or twenty-five elegantly clothed ladies. Racing charts hung against the walls, a ticker clicked in one corner; with a telephone receiver to his ear a man was calling out the various positions of the horses in a very exciting race. The occupants of the room looked up at the intruders; but, as if reassured by the sight of the captain's uniform, they reverted their attention to the man at the telephone.

"You see," said the captain to Turpin, "the value of an anonymous letter! No high-minded and self-respecting gentleman should consider one worthy of notice. Is your wife among this assembly, Mr. Turpin?"

"She is not," said Turpin.

"And if she was," continued the captain, "would she be within the reach of the tongue of slander? These ladies constitute a Browning Society. They meet to discuss the meaning of the great poet. The telephone is connected with Boston, whence the parent society transmits frequently its interpretations of the poems. Be ashamed of yer suspicions, Mr. Turpin."

"Go soak your shield," said Turpin. "Vivien knows how to take care of herself in a pool-room. She's not dropping anything on the ponies. There must be something queer going on here."

"Nothing but Browning," said the captain. "Hear that?"

"Thanatopsis by a nose," drawled the man at the telephone.

"That's not Browning; that's Longfellow," said Turpin, who sometimes read books.

"Back to the pasture!" exclaimed the captain. "Longfellow made the pacing-to-wagon record of 7.53 'way back in 1868."

"I believe there's something queer about this joint," repeated Turpin.

"I don't see it," said the captain.

"I know it looks like a pool-room, all right," persisted Turpin, "but that's all a blind. Vivien has been dropping a lot of coin somewhere. I believe there's some under-handed work going on here."

A number of racing sheets were tacked close together, covering a large space on one of the walls. Turpin, suspicious, tore several of them down. A door, previously hidden, was revealed. Turpin placed an ear to the crack and listened intently. He heard the soft hum of many voices, low and guarded laughter, and a sharp, metallic clicking and scraping as if from a multitude of tiny but busy objects.

"My God! It is as I feared!" whispered Turpin to himself. "Summon your men at once!" he called to the captain. "She is in there, I know."

At the blowing of the captain's whistle the uniformed plain-clothes men rushed up the stairs into the pool-room. When they saw the betting paraphernalia distributed around they halted, surprised and puzzled to know why they had been summoned.

But the captain pointed to the locked door and bade them break it down. In a few moments they demolished it with the axes they carried. Into the other room sprang Claude Turpin, with the captain at his heels.

The scene was one that lingered long in Turpin's mind. Nearly a score of women—women expensively and fashionably clothed, many beautiful and of refined appearance—had been seated at little marble-topped tables. When the police burst open the door they shrieked and ran here and there like gayly plumed birds that had been disturbed in a tropical grove. Some became hysterical; one or two fainted; several knelt at the feet of the officers and besought them for mercy on account of their families and social position.

A man who had been seated behind a desk had seized a roll of currency as large as the ankle of a Paradise Roof Gardens chorus girl and jumped out of the window. Half a dozen attendants huddled at one end of the room, breathless from fear.

Upon the tables remained the damning and incontrovertible evidences of the guilt of the habituées of that sinister room—dish after dish heaped high with ice cream, and surrounded by stacks of empty ones, scraped to the last spoonful.

"Ladies," said the captain to his weeping circle of prisoners, "I'll not hold any of yez. Some of yez I recognize as having fine houses and good standing in the community, with hard-working husbands and childer at home. But I'll read ye a bit of a lecture before ye go. In the next room there's a 20-to-1 shot just dropped in under the wire three lengths ahead of the field. Is this the way ye waste your husbands' money instead of helping earn it? Home wid yez! The lid's on the ice-cream freezer in this precinct."

Claude Turpin's wife was among the patrons of the raided room. He led her to their apartment in stern silence. There she wept so remorsefully and besought his forgiveness so pleadingly that he forgot his just anger, and soon he gathered his penitent golden-haired Vivien in his arms and forgave her.

"Darling," she murmured, half sobbingly, as the moonlight drifted through the open window, glorifying her sweet, upturned face, "I know I done wrong. I will never touch ice cream again. I forgot you were not a millionaire. I used to go there every day. But to-day I felt some strange, sad presentiment of evil, and I was not myself. I ate only eleven saucers."

"Say no more," said Claude, gently as he fondly caressed her waving curls.

"And you are sure that you fully forgive me?" asked Vivien, gazing at him entreatingly with dewy eyes of heavenly blue.

"Almost sure, little one," answered Claude, stooping and lightly touching her snowy forehead with his lips. "I'll let you know later on. I've got a month's salary down on Vanilla to win the three-year-old steeplechase to-morrow; and if the ice-cream hunch is to the good you are It again—see?"

XII

THE WHIRLIGIG OF LIFE

Justice-of-the-Peace Benaja Widdup sat in the door of his office smoking his elder-stem pipe. Half-way to the zenith the Cumberland range rose blue-gray in the afternoon haze. A speckled hen swaggered down the main street of the "settlement," cackling foolishly.

Up the road came a sound of creaking axles, and then a slow cloud of dust, and then a bull-cart bearing Ransie Bilbro and his wife. The cart stopped at the Justice's door, and the two climbed down. Ransie was a narrow six feet of sallow brown skin and yellow hair. The imperturbability of the mountains hung upon him like a suit of armour. The woman was calicoed, angled, snuff-brushed, and weary with unknown desires. Through it all gleamed a faint protest of cheated youth unconscious of its loss.

The Justice of the Peace slipped his feet into his shoes, for the sake of dignity, and moved to let them enter.

"We-all," said the woman, in a voice like the wind blowing through pine boughs, "wants a divo'ce." She looked at Ransie to see if he noted any flaw or ambiguity or evasion or partiality or self-partisanship in her statement of their business.

"A divo'ce," repeated Ransie, with a solemn nod. "We-all can't git along together nohow. It's lonesome enough fur to live in the mount'ins when a man and a woman keers fur one another. But when she's a-spittin' like a wildcat or a-sullenin' like a hoot-owl in the cabin, a man ain't got no call to live with her."

"When he's a no-'count varmint," said the woman, "without any especial warmth, a-traipsin' along of scalawags and moonshiners and a-layin' on his back pizen 'ith co'n whiskey, and a-pesterin' folks with a pack o' hungry, triflin' houn's to feed!"

"When she keeps a-throwin' skillet lids," came Ransie's antiphony, "and slings b'ilin' water on the best coon-dog in the Cumberlands, and sets herself agin' cookin' a man's victuals, and keeps him awake o' nights accusin' him of a sight of doin's!"

"When he's al'ays a-fightin' the revenues, and gits a hard name in the mount'ins fur a mean man, who's gwine to be able fur to sleep o' nights?"

The Justice of the Peace stirred deliberately to his duties. He placed his one chair and a wooden stool for his petitioners. He opened his book of statutes on the table and scanned the index. Presently he wiped his spectacles and shifted his inkstand.

"The law and the statutes," said he, "air silent on the subjeck of divo'ce as fur as the jurisdiction of this co't air concerned. But, accordin' to equity and the Constitution and the golden rule, it's a bad barg'in that can't run both ways. If a justice of the peace can marry a couple, it's plain that he is bound to be able to divo'ce 'em. This here office will issue a decree of divo'ce and abide by the decision of the Supreme Co't to hold it good."

Ransie Bilbro drew a small tobacco-bag from his trousers pocket. Out of this he shook upon the table a five-dollar note. "Sold a b'arskin and two foxes fur that," he remarked. "It's all the money we got."

"The regular price of a divo'ce in this co't," said the Justice, "air five dollars." He stuffed the bill into the pocket of his homespun vest with a deceptive air of indifference. With much bodily toil and mental travail he wrote the decree upon half a sheet of foolscap, and then copied it upon the other. Ransie Bilbro and his wife listened to his reading of the document that was to give them freedom:

"Know all men by these presents that Ransie Bilbro and his wife, Ariela Bilbro, this day personally appeared before me and promises that hereinafter they will neither love, honour, nor obey each other, neither for better nor worse, being of sound mind and body, and accept summons for divorce according to the peace and dignity of the State. Herein fail not, so help you God. Benaja Widdup, justice of the peace in and for the county of Piedmont, State of Tennessee."

The Justice was about to hand one of the documents to Ransie. The voice of Ariela delayed the transfer. Both men looked at her. Their dull masculinity was confronted by something sudden and unexpected in the woman.

"Judge, don't you give him that air paper yit. 'Tain't all settled, nohow. I got to have my rights first. I got to have my ali-money. 'Tain't no kind of a way to do fur a man to divo'ce his wife 'thout her havin' a cent fur to do with. I'm a-layin' off to be a-goin' up to brother Ed's up on Hogback Mount'in. I'm bound fur to hev a pa'r of shoes and some snuff and things besides. Ef Rance kin affo'd a divo'ce, let him pay me ali-money."

Ransie Bilbro was stricken to dumb perplexity. There had been no previous hint of alimony. Women were always bringing up startling and unlooked-for issues.

Justice Benaja Widdup felt that the point demanded judicial decision. The authorities were also silent on the subject of alimony. But the woman's feet were bare. The trail to Hogback Mountain was steep and flinty.

"Ariela Bilbro," he asked, in official tones, "how much did you 'low would be good and sufficient ali-money in the case befo' the co't."

"I 'lowed," she answered, "fur the shoes and all, to say five dollars. That ain't much fur ali-money, but I reckon that'll git me to up brother Ed's."

"The amount," said the Justice, "air not onreasonable. Ransie Bilbro, you air ordered by the co't to pay the plaintiff the sum of five dollars befo' the decree of divo'ce air issued."

"I hain't no mo' money," breathed Ransie, heavily. "I done paid you all I had."

"Otherwise," said the Justice, looking severely over his spectacles, "you air in contempt of co't."

"I reckon if you gimme till to-morrow," pleaded the husband, "I mout be able to rake or scrape it up somewhars. I never looked for to be a-payin' no ali-money."

"The case air adjourned," said Benaja Widdup, "till to-morrow, when you-all will present yo'selves and obey the order of the co't. Followin' of which the decrees of divo'ce will be delivered." He sat down in the door and began to loosen a shoestring.

"We mout as well go down to Uncle Ziah's," decided Ransie, "and spend the night." He climbed into the cart on one side, and Ariela climbed in on the other. Obeying the flap of his rope, the little red bull slowly came around on a tack, and the cart crawled away in the nimbus arising from its wheels.

Justice-of-the-peace Benaja Widdup smoked his elder-stem pipe. Late in the afternoon he got his weekly paper, and read it until the twilight dimmed its lines. Then he lit the tallow candle on his table, and read until the moon rose, marking the time for supper. He lived in the double log cabin on the slope near the girdled poplar. Going home to supper he crossed a little branch darkened by a laurel thicket. The dark figure of a man stepped from the laurels and pointed a rifle at his breast. His hat was pulled down low, and something covered most of his face.

"I want yo' money," said the figure, "'thout any talk. I'm gettin' nervous, and my finger's a-wabblin' on this here trigger."

"I've only got f-f-five dollars," said the Justice, producing it from his vest pocket.

"Roll it up," came the order, "and stick it in the end of this here gun-bar'l."

The bill was crisp and new. Even fingers that were clumsy and trembling found little difficulty in making a spill of it and inserting it (this with less ease) into the muzzle of the rifle.

"Now I reckon you kin be goin' along," said the robber.

The Justice lingered not on his way.

THE NEXT DAY CAME THE little red bull, drawing the cart to the office door. Justice Benaja Widdup had his shoes on, for he was expecting the visit. In his presence Ransie Bilbro handed to his wife a five-dollar bill. The official's eye sharply viewed it. It seemed to curl up as though it had been rolled and inserted into the end of a gun-barrel. But the Justice refrained from comment. It is true that other bills might be inclined to curl. He handed each one a decree of divorce. Each stood awkwardly silent, slowly folding the guarantee of freedom. The woman cast a shy glance full of constraint at Ransie.

"I reckon you'll be goin' back up to the cabin," she said, "along 'ith the bull-cart. There's bread in the tin box settin' on the shelf. I put the bacon in the b'ilin'-pot to keep the hounds from gittin' it. Don't forget to wind the clock to-night."

"You air a-goin' to your brother Ed's?" asked Ransie, with fine unconcern.

"I was 'lowin' to get along up thar afore night. I ain't sayin' as they'll pester theyselves any to make me welcome, but I hain't nowhar else fur to go. It's a right smart ways, and I reckon I better be goin'. I'll be a-sayin' good-bye, Ranse—that is, if you keer fur to say so."

"I don't know as anybody's a hound dog," said Ransie, in a martyr's voice, "fur to not want to say good-bye—'less you air so anxious to git away that you don't want me to say it."

Ariela was silent. She folded the five-dollar bill and her decree carefully, and placed them in the bosom of her dress. Benaja Widdup watched the money disappear with mournful eyes behind his spectacles.

And then with his next words he achieved rank (as his thoughts ran) with either the great crowd of the world's sympathizers or the little crowd of its great financiers.

"Be kind o' lonesome in the old cabin to-night, Ranse," he said.

Ransie Bilbro stared out at the Cumberlands, clear blue now in the sunlight. He did not look at Ariela.

"I 'low it might be lonesome," he said; "but when folks gits mad and wants a divo'ce, you can't make folks stay."

"There's others wanted a divo'ce," said Ariela, speaking to the wooden stool. "Besides, nobody don't want nobody to stay."

"Nobody never said they didn't."

"Nobody never said they did. I reckon I better start on now to brother Ed's."

"Nobody can't wind that old clock."

"Want me to go back along 'ith you in the cart and wind it fur you, Ranse?"

The mountaineer's countenance was proof against emotion. But he reached out a big hand and enclosed Ariela's thin brown one. Her soul peeped out once through her impassive face, hallowing it.

"Them hounds shan't pester you no more," said Ransie. "I reckon I been mean and low down. You wind that clock, Ariela."

"My heart hit's in that cabin, Ranse," she whispered, "along 'ith you. I ai'nt a-goin' to git mad no more. Le's be startin', Ranse, so's we kin git home by sundown."

Justice-of-the-peace Benaja Widdup interposed as they started for the door, forgetting his presence.

"In the name of the State of Tennessee," he said, "I forbid you-all to be a-defyin' of its laws and statutes. This co't is mo' than willin' and full of joy to see the clouds of discord and misunderstandin' rollin' away from two lovin' hearts, but it air the duty of the co't to p'eserve the morals and integrity of the State. The co't reminds you that you air no longer man and wife, but air divo'ced by regular decree, and as such air not entitled to the benefits and 'purtenances of the mattermonal estate."

Ariela caught Ransie's arm. Did those words mean that she must lose him now when they had just learned the lesson of life?

"But the co't air prepared," went on the Justice, "fur to remove the disabilities set up by the decree of divo'ce. The co't air on hand to perform the solemn ceremony of marri'ge, thus fixin' things up and enablin' the parties in the case to resume the honour'ble and elevatin' state of mattermony which they desires. The fee fur performin' said ceremony will be, in this case, to wit, five dollars."

Ariela caught the gleam of promise in his words. Swiftly her hand went to her bosom. Freely as an alighting dove the bill fluttered to the

Justice's table. Her sallow cheek coloured as she stood hand in hand with Ransie and listened to the reuniting words.

Ransie helped her into the cart, and climbed in beside her. The little red bull turned once more, and they set out, hand-clasped, for the mountains.

Justice-of-the-peace Benaja Widdup sat in his door and took off his shoes. Once again he fingered the bill tucked down in his vest pocket. Once again he smoked his elder-stem pipe. Once again the speckled hen swaggered down the main street of the "settlement," cackling foolishly.

XIII

A Sacrifice Hit

The editor of the *Hearthstone Magazine* has his own ideas about the selection of manuscript for his publication. His theory is no secret; in fact, he will expound it to you willingly sitting at his mahogany desk, smiling benignantly and tapping his knee gently with his gold-rimmed eye-glasses.

"The *Hearthstone*," he will say, "does not employ a staff of readers. We obtain opinions of the manuscripts submitted to us directly from types of the various classes of our readers."

That is the editor's theory; and this is the way he carries it out:

When a batch of Mss. is received the editor stuffs every one of his pockets full of them and distributes them as he goes about during the day. The office employees, the hall porter, the janitor, the elevator man, messenger boys, the waiters at the café where the editor has luncheon, the man at the news-stand where he buys his evening paper, the grocer and milkman, the guard on the 5.30 uptown elevated train, the ticket-chopper at Sixty ——th street, the cook and maid at his home—these are the readers who pass upon Mss. sent in to the *Hearthstone Magazine*. If his pockets are not entirely emptied by the time he reaches the bosom of his family the remaining ones are handed over to his wife to read after the baby goes to sleep. A few days later the editor gathers in the Mss. during his regular rounds and considers the verdict of his assorted readers.

This system of making up a magazine has been very successful; and the circulation, paced by the advertising rates, is making a wonderful record of speed.

The *Hearthstone* Company also publishes books, and its imprint is to be found on several successful works—all recommended, says the editor, by the *Hearthstone's* army of volunteer readers. Now and then (according to talkative members of the editorial staff) the *Hearthstone* has allowed manuscripts to slip through its fingers on the advice of its heterogeneous readers, that afterward proved to be famous sellers when brought out by other houses.

For instance (the gossips say), "The Rise and Fall of Silas Latham" was unfavourably passed upon by the elevator-man; the office-boy unanimously rejected "The Boss"; "In the Bishop's Carriage" was contemptuously looked upon by the street-car conductor; "The Deliverance" was turned down by a clerk in the subscription department whose wife's mother had just begun a two-months' visit at his home; "The Queen's Quair" came back from the janitor with the comment: "So is the book."

But nevertheless the *Hearthstone* adheres to its theory and system, and it will never lack volunteer readers; for each one of the widely scattered staff, from the young lady stenographer in the editorial office to the man who shovels in coal (whose adverse decision lost to the *Hearthstone* Company the manuscript of "The Under World"), has expectations of becoming editor of the magazine some day.

This method of the *Hearthstone* was well known to Allen Slayton when he wrote his novelette entitled "Love Is All." Slayton had hung about the editorial offices of all the magazines so persistently that he was acquainted with the inner workings of every one in Gotham.

He knew not only that the editor of the Hearthstone handed his Mss. around among different types of people for reading, but that the stories of sentimental love-interest went to Miss Puffkin, the editor's stenographer. Another of the editor's peculiar customs was to conceal invariably the name of the writer from his readers of Mss. so that a glittering name might not influence the sincerity of their reports.

Slayton made "Love Is All" the effort of his life. He gave it six months of the best work of his heart and brain. It was a pure love-story, fine, elevated, romantic, passionate—a prose poem that set the divine blessing of love (I am transposing from the manuscript) high above all earthly gifts and honours, and listed it in the catalogue of heaven's choicest rewards. Slayton's literary ambition was intense. He would have sacrificed all other worldly possessions to have gained fame in his chosen art. He would almost have cut off his right hand, or have offered himself to the knife of the appendicitis fancier to have realized his dream of seeing one of his efforts published in the *Hearthstone*.

Slayton finished "Love Is All," and took it to the *Hearthstone* in person. The office of the magazine was in a large, conglomerate building, presided under by a janitor.

As the writer stepped inside the door on his way to the elevator a potato masher flew through the hall, wrecking Slayton's hat, and smashing the glass of the door. Closely following in the wake of the utensil flew the janitor, a bulky, unwholesome man, suspenderless and sordid, panic-stricken and breathless. A frowsy, fat woman with flying hair followed the missile. The janitor's foot slipped on the tiled floor, he fell in a heap with an exclamation of despair. The woman pounced upon him and seized his hair. The man bellowed lustily.

Her vengeance wreaked, the virago rose and stalked triumphant as Minerva, back to some cryptic domestic retreat at the rear. The janitor got to his feet, blown and humiliated.

"This is married life," he said to Slayton, with a certain bruised humour. "That's the girl I used to lay awake of nights thinking about. Sorry about your hat, mister. Say, don't snitch to the tenants about this, will yer? I don't want to lose me job."

Slayton took the elevator at the end of the hall and went up to the offices of the *Hearthstone*. He left the Ms. of "Love Is All" with the editor, who agreed to give him an answer as to its availability at the end of a week.

Slayton formulated his great winning scheme on his way down. It struck him with one brilliant flash, and he could not refrain from admiring his own genius in conceiving the idea. That very night he set about carrying it into execution.

Miss Puffkin, the *Hearthstone* stenographer, boarded in the same house with the author. She was an oldish, thin, exclusive, languishing, sentimental maid; and Slayton had been introduced to her some time before.

The writer's daring and self-sacrificing project was this: He knew that the editor of the *Hearthstone* relied strongly upon Miss Puffkin's judgment in the manuscript of romantic and sentimental fiction. Her taste represented the immense average of mediocre women who devour novels and stories of that type. The central idea and keynote of "Love Is All" was love at first sight—the enrapturing, irresistible, soul-thrilling feeling that compels a man or a woman to recognize his or her spirit-mate as soon as heart speaks to heart. Suppose he should impress this divine truth upon Miss Puffkin personally!—would she not surely indorse her new and rapturous sensations by recommending highly to the editor of the *Hearthstone* the novelette "Love Is All"?

Slayton thought so. And that night he took Miss Puffkin to the theatre. The next night he made vehement love to her in the dim parlour of the boarding-house. He quoted freely from "Love Is All"; and he wound up with Miss Puffkin's head on his shoulder, and visions of literary fame dancing in his head.

But Slayton did not stop at love-making. This, he said to himself, was the turning point of his life; and, like a true sportsman, he "went the limit." On Thursday night he and Miss Puffkin walked over to the Big Church in the Middle of the Block and were married.

Brave Slayton! Châteaubriand died in a garret, Byron courted a widow, Keats starved to death, Poe mixed his drinks, De Quincey hit the pipe, Ade lived in Chicago, James kept on doing it, Dickens wore white socks, De Maupassant wore a strait-jacket, Tom Watson became a Populist, Jeremiah wept, all these authors did these things for the sake of literature, but thou didst cap them all; thou marriedst a wife for to carve for thyself a niche in the temple of fame!

On Friday morning Mrs. Slayton said she would go over to the *Hearthstone* office, hand in one or two manuscripts that the editor had given to her to read, and resign her position as stenographer.

"Was there anything—er—that—er—you particularly fancied in the stories you are going to turn in?" asked Slayton with a thumping heart.

"There was one—a novelette, that I liked so much," said his wife. "I haven't read anything in years that I thought was half as nice and true to life."

That afternoon Slayton hurried down to the *Hearthstone* office. He felt that his reward was close at hand. With a novelette in the *Hearthstone*, literary reputation would soon be his.

The office boy met him at the railing in the outer office. It was not for unsuccessful authors to hold personal colloquy with the editor except at rare intervals.

Slayton, hugging himself internally, was nursing in his heart the exquisite hope of being able to crush the office boy with his forthcoming success.

He inquired concerning his novelette. The office boy went into the sacred precincts and brought forth a large envelope, thick with more than the bulk of a thousand checks.

"The boss told me to tell you he's sorry," said the boy, "but your manuscript ain't available for the magazine."

Slayton stood, dazed. "Can you tell me," he stammered, "whether or no Miss Puff—that is my—I mean Miss Puffkin—handed in a novelette this morning that she had been asked to read?"

"Sure she did," answered the office boy wisely. "I heard the old man say that Miss Puffkin said it was a daisy. The name of it was, 'Married for the Mazuma, or a Working Girl's Triumph.'"

"Say, you!" said the office boy confidentially, "your name's Slayton, ain't it? I guess I mixed cases on you without meanin' to do it. The boss give me some manuscript to hand around the other day and I got the ones for Miss Puffkin and the janitor mixed. I guess it's all right, though."

And then Slayton looked closer and saw on the cover of his manuscript, under the title "Love Is All," the janitor's comment scribbled with a piece of charcoal:

"The—you say!"

XIV

THE ROADS WE TAKE

Twenty miles west of Tucson, the "Sunset Express" stopped at a tank to take on water. Besides the aqueous addition the engine of that famous flyer acquired some other things that were not good for it.

While the fireman was lowering the feeding hose, Bob Tidball, "Shark" Dodson and a quarter-bred Creek Indian called John Big Dog climbed on the engine and showed the engineer three round orifices in pieces of ordnance that they carried. These orifices so impressed the engineer with their possibilities that he raised both hands in a gesture such as accompanies the ejaculation "Do tell!"

At the crisp command of Shark Dodson, who was leader of the attacking force the engineer descended to the ground and uncoupled the engine and tender. Then John Big Dog, perched upon the coal, sportively held two guns upon the engine driver and the fireman, and suggested that they run the engine fifty yards away and there await further orders.

Shark Dodson and Bob Tidball, scorning to put such low-grade ore as the passengers through the mill, struck out for the rich pocket of the express car. They found the messenger serene in the belief that the "Sunset Express" was taking on nothing more stimulating and dangerous than aqua pura. While Bob was knocking this idea out of his head with the butt-end of his six-shooter Shark Dodson was already dosing the express-car safe with dynamite.

The safe exploded to the tune of $30,000, all gold and currency. The passengers thrust their heads casually out of the windows to look for the thunder-cloud. The conductor jerked at the bell-rope, which sagged down loose and unresisting, at his tug. Shark Dodson and Bob Tidball, with their booty in a stout canvas bag, tumbled out of the express car and ran awkwardly in their high-heeled boots to the engine.

The engineer, sullenly angry but wise, ran the engine, according to orders, rapidly away from the inert train. But before this was accomplished the express messenger, recovered from Bob Tidball's persuader to neutrality, jumped out of his car with a Winchester rifle and took a trick in the game. Mr. John Big Dog, sitting on the coal tender, unwittingly made a wrong lead by giving an imitation of a target, and the messenger trumped him. With a ball exactly between his shoulder blades the Creek chevalier of industry rolled off to the ground, thus increasing the share of his comrades in the loot by one-sixth each.

Two miles from the tank the engineer was ordered to stop.

The robbers waved a defiant adieu and plunged down the steep slope into the thick woods that lined the track. Five minutes of crashing through a thicket of chaparral brought them to open woods, where three horses were tied to low-hanging branches. One was waiting for John Big Dog, who would never ride by night or day again. This animal the robbers divested of saddle and bridle and set free. They mounted the other two with the bag across one pommel, and rode fast and with discretion through the forest and up a primeval, lonely gorge. Here the animal that bore Bob Tidball slipped on a mossy boulder and broke a foreleg. They shot him through the head at once and sat down to hold a council of flight. Made secure for the present by the tortuous trail they had travelled, the question of time was no longer so big. Many miles and hours lay between them and the spryest posse that could follow. Shark Dodson's horse, with trailing rope and dropped bridle, panted and cropped thankfully of the grass along the stream in the gorge. Bob Tidball opened the sack, drew out double handfuls of the neat packages of currency and the one sack of gold and chuckled with the glee of a child.

"Say, you old double-decked pirate," he called joyfully to Dodson, "you said we could do it—you got a head for financing that knocks the horns off of anything in Arizona."

"What are we going to do about a hoss for you, Bob? We ain't got long to wait here. They'll be on our trail before daylight in the mornin'."

"Oh, I guess that cayuse of yourn'll carry double for a while," answered the sanguine Bob. "We'll annex the first animal we come across. By jingoes, we made a haul, didn't we? Accordin' to the marks on this money there's $30,000—$15,000 apiece!"

"It's short of what I expected," said Shark Dodson, kicking softly at the packages with the toe of his boot. And then he looked pensively at the wet sides of his tired horse.

"Old Bolivar's mighty nigh played out," he said, slowly. "I wish that sorrel of yours hadn't got hurt."

"So do I," said Bob, heartily, "but it can't be helped. Bolivar's got plenty of bottom—he'll get us both far enough to get fresh mounts.

Dang it, Shark, I can't help thinkin' how funny it is that an Easterner like you can come out here and give us Western fellows cards and spades in the desperado business. What part of the East was you from, anyway?"

"New York State," said Shark Dodson, sitting down on a boulder and chewing a twig. "I was born on a farm in Ulster County. I ran away from home when I was seventeen. It was an accident my coming West. I was walkin' along the road with my clothes in a bundle, makin' for New York City. I had an idea of goin' there and makin' lots of money. I always felt like I could do it. I came to a place one evenin' where the road forked and I didn't know which fork to take. I studied about it for half an hour, and then I took the left-hand. That night I run into the camp of a Wild West show that was travellin' among the little towns, and I went West with it. I've often wondered if I wouldn't have turned out different if I'd took the other road."

"Oh, I reckon you'd have ended up about the same," said Bob Tidball, cheerfully philosophical. "It ain't the roads we take; it's what's inside of us that makes us turn out the way we do."

Shark Dodson got up and leaned against a tree.

"I'd a good deal rather that sorrel of yourn hadn't hurt himself, Bob," he said again, almost pathetically.

"Same here," agreed Bob; "he was sure a first-rate kind of a crowbait. But Bolivar, he'll pull us through all right. Reckon we'd better be movin' on, hadn't we, Shark? I'll bag this boodle ag'in and we'll hit the trail for higher timber."

Bob Tidball replaced the spoil in the bag and tied the mouth of it tightly with a cord. When he looked up the most prominent object that he saw was the muzzle of Shark Dodson's .45 held upon him without a waver.

"Stop your funnin'," said Bob, with a grin. "We got to be hittin' the breeze."

"Set still," said Shark. "You ain't goin' to hit no breeze, Bob. I hate to tell you, but there ain't any chance for but one of us. Bolivar, he's plenty tired, and he can't carry double."

"We been pards, me and you, Shark Dodson, for three year," Bob said quietly. "We've risked our lives together time and again. I've always give you a square deal, and I thought you was a man. I've heard some queer stories about you shootin' one or two men in a peculiar way, but I never believed 'em. Now if you're just havin' a little fun with me, Shark, put your gun up, and we'll get on Bolivar and vamose. If you mean to shoot—shoot, you blackhearted son of a tarantula!"

Shark Dodson's face bore a deeply sorrowful look. "You don't know how bad I feel," he sighed, "about that sorrel of yourn breakin' his leg, Bob."

The expression on Dodson's face changed in an instant to one of cold ferocity mingled with inexorable cupidity. The soul of the man showed itself for a moment like an evil face in the window of a reputable house.

Truly Bob Tidball was never to "hit the breeze" again. The deadly .45 of the false friend cracked and filled the gorge with a roar that the walls hurled back with indignant echoes. And Bolivar, unconscious accomplice, swiftly bore away the last of the holders-up of the "Sunset Express," not put to the stress of "carrying double."

But as "Shark" Dodson galloped away the woods seemed to fade from his view; the revolver in his right hand turned to the curved arm of a mahogany chair; his saddle was strangely upholstered, and he opened his eyes and saw his feet, not in stirrups, but resting quietly on the edge of a quartered-oak desk.

I AM TELLING YOU THAT Dodson, of the firm of Dodson & Decker, Wall Street brokers, opened his eyes. Peabody, the confidential clerk, was standing by his chair, hesitating to speak. There was a confused hum of wheels below, and the sedative buzz of an electric fan.

"Ahem! Peabody," said Dodson, blinking. "I must have fallen asleep. I had a most remarkable dream. What is it, Peabody?"

"Mr. Williams, sir, of Tracy & Williams, is outside. He has come to settle his deal in X. Y. Z. The market caught him short, sir, if you remember."

"Yes, I remember. What is X. Y. Z. quoted at to-day, Peabody?"

"One eighty-five, sir."

"Then that's his price."

"Excuse me," said Peabody, rather nervously "for speaking of it, but I've been talking to Williams. He's an old friend of yours, Mr. Dodson, and you practically have a corner in X. Y. Z. I thought you might—that is, I thought you might not remember that he sold you the stock at 98. If he settles at the market price it will take every cent he has in the world and his home too to deliver the shares."

The expression on Dodson's face changed in an instant to one of cold ferocity mingled with inexorable cupidity. The soul of the man showed itself for a moment like an evil face in the window of a reputable house.

"He will settle at one eighty-five," said Dodson. "Bolivar cannot carry double."

XV

A BLACKJACK BARGAINER

The most disreputable thing in Yancey Goree's law office was Goree himself, sprawled in his creaky old arm-chair. The rickety little office, built of red brick, was set flush with the street—the main street of the town of Bethel.

Bethel rested upon the foot-hills of the Blue Ridge. Above it the mountains were piled to the sky. Far below it the turbid Catawba gleamed yellow along its disconsolate valley.

The June day was at its sultriest hour. Bethel dozed in the tepid shade. Trade was not. It was so still that Goree, reclining in his chair, distinctly heard the clicking of the chips in the grand-jury room, where the "court-house gang" was playing poker. From the open back door of the office a well-worn path meandered across the grassy lot to the court-house. The treading out of that path had cost Goree all he ever had—first inheritance of a few thousand dollars, next the old family home, and, latterly the last shreds of his self-respect and manhood. The "gang" had cleaned him out. The broken gambler had turned drunkard and parasite; he had lived to see this day come when the men who had stripped him denied him a seat at the game. His word was no longer to be taken. The daily bouts at cards had arranged itself accordingly, and to him was assigned the ignoble part of the onlooker. The sheriff, the county clerk, a sportive deputy, a gay attorney, and a chalk-faced man hailing "from the valley," sat at table, and the sheared one was thus tacitly advised to go and grow more wool.

Soon wearying of his ostracism, Goree had departed for his office, muttering to himself as he unsteadily traversed the unlucky pathway. After a drink of corn whiskey from a demijohn under the table, he had flung himself into the chair, staring, in a sort of maudlin apathy, out at the mountains immersed in the summer haze. The little white patch he saw away up on the side of Blackjack was Laurel, the village near which he had been born and bred. There, also, was the birthplace of the feud between the Gorees and the Coltranes. Now no direct heir of the Gorees survived except this plucked and singed bird of misfortune. To the Coltranes, also, but one male supporter was left—Colonel Abner Coltrane, a man of substance and standing, a member of the State Legislature, and a contemporary with Goree's father. The feud had been a typical one of the region; it had left a red record of hate, wrong and slaughter.

But Yancey Goree was not thinking of feuds. His befuddled brain was hopelessly attacking the problem of the future maintenance of himself and his favourite follies. Of late, old friends of the family had seen to it that he had whereof to eat and a place to sleep—but whiskey they would not buy for him, and he must have whiskey. His law business was extinct; no case had been intrusted to him in two years. He had been a borrower and a sponge, and it seemed that if he fell no lower it would be from lack of opportunity. One more chance—he was saying to himself—if he had one more stake at the game, he thought he could win; but he had nothing left to sell, and his credit was more than exhausted.

He could not help smiling, even in his misery, as he thought of the man to whom, six months before, he had sold the old Goree homestead. There had come from "back yan'" in the mountains two of the strangest creatures, a man named Pike Garvey and his wife. "Back yan'," with a wave of the hand toward the hills, was understood among the mountaineers to designate the remotest fastnesses, the unplumbed gorges, the haunts of lawbreakers, the wolf's den, and the boudoir of the bear. In the cabin far up on Blackjack's shoulder, in the wildest part of these retreats, this odd couple had lived for twenty years. They had neither dog nor children to mitigate the heavy silence of the hills. Pike Garvey was little known in the settlements, but all who had dealt with him pronounced him "crazy as a loon." He acknowledged no occupation save that of a squirrel hunter, but he "moonshined" occasionally by way of diversion. Once the "revenues" had dragged him from his lair, fighting silently and desperately like a terrier, and he had been sent to state's prison for two years. Released, he popped back into his hole like an angry weasel.

Fortune, passing over many anxious wooers, made a freakish flight into Blackjack's bosky pockets to smile upon Pike and his faithful partner.

One day a party of spectacled, knickerbockered, and altogether absurd prospectors invaded the vicinity of the Garvey's cabin. Pike lifted his squirrel rifle off the hooks and took a shot at them at long range on the chance of their being revenues. Happily he missed, and the unconscious agents of good luck drew nearer, disclosing their innocence of anything resembling law or justice. Later on, they offered the Garveys an enormous quantity of ready, green, crisp money for their thirty-acre patch of cleared land, mentioning, as an excuse for such a mad action, some irrelevant and inadequate nonsense about a bed of mica underlying the said property.

When the Garveys became possessed of so many dollars that they faltered in computing them, the deficiencies of life on Blackjack began to grow prominent. Pike began to talk of new shoes, a hogshead of tobacco to set in the corner, a new lock to his rifle; and, leading Martella to a certain spot on the mountain-side, he pointed out to her how a small cannon—doubtless a thing not beyond the scope of their fortune in price—might be planted so as to command and defend the sole accessible trail to the cabin, to the confusion of revenues and meddling strangers forever.

But Adam reckoned without his Eve. These things represented to him the applied power of wealth, but there slumbered in his dingy cabin an ambition that soared far above his primitive wants. Somewhere in Mrs. Garvey's bosom still survived a spot of femininity unstarved by twenty years of Blackjack. For so long a time the sounds in her ears had been the scaly-barks dropping in the woods at noon, and the wolves singing among the rocks at night, and it was enough to have purged her of vanities. She had grown fat and sad and yellow and dull. But when the means came, she felt a rekindled desire to assume the perquisites of her sex—to sit at tea tables; to buy futile things; to whitewash the hideous veracity of life with a little form and ceremony. So she coldly vetoed Pike's proposed system of fortifications, and announced that they would descend upon the world, and gyrate socially.

And thus, at length, it was decided, and the thing done. The village of Laurel was their compromise between Mrs. Garvey's preference for one of the large valley towns and Pike's hankering for primeval solitudes. Laurel yielded a halting round of feeble social distractions comportable with Martella's ambitions, and was not entirely without recommendation to Pike, its contiguity to the mountains presenting advantages for sudden retreat in case fashionable society should make it advisable.

Their descent upon Laurel had been coincident with Yancey Goree's feverish desire to convert property into cash, and they bought the old Goree homestead, paying four thousand dollars ready money into the spendthrift's shaking hands.

Thus it happened that while the disreputable last of the Gorees sprawled in his disreputable office, at the end of his row, spurned by the cronies whom he had gorged, strangers dwelt in the halls of his fathers.

A cloud of dust was rolling, slowly up the parched street, with something travelling in the midst of it. A little breeze wafted the cloud to one side, and a new, brightly painted carryall, drawn by a slothful gray horse, became visible. The vehicle deflected from the middle of the street as it neared Goree's office, and stopped in the gutter directly in front of his door.

On the front seat sat a gaunt, tall man, dressed in black broadcloth, his rigid hands incarcerated in yellow kid gloves. On the back seat was a lady who triumphed over the June heat. Her stout form was armoured in a skin-tight silk dress of the description known as "changeable," being a gorgeous combination of shifting hues. She sat erect, waving a much-ornamented fan, with her eyes fixed stonily far down the street. However Martella Garvey's heart might be rejoicing at the pleasures of her new life, Blackjack had done his work with her exterior. He had carved her countenance to the image of emptiness and inanity; had imbued her with the stolidity of his crags, and the reserve of his hushed interiors. She always seemed to hear, whatever her surroundings were, the scaly-barks falling and pattering down the mountain-side. She could always hear the awful silence of Blackjack sounding through the stillest of nights.

Goree watched this solemn equipage, as it drove to his door, with only faint interest; but when the lank driver wrapped the reins about his whip, awkwardly descended, and stepped into the office, he rose unsteadily to receive him, recognizing Pike Garvey, the new, the transformed, the recently civilized.

The mountaineer took the chair Goree offered him. They who cast doubts upon Garvey's soundness of mind had a strong witness in the man's countenance. His face was too long, a dull saffron in hue, and immobile as a statue's. Pale-blue, unwinking round eyes without lashes added to the singularity of his gruesome visage. Goree was at a loss to account for the visit.

"Everything all right at Laurel, Mr. Garvey?" he inquired.

"Everything all right, sir, and mighty pleased is Missis Garvey and me with the property. Missis Garvey likes yo' old place, and she likes the neighbourhood. Society is what she 'lows she wants, and she is gettin' of it. The Rogerses, the Hapgoods, the Pratts and the Troys hev been to see Missis Garvey, and she hev et meals to most of thar houses. The best folks hev axed her to differ'nt kinds of doin's. I cyan't say, Mr. Goree, that sech things suits me—fur me, give me them thar." Garvey's huge, yellow-gloved hand flourished in the direction of the mountains. "That's whar I b'long, 'mongst the wild honey bees and the b'ars. But that ain't what I come fur to say, Mr. Goree. Thar's somethin' you got what me and Missis Garvey wants to buy."

"Buy!" echoed Goree. "From me?" Then he laughed harshly. "I reckon you are mistaken about that. I reckon you are mistaken about that. I sold out to you, as you yourself expressed it, 'lock, stock and barrel.' There isn't even a ramrod left to sell."

"You've got it; and we 'uns want it. 'Take the money,' says Missis Garvey, 'and buy it fa'r and squar'.'"

Goree shook his head. "The cupboard's bare," he said.

"We've riz," pursued the mountaineer, undeflected from his object, "a heap. We was pore as possums, and now we could hev folks to dinner every day. We been recognized, Missis Garvey says, by the best society. But there's somethin' we need we ain't got. She says it ought to been put in the 'ventory ov the sale, but it tain't thar. 'Take the money, then,' says she, 'and buy it fa'r and squar'.'"

"Out with it," said Goree, his racked nerves growing impatient.

Garvey threw his slouch hat upon the table, and leaned forward, fixing his unblinking eyes upon Goree's.

"There's a old feud," he said distinctly and slowly, "'tween you 'uns and the Coltranes."

Goree frowned ominously. To speak of his feud to a feudist is a serious breach of the mountain etiquette. The man from "back yan'" knew it as well as the lawyer did.

"Na offense," he went on "but purely in the way of business. Missis Garvey hev studied all about feuds. Most of the quality folks in the mountains hev 'em. The Settles and the Goforths, the Rankins and the Boyds, the Silers and the Galloways, hev all been cyarin' on feuds f'om twenty to a hundred year. The last man to drap was when yo' uncle, Jedge Paisley Goree, 'journed co't and shot Len Coltrane f'om the bench. Missis Garvey and me, we come f'om the po' white trash. Nobody wouldn't pick a feud with we 'uns, no mo'n with a fam'ly of tree-toads. Quality people everywhar, says Missis Garvey, has feuds. We 'uns ain't quality, but we're buyin' into it as fur as we can. 'Take the money, then,' says Missis Garvey, 'and buy Mr. Goree's feud, fa'r and squar'.'"

The squirrel hunter straightened a leg half across the room, drew a roll of bills from his pocket, and threw them on the table.

"Thar's two hundred dollars, Mr. Goree; what you would call a fa'r price for a feud that's been 'lowed to run down like yourn hev. Thar's only you left to cyar' on yo' side of it, and you'd make mighty po' killin'. I'll take it off yo' hands, and it'll set me and Missis Garvey up among the quality. Thar's the money."

The little roll of currency on the table slowly untwisted itself, writhing and jumping as its folds relaxed. In the silence that followed Garvey's last speech the rattling of the poker chips in the court-house could be plainly heard. Goree knew that the sheriff had just won a pot, for the subdued whoop with which he always greeted a victory floated across the square upon the crinkly heat waves. Beads of moisture stood on Goree's brow. Stooping, he drew the wicker-covered demijohn from under the table, and filled a tumbler from it.

"A little corn liquor, Mr. Garvey? Of course you are joking about—what you spoke of? Opens quite a new market, doesn't it? Feuds. Prime, two-fifty to three. Feuds, slightly damaged—two hundred, I believe you said, Mr. Garvey?"

Goree laughed self-consciously.

The mountaineer took the glass Goree handed him, and drank the whisky without a tremor of the lids of his staring eyes. The lawyer applauded the feat by a look of envious admiration. He poured his own drink, and took it like a drunkard, by gulps, and with shudders at the smell and taste.

"Two hundred," repeated Garvey. "Thar's the money."

A sudden passion flared up in Goree's brain. He struck the table with his fist. One of the bills flipped over and touched his hand. He flinched as if something had stung him.

"Do you come to me," he shouted, "seriously with such a ridiculous, insulting, darned-fool proposition?"

"It's fa'r and squar'," said the squirrel hunter, but he reached out his hand as if to take back the money; and then Goree knew that his own flurry of rage had not been from pride or resentment, but from anger at himself, knowing that he would set foot in the deeper depths that were being opened to him. He turned in an instant from an outraged gentleman to an anxious chafferer recommending his goods.

"Don't be in a hurry, Garvey," he said, his face crimson and his speech thick. "I accept your p-p-proposition, though it's dirt cheap at two hundred. A t-trade's all right when both p-purchaser and b-buyer are s-satisfied. Shall I w-wrap it up for you, Mr. Garvey?"

Garvey rose, and shook out his broadcloth. "Missis Garvey will be pleased. You air out of it, and it stands Coltrane and Garvey. Just a scrap ov writin', Mr. Goree, you bein' a lawyer, to show we traded."

Goree seized a sheet of paper and a pen. The money was clutched in his moist hand. Everything else suddenly seemed to grow trivial and light.

"Bill of sale, by all means. 'Right, title, and interest in and to' . . . 'forever warrant and—' No, Garvey, we'll have to leave out that 'defend,'" said Goree with a loud laugh. "You'll have to defend this title yourself."

The mountaineer received the amazing screed that the lawyer handed him, folded it with immense labour, and laced it carefully in his pocket.

Goree was standing near the window. "Step here," he said, raising his finger, "and I'll show you your recently purchased enemy. There he goes, down the other side of the street."

The mountaineer crooked his long frame to look through the window in the direction indicated by the other. Colonel Abner Coltrane, an erect, portly gentleman of about fifty, wearing the inevitable long, double-breasted frock coat of the Southern lawmaker, and an old high silk hat, was passing on the opposite sidewalk. As Garvey looked, Goree glanced at his face. If there be such a thing as a yellow wolf, here was its counterpart. Garvey snarled as his unhuman eyes followed the moving figure, disclosing long, amber-coloured fangs.

"Is that him? Why, that's the man who sent me to the pen'tentiary once!"

"He used to be district attorney," said Goree carelessly. "And, by the way, he's a first-class shot."

"I kin hit a squirrel's eye at a hundred yard," said Garvey. "So that thar's Coltrane! I made a better trade than I was thinkin'. I'll take keer ov this feud, Mr. Goree, better'n you ever did!"

He moved toward the door, but lingered there, betraying a slight perplexity.

"Anything else to-day?" inquired Goree with frothy sarcasm. "Any family traditions, ancestral ghosts, or skeletons in the closet? Prices as low as the lowest."

"Thar was another thing," replied the unmoved squirrel hunter, "that Missis Garvey was thinkin' of. 'Tain't so much in my line as t'other, but she wanted partic'lar that I should inquire, and ef you was willin', 'pay fur it,' she says, 'fa'r and squar'.' Thar's a buryin' groun', as you know, Mr. Goree, in the yard of yo' old place, under the cedars. Them that lies thar is yo' folks what was killed by the Coltranes. The monyments has the names on 'em. Missis Garvey says a fam'ly buryin' groun' is a sho' sign of quality. She says ef we git the feud, thar's somethin' else ought to go with it. The names on them monyments is 'Goree,' but they can be changed to ourn by—"

"Go! Go!" screamed Goree, his face turning purple. He stretched out both hands toward the mountaineer, his fingers hooked and shaking. "Go, you ghoul! Even a Ch-Chinaman protects the g-graves of his ancestors—go!"

The squirrel hunter slouched out of the door to his carryall. While he was climbing over the wheel Goree was collecting, with feverish celerity, the money that had fallen from his hand to the floor. As the vehicle slowly turned about, the sheep, with a coat of newly grown wool, was hurrying, in indecent haste, along the path to the court-house.

At three o'clock in the morning they brought him back to his office, shorn and unconscious. The sheriff, the sportive deputy, the county clerk, and the gay attorney carried him, the chalk-faced man "from the valley" acting as escort.

"On the table," said one of them, and they deposited him there among the litter of his unprofitable books and papers.

"Yance thinks a lot of a pair of deuces when he's liquored up," sighed the sheriff reflectively.

"Too much," said the gay attorney. "A man has no business to play poker who drinks as much as he does. I wonder how much he dropped to-night."

"Close to two hundred. What I wonder is whar he got it. Yance ain't had a cent fur over a month, I know."

"Struck a client, maybe. Well, let's get home before daylight. He'll be all right when he wakes up, except for a sort of beehive about the cranium."

The gang slipped away through the early morning twilight. The next eye to gaze upon the miserable Goree was the orb of day. He peered through the uncurtained window, first deluging the sleeper in a flood of faint gold, but soon pouring upon the mottled red of his flesh a searching, white, summer heat. Goree stirred, half unconsciously, among the table's débris, and turned his face from the window. His movement dislodged a heavy law book, which crashed upon the floor. Opening his eyes, he saw, bending over him, a man in a black frock coat. Looking higher, he discovered a well-worn silk hat, and beneath it the kindly, smooth face of Colonel Abner Coltrane.

A little uncertain of the outcome, the colonel waited for the other to make some sign of recognition. Not in twenty years had male members of these two families faced each other in peace. Goree's eyelids puckered as he strained his blurred sight toward this visitor, and then he smiled serenely.

"Have you brought Stella and Lucy over to play?" he said calmly.

"Do you know me, Yancey?" asked Coltrane.

"Of course I do. You brought me a whip with a whistle in the end."

So he had—twenty-four years ago; when Yancey's father was his best friend.

Goree's eyes wandered about the room. The colonel understood. "Lie still, and I'll bring you some," said he. There was a pump in the yard at the rear, and Goree closed his eyes, listening with rapture to the click of its handle, and the bubbling of the falling stream. Coltrane brought a pitcher of the cool water, and held it for him to drink. Presently Goree sat up—a most forlorn object, his summer suit of flax soiled and crumpled, his discreditable head tousled and unsteady. He tried to wave one of his hands toward the colonel.

"Ex-excuse—everything, will you?" he said. "I must have drunk too much whiskey last night, and gone to bed on the table." His brows knitted into a puzzled frown.

"Out with the boys awhile?" asked Coltrane kindly.

"No, I went nowhere. I haven't had a dollar to spend in the last two months. Struck the demijohn too often, I reckon, as usual."

Colonel Coltrane touched him on the shoulder.

"A little while ago, Yancey," he began, "you asked me if I had brought Stella and Lucy over to play. You weren't quite awake then, and must have been dreaming you were a boy again. You are awake now, and I want you to listen to me. I have come from Stella and Lucy to their old playmate, and to my old friend's son. They know that I am going to bring you home with me, and you will find them as ready with a welcome as they were in the old days. I want you to come to my house and stay until you are yourself again, and as much longer as you will. We heard of your being down in the world, and in the midst of temptation, and we agreed that you should come over and play at our house once more. Will you come, my boy? Will you drop our old family trouble and come with me?"

"Trouble!" said Goree, opening his eyes wide. "There was never any trouble between us that I know of. I'm sure we've always been the best friends. But, good Lord, Colonel, how could I go to your home as I am—a drunken wretch, a miserable, degraded spendthrift and gambler—"

He lurched from the table into his armchair, and began to weep maudlin tears, mingled with genuine drops of remorse and shame. Coltrane talked to him persistently and reasonably, reminding him of the simple mountain pleasures of which he had once been so fond, and insisting upon the genuineness of the invitation.

Finally he landed Goree by telling him he was counting upon his help in the engineering and transportation of a large amount of felled timber from a high mountain-side to a waterway. He knew that Goree had once invented a device for this purpose—a series of slides and chutes upon which he had justly prided himself. In an instant the poor fellow, delighted at the idea of his being of use to any one, had paper spread upon the table, and was drawing rapid but pitifully shaky lines in demonstration of what he could and would do.

The man was sickened of the husks; his prodigal heart was turning again toward the mountains. His mind was yet strangely clogged, and his thoughts and memories were returning to his brain one by one, like carrier pigeons over a stormy sea. But Coltrane was satisfied with the progress he had made.

Bethel received the surprise of its existence that afternoon when a Coltrane and a Goree rode amicably together through the town. Side by side they rode, out from the dusty streets and gaping townspeople, down across the creek bridge, and up toward the mountain. The prodigal had brushed and washed and combed himself to a more decent figure, but he was unsteady in the saddle, and he seemed to be deep in the contemplation of some vexing problem. Coltrane left him in his mood, relying upon the influence of changed surroundings to restore his equilibrium.

Once Goree was seized with a shaking fit, and almost came to a collapse. He had to dismount and rest at the side of the road. The colonel, foreseeing such a condition, had provided a small flask of whisky for the journey but when it was offered to him Goree refused it almost with violence, declaring he would never touch it again. By and by he was recovered, and went quietly enough for a mile or two. Then he pulled up his horse suddenly, and said:

"I lost two hundred dollars last night, playing poker. Now, where did I get that money?"

"Take it easy, Yancey. The mountain air will soon clear it up. We'll go fishing, first thing, at the Pinnacle Falls. The trout are jumping there like bullfrogs. We'll take Stella and Lucy along, and have a picnic on Eagle Rock. Have you forgotten how a hickory-cured-ham sandwich tastes, Yancey, to a hungry fisherman?"

Evidently the colonel did not believe the story of his lost wealth; so Goree retired again into brooding silence.

By late Afternoon they had travelled ten of the twelve miles between Bethel and Laurel. Half a mile this side of Laurel lay the old Goree place; a mile or two beyond the village lived the Coltranes. The road was now steep and laborious, but the compensations were many. The tilted aisles of the forest were opulent with leaf and bird and bloom. The tonic air put to shame the pharmacopæia. The glades were dark with mossy shade, and bright with shy rivulets winking from the ferns and laurels. On the lower side they viewed, framed in the near foliage, exquisite sketches of the far valley swooning in its opal haze.

Coltrane was pleased to see that his companion was yielding to the spell of the hills and woods. For now they had but to skirt the base of Painter's Cliff; to cross Elder Branch and mount the hill beyond, and Goree would have to face the squandered home of his fathers. Every rock he passed, every tree, every foot of the rocky way, was familiar to him. Though he had forgotten the woods, they thrilled him like the music of "Home, Sweet Home."

They rounded the cliff, descended into Elder Branch, and paused there to let the horses drink and splash in the swift water. On the right was a rail fence that cornered there, and followed the road and stream. Inclosed by it was the old apple orchard of the home place; the house was yet concealed by the brow of the steep hill. Inside and along the fence, pokeberries, elders, sassafras, and sumac grew high and dense. At a rustle of their branches, both Goree and Coltrane glanced up, and saw a long, yellow, wolfish face above the fence, staring at them with pale, unwinking eyes. The head quickly disappeared; there was a violent swaying of the bushes, and an ungainly figure ran up through the apple orchard in the direction of the house, zig-zagging among the trees.

"That's Garvey," said Coltrane; "the man you sold out to. There's no doubt but he's considerably cracked. I had to send him up for moonshining once, several years ago, in spite of the fact that I believed him irresponsible. Why, what's the matter, Yancey?"

Goree was wiping his forehead, and his face had lost its colour. "Do I look queer, too?" he asked, trying to smile. "I'm just remembering a few more things." Some of the alcohol had evaporated from his brain. "I recollect now where I got that two hundred dollars."

"Don't think of it," said Coltrane cheerfully. "Later on we'll figure it all out together."

They rode out of the branch, and when they reached the foot of the hill Goree stopped again.

"Did you ever suspect I was a very vain kind of fellow, Colonel?" he asked. "Sort of foolish proud about appearances?"

The colonel's eyes refused to wander to the soiled, sagging suit of flax and the faded slouch hat.

"It seems to me," he replied, mystified, but humouring him, "I remember a young buck about twenty, with the tightest coat, the sleekest hair, and the prancingest saddle horse in the Blue Ridge."

"Right you are," said Goree eagerly. "And it's in me yet, though it don't show. Oh, I'm as vain as a turkey gobbler, and as proud as Lucifer. I'm going to ask you to indulge this weakness of mine in a little matter."

"Speak out, Yancey. We'll create you Duke of Laurel and Baron of Blue Ridge, if you choose; and you shall have a feather out of Stella's peacock's tail to wear in your hat."

"I'm in earnest. In a few minutes we'll pass the house up there on the hill where I was born, and where my people have lived for nearly a century. Strangers live there now—and look at me! I am about to show myself to them ragged and poverty-stricken, a wastrel and a beggar. Colonel Coltrane, I'm ashamed to do it. I want you to let me wear your coat and hat until we are out of sight beyond. I know you think it a foolish pride, but I want to make as good a showing as I can when I pass the old place."

"Now, what does this mean?" said Coltrane to himself, as he compared his companion's sane looks and quiet demeanour with his strange request. But he was already unbuttoning the coat, assenting readily, as if the fancy were in no wise to be considered strange.

The coat and hat fitted Goree well. He buttoned the former about him with a look of satisfaction and dignity. He and Coltrane were nearly the same size—rather tall, portly, and erect. Twenty-five years were between them, but in appearance they might have been brothers. Goree looked older than his age; his face was puffy and lined; the colonel had the smooth, fresh complexion of a temperate liver. He put on Goree's disreputable old flax coat and faded slouch hat.

"Now," said Goree, taking up the reins, "I'm all right. I want you to ride about ten feet in the rear as we go by, Colonel, so that they can get a good look at me. They'll see I'm no back number yet, by any means. I guess I'll show up pretty well to them once more, anyhow. Let's ride on."

He set out up the hill at a smart trot, the colonel following, as he had been requested.

Goree sat straight in the saddle, with head erect, but his eyes were turned to the right, sharply scanning every shrub and fence and hiding-place in the old homestead yard. Once he muttered to himself, "Will the crazy fool try it, or did I dream half of it?"

It was when he came opposite the little family burying ground that he saw what he had been looking for—a puff of white smoke, coming from the thick cedars in one corner. He toppled so slowly to the left that Coltrane had time to urge his horse to that side, and catch him with one arm.

The squirrel hunter had not overpraised his aim. He had sent the bullet where he intended, and where Goree had expected that it would pass—through the breast of Colonel Abner Coltrane's black frock coat.

Goree leaned heavily against Coltrane, but he did not fall. The horses kept pace, side by side, and the Colonel's arm kept him steady. The little white houses of Laurel shone through the trees, half a mile away. Goree reached out one hand and groped until it rested upon Coltrane's fingers, which held his bridle.

"Good friend," he said, and that was all.

Thus did Yancey Goree, as he rode past his old home, make, considering all things, the best showing that was in his power.

XVI

The Song and the Sergeant

Half a dozen people supping at a table in one of the upper-Broadway all-night restaurants were making too much noise. Three times the manager walked past them with a politely warning glance; but their argument had waxed too warm to be quelled by a manager's gaze. It was midnight, and the restaurant was filled with patrons from the theatres of that district. Some among the dispersed audiences must have recognized among the quarrelsome sextet the faces of the players belonging to the Carroll Comedy Company.

Four of the six made up the company. Another was the author of the comedietta, "A Gay Coquette," which the quartette of players had been presenting with fair success at several vaudeville houses in the city. The sixth at the table was a person inconsequent in the realm of art, but one at whose bidding many lobsters had perished.

Loudly the six maintained their clamorous debate. No one of the Party was silent except when answers were stormed from him by the excited ones. That was the comedian of "A Gay Coquette." He was a young man with a face even too melancholy for his profession.

The oral warfare of four immoderate tongues was directed at Miss Clarice Carroll, the twinkling star of the small aggregation. Excepting the downcast comedian, all members of the party united in casting upon her with vehemence the blame of some momentous misfortune. Fifty times they told her: "It is your fault, Clarice—it is you alone who spoilt the scene. It is only of late that you have acted this way. At this rate the sketch will have to be taken off."

Miss Carroll was a match for any four. Gallic ancestry gave her a vivacity that could easily mount to fury. Her large eyes flashed a scorching denial at her accusers. Her slender, eloquent arms constantly menaced the tableware. Her high, clear soprano voice rose to what would have been a scream had it not possessed so pure a musical quality. She hurled back at the attacking four their denunciations in tones sweet, but of too great carrying power for a Broadway restaurant.

Finally they exhausted her patience both as a woman and an artist. She sprang up like a panther, managed to smash half a dozen plates and glasses with one royal sweep of her arm, and defied her critics. They rose and wrangled more loudly. The comedian sighed and looked a trifle sadder and disinterested. The manager came tripping and suggested peace. He was told to go to the popular synonym for war so promptly that the affair might have happened at The Hague.

Thus was the manager angered. He made a sign with his hand and a waiter slipped out of the door. In twenty minutes the party of six was in a police station facing a grizzled and philosophical desk sergeant.

"Disorderly conduct in a restaurant," said the policeman who had brought the party in.

The author of "A Gay Coquette" stepped to the front. He wore nose-glasses and evening clothes, even if his shoes had been tans before they met the patent-leather-polish bottle.

"Mr. Sergeant," said he, out of his throat, like Actor Irving, "I would like to protest against this arrest. The company of actors who are performing in a little play that I have written, in company with a friend and myself were having a little supper. We became deeply interested in the discussion as to which one of the cast is responsible for a scene in the sketch that lately has fallen so flat that the piece is about to become a failure. We may have been rather noisy and intolerant of interruption by the restaurant people; but the matter was of considerable importance to all of us. You see that we are sober and are not the kind of people who desire to raise disturbances. I hope that the case will not be pressed and that we may be allowed to go."

"Who makes the charge?" asked the sergeant.

"Me," said a white-aproned voice in the rear. "De restaurant sent me to. De gang was raisin' a rough-house and breakin' dishes."

"The dishes were paid for," said the playwright. "They were not broken purposely. In her anger, because we remonstrated with her for spoiling the scene, Miss—"

"It's not true, sergeant," cried the clear voice of Miss Clarice Carroll. In a long coat of tan silk and a red-plumed hat, she bounded before the desk.

"It's not my fault," she cried indignantly. "How dare they say such a thing! I've played the title rôle ever since it was staged, and if you want to know who made it a success, ask the public—that's all."

"What Miss Carroll says is true in part," said the author. "For five months the comedietta was a drawing-card in the best houses. But during the last two weeks it has lost favour. There is one scene in it in which Miss Carroll made a big hit. Now she hardly gets a hand out of it. She spoils it by acting it entirely different from her old way."

"It is not my fault," reiterated the actress.

"There are only two of you on in the scene," argued the playwright hotly, "you and Delmars, here—"

"Then it's his fault," declared Miss Carroll, with a lightning glance of scorn from her dark eyes. The comedian caught it, and gazed with increased melancholy at the panels of the sergeant's desk.

The night was a dull one in that particular police station.

The sergeant's long-blunted curiosity awoke a little.

"I've heard you," he said to the author. And then he addressed the thin-faced and ascetic-looking lady of the company who played "Aunt Turnip-top" in the little comedy.

"Who do you think spoils the scene you are fussing about?" he asked.

"I'm no knocker," said that lady, "and everybody knows it. So, when I say that Clarice falls down every time in that scene I'm judging her art and not herself. She was great in it once. She does it something fierce now. It'll dope the show if she keeps it up."

The sergeant looked at the comedian.

"You and the lady have this scene together, I understand. I suppose there's no use asking you which one of you queers it?"

The comedian avoided the direct rays from the two fixed stars of Miss Carroll's eyes.

"I don't know," he said, looking down at his patent-leather toes.

"Are you one of the actors?" asked the sergeant of a dwarfish youth with a middle-aged face.

"Why, say!" replied the last Thespian witness, "you don't notice any tin spear in my hands, do you? You haven't heard me shout: 'See, the Emperor comes!' since I've been in here, have you? I guess I'm on the stage long enough for 'em not to start a panic by mistaking me for a thin curl of smoke rising above the footlights."

"In your opinion, if you've got one," said the sergeant, "is the frost that gathers on the scene in question the work of the lady or the gentleman who takes part in it?"

The middle-aged youth looked pained.

"I regret to say," he answered, "that Miss Carroll seems to have lost her grip on that scene. She's all right in the rest of the play, but—but I tell you, sergeant, she can do it—she has done it equal to any of 'em— and she can do it again."

Miss Carroll ran forward, glowing and palpitating.

"Thank you, Jimmy, for the first good word I've had in many a day," she cried. And then she turned her eager face toward the desk.

"I'll show you, sergeant, whether I am to blame. I'll show them whether I can do that scene. Come, Mr. Delmars; let us begin. You will let us, won't you, sergeant?"

"How long will it take?" asked the sergeant, dubiously.

"Eight minutes," said the playwright. "The entire play consumes but thirty."

"You may go ahead," said the sergeant. "Most of you seem to side against the little lady. Maybe she had a right to crack up a saucer or two in that restaurant. We'll see how she does the turn before we take that up."

The matron of the police station had been standing near, listening to the singular argument. She came nigher and stood near the sergeant's chair. Two or three of the reserves strolled in, big and yawning.

"Before beginning the scene," said the playwright, "and assuming that you have not seen a production of 'A Gay Coquette,' I will make a brief but necessary explanation. It is a musical-farce-comedy—burlesque-comedietta. As the title implies, Miss Carroll's rôle is that of a gay, rollicking, mischievous, heartless coquette. She sustains that character throughout the entire comedy part of the production. And I have designed the extravaganza features so that she may preserve and present the same coquettish idea.

"Now, the scene in which we take exception to Miss Carroll's acting is called the 'gorilla dance.' She is costumed to represent a wood nymph, and there is a great song-and-dance scene with a gorilla—played by Mr. Delmars, the comedian. A tropical-forest stage is set.

"That used to get four and five recalls. The main thing was the acting and the dance—it was the funniest thing in New York for five months. Delmars's song, 'I'll Woo Thee to My Sylvan Home,' while he and Miss Carroll were cutting hide-and-seek capers among the tropical plants, was a winner."

"What's the trouble with the scene now?" asked the sergeant.

"Miss Carroll spoils it right in the middle of it," said the playwright wrathfully.

With a wide gesture of her ever-moving arms the actress waved back the little group of spectators, leaving a space in front of the desk for the scene of her vindication or fall. Then she whipped off her long tan cloak and tossed it across the arm of the policeman who still stood officially among them.

Miss Carroll had gone to supper well cloaked, but in the costume of the tropic wood nymph. A skirt of fern leaves touched her knee; she was like a humming-bird—green and golden and purple.

And then she danced a fluttering, fantastic dance, so agile and light and mazy in her steps that the other three members of the Carroll Comedy Company broke into applause at the art of it.

And at the proper time Delmars leaped out at her side, mimicking the uncouth, hideous bounds of the gorilla so funnily that the grizzled sergeant himself gave a short laugh like the closing of a padlock. They danced together the gorilla dance, and won a hand from all.

Then began the most fantastic part of the scene—the wooing of the nymph by the gorilla. It was a kind of dance itself—eccentric and prankish, with the nymph in coquettish and seductive retreat, followed by the gorilla as he sang "I'll Woo Thee to My Sylvan Home."

The song was a lyric of merit. The words were non-sense, as befitted the play, but the music was worthy of something better. Delmars struck into it in a rich tenor that owned a quality that shamed the flippant words.

During one verse of the song the wood nymph performed the grotesque evolutions designed for the scene. At the middle of the second verse she stood still, with a strange look on her face, seeming to gaze dreamily into the depths of the scenic forest. The gorilla's last leap had brought him to her feet, and there he knelt, holding her hand, until he had finished the haunting-lyric that was set in the absurd comedy like a diamond in a piece of putty.

When Delmars ceased Miss Carroll started, and covered a sudden flow of tears with both hands.

"There!" cried the playwright, gesticulating with violence; "there you have it, sergeant. For two weeks she has spoiled that scene in just that manner at every performance. I have begged her to consider that it is not Ophelia or Juliet that she is playing. Do you wonder now at our impatience? Tears for the gorilla song! The play is lost!"

Out of her bewitchment, whatever it was, the wood nymph flared suddenly, and pointed a desperate finger at Delmars.

"It is you—you who have done this," she cried wildly. "You never sang that song that way until lately. It is your doing."

"I give it up," said the sergeant.

And then the gray-haired matron of the police station came forward from behind the sergeant's chair.

"Must an old woman teach you all?" she said. She went up to Miss Carroll and took her hand.

"The man's wearing his heart out for you, my dear. Couldn't you tell it the first note you heard him sing? All of his monkey flip-flops wouldn't have kept it from me. Must you be deaf as well as blind? That's why you couldn't act your part, child. Do you love him or must he be a gorilla for the rest of his days?"

Miss Carroll whirled around and caught Delmars with a lightning glance of her eye. He came toward her, melancholy.

"Did you hear, Mr. Delmars?" she asked, with a catching breath.

"I did," said the comedian. "It is true. I didn't think there was any use. I tried to let you know with the song."

"Silly!" said the matron; "why didn't you speak?"

"No, no," cried the wood nymph, "his way was the best. I didn't know, but—it was just what I wanted, Bobby."

She sprang like a green grasshopper; and the comedian opened his arms, and—smiled.

"Get out of this," roared the desk sergeant to the waiting waiter from the restaurant. "There's nothing doing here for you."

XVII

One Dollar's Worth

The judge of the United States court of the district lying along the Rio Grande border found the following letter one morning in his mail:

JUDGE:

When you sent me up for four years you made a talk. Among other hard things, you called me a rattlesnake. Maybe I am one—anyhow, you hear me rattling now. One year after I got to the pen, my daughter died of—well, they said it was poverty and the disgrace together. You've got a daughter, Judge, and I'm going to make you know how it feels to lose one. And I'm going to bite that district attorney that spoke against me. I'm free now, and I guess I've turned to rattlesnake all right. I feel like one. I don't say much, but this is my rattle. Look out when I strike.

Yours respectfully,
RATTLESNAKE

Judge Derwent threw the letter carelessly aside. It was nothing new to receive such epistles from desperate men whom he had been called upon to judge. He felt no alarm. Later on he showed the letter to Littlefield, the young district attorney, for Littlefield's name was included in the threat, and the judge was punctilious in matters between himself and his fellow men.

Littlefield honoured the rattle of the writer, as far as it concerned himself, with a smile of contempt; but he frowned a little over the reference to the Judge's daughter, for he and Nancy Derwent were to be married in the fall.

Littlefield went to the clerk of the court and looked over the records with him. They decided that the letter might have been sent by Mexico Sam, a half-breed border desperado who had been imprisoned for manslaughter four years before. Then official duties crowded the matter from his mind, and the rattle of the revengeful serpent was forgotten.

Court was in session at Brownsville. Most of the cases to be tried were charges of smuggling, counterfeiting, post-office robberies, and violations of Federal laws along the border. One case was that of a young Mexican, Rafael Ortiz, who had been rounded up by a clever deputy marshal in the act of passing a counterfeit silver dollar. He had been suspected of many such deviations from rectitude, but this was the first time that anything provable had been fixed upon him. Ortiz languished cozily in jail, smoking brown cigarettes and waiting for trial. Kilpatrick, the deputy, brought the counterfeit dollar and handed it to the district attorney in his office in the court-house. The deputy and a reputable druggist were prepared to swear that Ortiz paid for a bottle of medicine with it. The coin was a poor counterfeit, soft, dull-looking, and made principally of lead. It was the day before the morning on which the docket would reach the case of Ortiz, and the district attorney was preparing himself for trial.

"Not much need of having in high-priced experts to prove the coin's queer, is there, Kil?" smiled Littlefield, as he thumped the dollar down upon the table, where it fell with no more ring than would have come from a lump of putty.

"I guess the Greaser's as good as behind the bars," said the deputy, easing up his holsters. "You've got him dead. If it had been just one time, these Mexicans can't tell good money from bad; but this little yaller rascal belongs to a gang of counterfeiters, I know. This is the first time I've been able to catch him doing the trick. He's got a girl down there in them Mexican jacals on the river bank. I seen her one day when I was watching him. She's as pretty as a red heifer in a flower bed."

Littlefield shoved the counterfeit dollar into his pocket, and slipped his memoranda of the case into an envelope. Just then a bright, winsome face, as frank and jolly as a boy's, appeared in the doorway, and in walked Nancy Derwent.

"Oh, Bob, didn't court adjourn at twelve to-day until to-morrow?" she asked of Littlefield.

"It did," said the district attorney, "and I'm very glad of it. I've got a lot of rulings to look up, and—"

"Now, that's just like you. I wonder you and father don't turn to law books or rulings or something! I want you to take me out plover-shooting this afternoon. Long Prairie is just alive with them. Don't say no, please! I want to try my new twelve-bore hammerless. I've sent to the livery stable to engage Fly and Bess for the buckboard; they stand fire so nicely. I was sure you would go."

They were to be married in the fall. The glamour was at its height. The plovers won the day—or, rather, the afternoon—over the calf-bound authorities. Littlefield began to put his papers away.

There was a knock at the door. Kilpatrick answered it. A beautiful, dark-eyed girl with a skin tinged with the faintest lemon colour walked into the room. A black shawl was thrown over her head and wound once around her neck.

She began to talk in Spanish, a voluble, mournful stream of melancholy music. Littlefield did not understand Spanish. The deputy did, and he translated her talk by portions, at intervals holding up his hand to check the flow of her words.

"She came to see you, Mr. Littlefield. Her name's Joya Treviñas. She wants to see you about—well, she's mixed up with that Rafael Ortiz. She's his—she's his girl. She says he's innocent. She says she made the money and got him to pass it. Don't you believe her, Mr. Littlefield. That's the way with these Mexican girls; they'll lie, steal, or kill for a fellow when they get stuck on him. Never trust a woman that's in love!"

"Mr. Kilpatrick!"

Nancy Derwent's indignant exclamation caused the deputy to flounder for a moment in attempting to explain that he had misquoted his own sentiments, and then he went on with the translation:

"She says she's willing to take his place in the jail if you'll let him out. She says she was down sick with the fever, and the doctor said she'd die if she didn't have medicine. That's why he passed the lead dollar on the drug store. She says it saved her life. This Rafael seems to be her honey, all right; there's a lot of stuff in her talk about love and such things that you don't want to hear."

It was an old story to the district attorney.

"Tell her," said he, "that I can do nothing. The case comes up in the morning, and he will have to make his fight before the court."

Nancy Derwent was not so hardened. She was looking with sympathetic interest at Joya Treviñas and at Littlefield alternately. The deputy repeated the district attorney's words to the girl. She spoke a sentence or two in a low voice, pulled her shawl closely about her face, and left the room.

"What did she say then?" asked the district attorney.

"Nothing special," said the deputy. "She said: 'If the life of the one'—let's see how it went—'*Si la vida de ella a quien tu amas*—if the life of the girl you love is ever in danger, remember Rafael Ortiz.'"

Kilpatrick strolled out through the corridor in the direction of the marshal's office.

"Can't you do anything for them, Bob?" asked Nancy. "It's such a little thing—just one counterfeit dollar—to ruin the happiness of two lives! She was in danger of death, and he did it to save her. Doesn't the law know the feeling of pity?"

"It hasn't a place in jurisprudence, Nan," said Littlefield, "especially *in re* the district attorney's duty. I'll promise you that the prosecution will not be vindictive; but the man is as good as convicted when the case is called. Witnesses will swear to his passing the bad dollar which I have in my pocket at this moment as 'Exhibit A.' There are no Mexicans on the jury, and it will vote Mr. Greaser guilty without leaving the box."

THE PLOVER-SHOOTING WAS FINE THAT afternoon, and in the excitement of the sport the case of Rafael and the grief of Joya Treviñas was forgotten. The district attorney and Nancy Derwent drove out from the town three miles along a smooth, grassy road, and then struck across a rolling prairie toward a heavy line of timber on Piedra Creek. Beyond this creek lay Long Prairie, the favourite haunt of the plover. As they were nearing the creek they heard the galloping of a horse to their right, and saw a man with black hair and a swarthy face riding toward the woods at a tangent, as if he had come up behind them.

"I've seen that fellow somewhere," said Littlefield, who had a memory for faces, "but I can't exactly place him. Some ranchman, I suppose, taking a short cut home."

They spent an hour on Long Prairie, shooting from the buckboard. Nancy Derwent, an active, outdoor Western girl, was pleased with her twelve-bore. She had bagged within two brace of her companion's score.

They started homeward at a gentle trot. When within a hundred yards of Piedra Creek a man rode out of the timber directly toward them.

"It looks like the man we saw coming over," remarked Miss Derwent.

As the distance between them lessened, the district attorney suddenly pulled up his team sharply, with his eyes fixed upon the advancing horseman. That individual had drawn a Winchester from its scabbard on his saddle and thrown it over his arm.

"Now I know you, Mexico Sam!" muttered Littlefield to himself. "It was you who shook your rattles in that gentle epistle."

Mexico Sam did not leave things long in doubt. He had a nice eye in all matters relating to firearms, so when he was within good rifle range, but outside of danger from No. 8 shot, he threw up his Winchester and opened fire upon the occupants of the buckboard.

The first shot cracked the back of the seat within the two-inch space between the shoulders of Littlefield and Miss Derwent. The next went through the dashboard and Littlefield's trouser leg.

The district attorney hustled Nancy out of the buck-board to the ground. She was a little pale, but asked no questions. She had the frontier instinct that accepts conditions in an emergency without superfluous argument. They kept their guns in hand, and Littlefield hastily gathered some handfuls of cartridges from the pasteboard box on the seat and crowded them into his pockets.

"Keep behind the horses, Nan," he commanded. "That fellow is a ruffian I sent to prison once. He's trying to get even. He knows our shot won't hurt him at that distance."

"All right, Bob," said Nancy steadily. "I'm not afraid. But you come close, too. Whoa, Bess; stand still, now!"

She stroked Bess's mane. Littlefield stood with his gun ready, praying that the desperado would come within range.

But Mexico Sam was playing his vendetta along safe lines. He was a bird of different feather from the plover. His accurate eye drew an imaginary line of circumference around the area of danger from bird-shot, and upon this line lie rode. His horse wheeled to the right, and as his victims rounded to the safe side of their equine breast-work he sent a ball through the district attorney's hat. Once he miscalculated in making a détour, and over-stepped his margin. Littlefield's gun flashed, and Mexico Sam ducked his head to the harmless patter of the shot. A few of them stung his horse, which pranced promptly back to the safety line.

The desperado fired again. A little cry came from Nancy Derwent. Littlefield whirled, with blazing eyes, and saw the blood trickling down her cheek.

"I'm not hurt, Bob—only a splinter struck me. I think he hit one of the wheel-spokes."

"Lord!" groaned Littlefield. "If I only had a charge of buckshot!"

The ruffian got his horse still, and took careful aim. Fly gave a snort and fell in the harness, struck in the neck. Bess, now disabused of the idea that plover were being fired at, broke her traces and galloped wildly away. Mexican Sam sent a ball neatly through the fulness of Nancy Derwent's shooting jacket.

"Lie down—lie down!" snapped Littlefield. "Close to the horse—flat on the ground—so." He almost threw her upon the grass against the back of the recumbent Fly. Oddly enough, at that moment the words of the Mexican girl returned to his mind:

"If the life of the girl you love is ever in danger, remember Rafael Ortiz."

Littlefield uttered an exclamation.

"Open fire on him, Nan, across the horse's back. Fire as fast as you can! You can't hurt him, but keep him dodging shot for one minute while I try to work a little scheme."

Nancy gave a quick glance at Littlefield, and saw him take out his pocket-knife and open it. Then she turned her face to obey orders, keeping up a rapid fire at the enemy.

Mexico Sam waited patiently until this innocuous fusillade ceased. He had plenty of time, and he did not care to risk the chance of a bird-shot in his eye when it could be avoided by a little caution. He pulled his heavy Stetson low down over his face until the shots ceased. Then he drew a little nearer, and fired with careful aim at what he could see of his victims above the fallen horse.

Neither of them moved. He urged his horse a few steps nearer. He saw the district attorney rise to one knee and deliberately level his shotgun. He pulled his hat down and awaited the harmless rattle of the tiny pellets.

The shotgun blazed with a heavy report. Mexico Sam sighed, turned limp all over, and slowly fell from his horse—a dead rattlesnake.

AT TEN O'CLOCK THE NEXT morning court opened, and the case of the United States versus Rafael Ortiz was called. The district attorney, with his arm in a sling, rose and addressed the court.

"May it please your honour," he said, "I desire to enter a *nolle pros.* in this case. Even though the defendant should be guilty, there is not sufficient evidence in the hands of the government to secure a conviction. The piece of counterfeit coin upon the identity of which the case was built is not now available as evidence. I ask, therefore, that the case be stricken off."

At the noon recess Kilpatrick strolled into the district attorney's office.

"I've just been down to take a squint at old Mexico Sam," said the deputy. "They've got him laid out. Old Mexico was a tough outfit, I reckon. The boys was wonderin' down there what you shot him with. Some said it must have been nails. I never see a gun carry anything to make holes like he had."

"I shot him," said the district attorney, "with Exhibit A of your counterfeiting case. Lucky thing for me—and somebody else—that it was as bad money as it was! It sliced up into slugs very nicely. Say, Kil, can't you go down to the jacals and find where that Mexican girl lives? Miss Derwent wants to know."

XVIII

A Newspaper Story

At 8 a.m. it lay on Giuseppi's news-stand, still damp from the presses. Giuseppi, with the cunning of his ilk, philandered on the opposite corner, leaving his patrons to help themselves, no doubt on a theory related to the hypothesis of the watched pot.

This particular newspaper was, according to its custom and design, an educator, a guide, a monitor, a champion and a household counsellor and *vade mecum*.

From its many excellencies might be selected three editorials. One was in simple and chaste but illuminating language directed to parents and teachers, deprecating corporal punishment for children.

Another was an accusive and significant warning addressed to a notorious labour leader who was on the point of instigating his clients to a troublesome strike.

The third was an eloquent demand that the police force be sustained and aided in everything that tended to increase its efficiency as public guardians and servants.

Besides these more important chidings and requisitions upon the store of good citizenship was a wise prescription or form of procedure laid out by the editor of the heart-to-heart column in the specific case of a young man who had complained of the obduracy of his lady love, teaching him how he might win her.

Again, there was, on the beauty page, a complete answer to a young lady inquirer who desired admonition toward the securing of bright eyes, rosy cheeks and a beautiful countenance.

One other item requiring special cognizance was a brief "personal," running thus:

Dear Jack:
   Forgive me. You were right. Meet me corner Madison and ——th at 8.30 this morning. We leave at noon.
                                                              Penitent

At 8 o'clock a young man with a haggard look and the feverish gleam of unrest in his eye dropped a penny and picked up the top paper as he passed Giuseppi's stand. A sleepless night had left him a late riser. There was an office to be reached by nine, and a shave and a hasty cup of coffee to be crowded into the interval.

He visited his barber shop and then hurried on his way. He pocketed his paper, meditating a belated perusal of it at the luncheon hour. At the next corner it fell from his pocket, carrying with it his pair of new gloves. Three blocks he walked, missed the gloves and turned back fuming.

Just on the half-hour he reached the corner where lay the gloves and the paper. But he strangely ignored that which he had come to seek. He was holding two little hands as tightly as ever he could and looking into two penitent brown eyes, while joy rioted in his heart.

"Dear Jack," she said, "I knew you would be here on time."

"I wonder what she means by that," he was saying to himself; "but it's all right, it's all right."

A big wind puffed out of the west, picked up the paper from the sidewalk, opened it out and sent it flying and whirling down a side street. Up that street was driving a skittish bay to a spider-wheel buggy, the young man who had written to the heart-to-heart editor for a recipe that he might win her for whom he sighed.

The wind, with a prankish flurry, flapped the flying newspaper against the face of the skittish bay. There was a lengthened streak of bay mingled with the red of running gear that stretched itself out for four blocks. Then a water-hydrant played its part in the cosmogony, the buggy became matchwood as foreordained, and the driver rested very quietly where he had been flung on the asphalt in front of a certain brownstone mansion.

They came out and had him inside very promptly. And there was one who made herself a pillow for his head, and cared for no curious eyes, bending over and saying, "Oh, it was you; it was you all the time, Bobby! Couldn't you see it? And if you die, why, so must I, and—"

But in all this wind we must hurry to keep in touch with our paper.

Policeman O'Brine arrested it as a character dangerous to traffic. Straightening its dishevelled leaves with his big, slow fingers, he stood a few feet from the family entrance of the Shandon Bells Café. One headline he spelled out ponderously: "The Papers to the Front in a Move to Help the Police."

But, whisht! The voice of Danny, the head bartender, through the crack of the door: "Here's a nip for ye, Mike, ould man."

Behind the widespread, amicable columns of the press Policeman O'Brine receives swiftly his nip of the real stuff. He moves away, stalwart, refreshed, fortified, to his duties. Might not the editor man view with pride the early, the spiritual, the literal fruit that had blessed his labours.

Policeman O'Brine folded the paper and poked it playfully under the arm of a small boy that was passing. That boy was named Johnny, and he took the paper home with him. His sister was named Gladys, and she had written to the beauty editor of the paper asking for the practicable touchstone of beauty. That was weeks ago, and she had ceased to look for an answer. Gladys was a pale girl, with dull eyes and a discontented expression. She was dressing to go up to the avenue to get some braid. Beneath her skirt she pinned two leaves of the paper Johnny had brought. When she walked the rustling sound was an exact imitation of the real thing.

On the street she met the Brown girl from the flat below and stopped to talk. The Brown girl turned green. Only silk at $5 a yard could make the sound that she heard when Gladys moved. The Brown girl, consumed by jealousy, said something spiteful and went her way, with pinched lips.

Gladys proceeded toward the avenue. Her eyes now sparkled like jagerfonteins. A rosy bloom visited her cheeks; a triumphant, subtle, vivifying, smile transfigured her face. She was beautiful. Could the beauty editor have seen her then! There was something in her answer in the paper, I believe, about cultivating kind feelings toward others in order to make plain features attractive.

The labour leader against whom the paper's solemn and weighty editorial injunction was laid was the father of Gladys and Johnny. He picked up the remains of the journal from which Gladys had ravished a cosmetic of silken sounds. The editorial did not come under his eye, but instead it was greeted by one of those ingenious and specious puzzle problems that enthrall alike the simpleton and the sage.

The labour leader tore off half of the page, provided himself with table, pencil and paper and glued himself to his puzzle.

Three hours later, after waiting vainly for him at the appointed place, other more conservative leaders declared and ruled in favour of arbitration, and the strike with its attendant dangers was averted. Subsequent editions of the paper referred, in coloured inks, to the clarion tone of its successful denunciation of the labour leader's intended designs.

The remaining leaves of the active journal also went loyally to the proving of its potency.

When Johnny returned from school he sought a secluded spot and removed the missing columns from the inside of his clothing, where they had been artfully distributed so as to successfully defend such areas as are generally attacked during scholastic castigations. Johnny attended a private school and had had trouble with his teacher. As has been said, there was an excellent editorial against corporal punishment in that morning's issue, and no doubt it had its effect.

After this can any one doubt the power of the press?

XIX

Tommy's Burglar

At ten o'clock P.M. Felicia, the maid, left by the basement door with the policeman to get a raspberry phosphate around the corner. She detested the policeman and objected earnestly to the arrangement. She pointed out, not unreasonably, that she might have been allowed to fall asleep over one of St. George Rathbone's novels on the third floor, but she was overruled. Raspberries and cops were not created for nothing.

The burglar got into the house without much difficulty; because we must have action and not too much description in a 2,000-word story.

In the dining room he opened the slide of his dark lantern. With a brace and centrebit he began to bore into the lock of the silver-closet.

Suddenly a click was heard. The room was flooded with electric light. The dark velvet portières parted to admit a fair-haired boy of eight in pink pajamas, bearing a bottle of olive oil in his hand.

"Are you a burglar?" he asked, in a sweet, childish voice.

"Listen to that," exclaimed the man, in a hoarse voice. "Am I a burglar? Wot do you suppose I have a three-days' growth of bristly beard on my face for, and a cap with flaps? Give me the oil, quick, and let me grease the bit, so I won't wake up your mamma, who is lying down with a headache, and left you in charge of Felicia who has been faithless to her trust."

"Oh, dear," said Tommy, with a sigh. "I thought you would be more up-to-date. This oil is for the salad when I bring lunch from the pantry for you. And mamma and papa have gone to the Metropolitan to hear De Reszke. But that isn't my fault. It only shows how long the story has been knocking around among the editors. If the author had been wise he'd have changed it to Caruso in the proofs."

"Be quiet," hissed the burglar, under his breath. "If you raise an alarm I'll wring your neck like a rabbit's."

"Like a chicken's," corrected Tommy. "You had that wrong. You don't wring rabbits' necks."

"Aren't you afraid of me?" asked the burglar.

"You know I'm not," answered Tommy. "Don't you suppose I know fact from fiction. If this wasn't a story I'd yell like an Indian when I saw you; and you'd probably tumble downstairs and get pinched on the sidewalk."

"I see," said the burglar, "that you're on to your job. Go on with the performance."

Tommy seated himself in an armchair and drew his toes up under him.

"Why do you go around robbing strangers, Mr. Burglar? Have you no friends?"

"I see what you're driving at," said the burglar, with a dark frown. "It's the same old story. Your innocence and childish insouciance is going to lead me back into an honest life. Every time I crack a crib where there's a kid around, it happens."

"Would you mind gazing with wolfish eyes at the plate of cold beef that the butler has left on the dining table?" said Tommy. "I'm afraid it's growing late."

The burglar accommodated.

"Poor man," said Tommy. "You must be hungry. If you will please stand in a listless attitude I will get you something to eat."

The boy brought a roast chicken, a jar of marmalade and a bottle of wine from the pantry. The burglar seized a knife and fork sullenly.

"It's only been an hour," he grumbled, "since I had a lobster and a pint of musty ale up on Broadway. I wish these story writers would let a fellow have a pepsin tablet, anyhow, between feeds."

"My papa writes books," remarked Tommy.

The burglar jumped to his feet quickly.

"You said he had gone to the opera," he hissed, hoarsely and with immediate suspicion.

"I ought to have explained," said Tommy. "He didn't buy the tickets." The burglar sat again and toyed with the wishbone.

"Why do you burgle houses?" asked the boy, wonderingly.

"Because," replied the burglar, with a sudden flow of tears. "God bless my little brown-haired boy Bessie at home."

"Ah," said Tommy, wrinkling his nose, "you got that answer in the wrong place. You want to tell your hard-luck story before you pull out the child stop."

"Oh, yes," said the burglar, "I forgot. Well, once I lived in Milwaukee, and—"

"Take the silver," said Tommy, rising from his chair.

"Hold on," said the burglar. "But I moved away. I could find no other employment. For a while I managed to support my wife and child by passing confederate money; but, alas! I was forced to give that up because it did not belong to the union. I became desperate and a burglar."

"Have you ever fallen into the hands of the police?" asked Tommy.

"I said 'burglar,' not 'beggar,'" answered the cracksman.

"After you finish your lunch," said Tommy, "and experience the usual change of heart, how shall we wind up the story?"

"Suppose," said the burglar, thoughtfully, "that Tony Pastor turns out earlier than usual to-night, and your father gets in from 'Parsifal' at 10.30. I am thoroughly repentant because you have made me think of my own little boy Bessie, and—"

"Say," said Tommy, "haven't you got that wrong?"

"Not on your coloured crayon drawings by B. Cory Kilvert," said the burglar. "It's always a Bessie that I have at home, artlessly prattling to the pale-cheeked burglar's bride. As I was saying, your father opens the front door just as I am departing with admonitions and sandwiches that you have wrapped up for me. Upon recognizing me as an old Harvard classmate he starts back in—"

"Not in surprise?" interrupted Tommy, with wide, open eyes.

"He starts back in the doorway," continued the burglar. And then he rose to his feet and began to shout "Rah, rah, rah! rah, rah, rah! rah, rah, rah!"

"Well," said Tommy, wonderingly, "that's the first time I ever knew a burglar to give a college yell when he was burglarizing a house, even in a story."

"That's one on you," said the burglar, with a laugh. "I was practising the dramatization. If this is put on the stage that college touch is about the only thing that will make it go."

Tommy looked his admiration.

"You're on, all right," he said.

"And there's another mistake you've made," said the burglar. "You should have gone some time ago and brought me the $9 gold piece your mother gave you on your birthday to take to Bessie."

"But she didn't give it to me to take to Bessie," said Tommy, pouting.

"Come, come!" said the burglar, sternly. "It's not nice of you to take advantage because the story contains an ambiguous sentence. You know what I mean. It's mighty little I get out of these fictional jobs, anyhow. I lose all the loot, and I have to reform every time; and all the swag I'm allowed is the blamed little fol-de-rols and luck-pieces that you kids hand over. Why, in one story, all I got was a kiss from a little girl who came in on me when I was opening a safe. And it tasted of molasses candy, too. I've a good notion to tie this table cover over your head and keep on into the silver-closet."

"Oh, no, you haven't," said Tommy, wrapping his arms around his knees. "Because if you did no editor would buy the story. You know you've got to preserve the unities."

"So've you," said the burglar, rather glumly. "Instead of sitting here talking impudence and taking the bread out of a poor man's mouth, what you'd like to be doing is hiding under the bed and screeching at the top of your voice."

"You're right, old man," said Tommy, heartily. "I wonder what they make us do it for? I think the S. P. C. C. ought to interfere. I'm sure it's neither agreeable nor usual for a kid of my age to butt in when a full-grown burglar is at work and offer him a red sled and a pair of skates not to awaken his sick mother. And look how they make the burglars act! You'd think editors would know—but what's the use?"

The burglar wiped his hands on the tablecloth and arose with a yawn.

"Well, let's get through with it," he said. "God bless you, my little boy! you have saved a man from committing a crime this night. Bessie shall pray for you as soon as I get home and give her her orders. I shall never burglarize another house—at least not until the June magazines are out. It'll be your little sister's turn then to run in on me while I am abstracting the U. S. 4 per cent. from the tea urn and buy me off with her coral necklace and a falsetto kiss."

"You haven't got all the kicks coming to you," sighed Tommy, crawling out of his chair. "Think of the sleep I'm losing. But it's tough on both of us, old man. I wish you could get out of the story and really rob somebody. Maybe you'll have the chance if they dramatize us."

"Never!" said the burglar, gloomily. "Between the box office and my better impulses that your leading juveniles are supposed to awaken and the magazines that pay on publication, I guess I'll always be broke."

"I'm sorry," said Tommy, sympathetically. "But I can't help myself any more than you can. It's one of the canons of household fiction that no burglar shall be successful. The burglar must be foiled by a kid like me, or by a young lady heroine, or at the last moment by his old pal, Red Mike, who recognizes the house as one in which he used to be the coachman. You have got the worst end of it in any kind of a story."

"Well, I suppose I must be clearing out now," said the burglar, taking up his lantern and bracebit.

"You have to take the rest of this chicken and the bottle of wine with you for Bessie and her mother," said Tommy, calmly.

"But confound it," exclaimed the burglar, in an annoyed tone, "they don't want it. I've got five cases of Château de Beychsvelle at home that was bottled in 1853. That claret of yours is corked. And you couldn't get either of them to look at a chicken unless it was stewed in champagne. You know, after I get out of the story I don't have so many limitations. I make a turn now and then."

"Yes, but you must take them," said Tommy, loading his arms with the bundles.

"Bless you, young master!" recited the burglar, obedient. "Second-Story Saul will never forget you. And now hurry and let me out, kid. Our 2,000 words must be nearly up."

Tommy led the way through the hall toward the front door. Suddenly the burglar stopped and called to him softly: "Ain't there a cop out there in front somewhere sparking the girl?"

"Yes," said Tommy, "but what—"

"I'm afraid he'll catch me," said the burglar. "You mustn't forget that this is fiction."

"Great head!" said Tommy, turning. "Come out by the back door."

XX

A Chaparral Christmas Gift

The original cause of the trouble was about twenty years in growing. At the end of that time it was worth it.

Had you lived anywhere within fifty miles of Sundown Ranch you would have heard of it. It possessed a quantity of jet-black hair, a pair of extremely frank, deep-brown eyes and a laugh that rippled across the prairie like the sound of a hidden brook. The name of it was Rosita McMullen; and she was the daughter of old man McMullen of the Sundown Sheep Ranch.

There came riding on red roan steeds—or, to be more explicit, on a paint and a flea-bitten sorrel—two wooers. One was Madison Lane, and the other was the Frio Kid. But at that time they did not call him the Frio Kid, for he had not earned the honours of special nomenclature. His name was simply Johnny McRoy.

It must not be supposed that these two were the sum of the agreeable Rosita's admirers. The bronchos of a dozen others champed their bits at the long hitching rack of the Sundown Ranch. Many were the sheeps'-eyes that were cast in those savannas that did not belong to the flocks of Dan McMullen. But of all the cavaliers, Madison Lane and Johnny McRoy galloped far ahead, wherefore they are to be chronicled.

Madison Lane, a young cattleman from the Nueces country, won the race. He and Rosita were married one Christmas day. Armed, hilarious, vociferous, magnanimous, the cowmen and the sheepmen, laying aside their hereditary hatred, joined forces to celebrate the occasion.

Sundown Ranch was sonorous with the cracking of jokes and sixshooters, the shine of buckles and bright eyes, the outspoken congratulations of the herders of kine.

But while the wedding feast was at its liveliest there descended upon it Johnny McRoy, bitten by jealousy, like one possessed.

"I'll give you a Christmas present," he yelled, shrilly, at the door, with his .45 in his hand. Even then he had some reputation as an offhand shot.

His first bullet cut a neat underbit in Madison Lane's right ear. The barrel of his gun moved an inch. The next shot would have been the bride's had not Carson, a sheepman, possessed a mind with triggers somewhat well oiled and in repair. The guns of the wedding party had been hung, in their belts, upon nails in the wall when they sat at table, as a concession to good taste. But Carson, with great promptness, hurled his plate of roast venison and frijoles at McRoy, spoiling his aim. The second bullet, then, only shattered the white petals of a Spanish dagger flower suspended two feet above Rosita's head.

The guests spurned their chairs and jumped for their weapons. It was considered an improper act to shoot the bride and groom at a wedding. In about six seconds there were twenty or so bullets due to be whizzing in the direction of Mr. McRoy.

"I'll shoot better next time," yelled Johnny; "and there'll be a next time." He backed rapidly out the door.

Carson, the sheepman, spurred on to attempt further exploits by the success of his plate-throwing, was first to reach the door. McRoy's bullet from the darkness laid him low.

The cattlemen then swept out upon him, calling for vengeance, for, while the slaughter of a sheepman has not always lacked condonement, it was a decided misdemeanour in this instance. Carson was innocent; he was no accomplice at the matrimonial proceedings; nor had any one heard him quote the line "Christmas comes but once a year" to the guests.

But the sortie failed in its vengeance. McRoy was on his horse and away, shouting back curses and threats as he galloped into the concealing chaparral.

That night was the birthnight of the Frio Kid. He became the "bad man" of that portion of the State. The rejection of his suit by Miss McMullen turned him to a dangerous man. When officers went after him for the shooting of Carson, he killed two of them, and entered upon the life of an outlaw. He became a marvellous shot with either hand. He would turn up in towns and settlements, raise a quarrel at the slightest opportunity, pick off his man and laugh at the officers of the law. He was so cool, so deadly, so rapid, so inhumanly blood-thirsty that none but faint attempts were ever made to capture him. When he was at last shot and killed by a little one-armed Mexican who was nearly dead himself from fright, the Frio Kid had the deaths of eighteen men on his head. About half of these were killed in fair duels depending upon the quickness of the draw. The other half were men whom he assassinated from absolute wantonness and cruelty.

Many tales are told along the border of his impudent courage and daring. But he was not one of the breed of desperadoes who have seasons of generosity and even of softness. They say he never had mercy on the object of his anger. Yet at this and every Christmastide it is well to give each one credit, if it can be done, for whatever speck of good he may have possessed. If the Frio Kid ever did a kindly act or felt a throb of generosity in his heart it was once at such a time and season, and this is the way it happened.

ONE WHO HAS BEEN CROSSED in love should never breathe the odour from the blossoms of the ratama tree. It stirs the memory to a dangerous degree.

One December in the Frio country there was a ratama tree in full bloom, for the winter had been as warm as springtime. That way rode the Frio Kid and his satellite and co-murderer, Mexican Frank. The kid reined in his mustang, and sat in his saddle, thoughtful and grim, with dangerously narrowing eyes. The rich, sweet scent touched him somewhere beneath his ice and iron.

"I don't know what I've been thinking about, Mex," he remarked in his usual mild drawl, "to have forgot all about a Christmas present I got to give. I'm going to ride over to-morrow night and shoot Madison Lane in his own house. He got my girl—Rosita would have had me if he hadn't cut into the game. I wonder why I happened to overlook it up to now?"

"Ah, shucks, Kid," said Mexican, "don't talk foolishness. You know you can't get within a mile of Mad Lane's house to-morrow night. I see old man Allen day before yesterday, and he says Mad is going to have Christmas doings at his house. You remember how you shot up the festivities when Mad was married, and about the threats you made? Don't you suppose Mad Lane'll kind of keep his eye open for a certain Mr. Kid? You plumb make me tired, Kid, with such remarks."

"I'm going," repeated the Frio Kid, without heat, "to go to Madison Lane's Christmas doings, and kill him. I ought to have done it a long time ago. Why, Mex, just two weeks ago I dreamed me and Rosita was married instead of her and him; and we was living in a house, and I could see her smiling at me, and—oh! h——l, Mex, he got her; and I'll get him—yes, sir, on Christmas Eve he got her, and then's when I'll get him."

"There's other ways of committing suicide," advised Mexican. "Why don't you go and surrender to the sheriff?"

"I'll get him," said the Kid.

Christmas Eve fell as balmy as April. Perhaps there was a hint of far-away frostiness in the air, but it tingles like seltzer, perfumed faintly with late prairie blossoms and the mesquite grass.

When night came the five or six rooms of the ranch-house were brightly lit. In one room was a Christmas tree, for the Lanes had a boy of three, and a dozen or more guests were expected from the nearer ranches.

At nightfall Madison Lane called aside Jim Belcher and three other cowboys employed on his ranch.

"Now, boys," said Lane, "keep your eyes open. Walk around the house and watch the road well. All of you know the 'Frio Kid,' as they call him now, and if you see him, open fire on him without asking any questions. I'm not afraid of his coming around, but Rosita is. She's been afraid he'd come in on us every Christmas since we were married."

The guests had arrived in buckboards and on horseback, and were making themselves comfortable inside.

The evening went along pleasantly. The guests enjoyed and praised Rosita's excellent supper, and afterward the men scattered in groups about the rooms or on the broad "gallery," smoking and chatting.

The Christmas tree, of course, delighted the youngsters, and above all were they pleased when Santa Claus himself in magnificent white beard and furs appeared and began to distribute the toys.

"It's my papa," announced Billy Sampson, aged six. "I've seen him wear 'em before."

Berkly, a sheepman, an old friend of Lane, stopped Rosita as she was passing by him on the gallery, where he was sitting smoking.

"Well, Mrs. Lane," said he, "I suppose by this Christmas you've gotten over being afraid of that fellow McRoy, haven't you? Madison and I have talked about it, you know."

"Very nearly," said Rosita, smiling, "but I am still nervous sometimes. I shall never forget that awful time when he came so near to killing us."

"He's the most cold-hearted villain in the world," said Berkly. "The citizens all along the border ought to turn out and hunt him down like a wolf."

"He has committed awful crimes," said Rosita, "but—I—don't—know. I think there is a spot of good somewhere in everybody. He was not always bad—that I know."

Rosita turned into the hallway between the rooms. Santa Claus, in muffling whiskers and furs, was just coming through.

"I heard what you said through the window, Mrs. Lane," he said. "I was just going down in my pocket for a Christmas present for your husband. But I've left one for you, instead. It's in the room to your right."

"Oh, thank you, kind Santa Claus," said Rosita, brightly.

Rosita went into the room, while Santa Claus stepped into the cooler air of the yard.

She found no one in the room but Madison.

"Where is my present that Santa said he left for me in here?" she asked.

"Haven't seen anything in the way of a present," said her husband, laughing, "unless he could have meant me."

THE NEXT DAY GABRIEL RADD, the foreman of the X O Ranch, dropped into the post-office at Loma Alta.

"Well, the Frio Kid's got his dose of lead at last," he remarked to the postmaster.

"That so? How'd it happen?"

"One of old Sanchez's Mexican sheep herders did it!—think of it! the Frio Kid killed by a sheep herder! The Greaser saw him riding along past his camp about twelve o'clock last night, and was so skeered that he up with a Winchester and let him have it. Funniest part of it was that the Kid was dressed all up with white Angora-skin whiskers and a regular Santy Claus rig-out from head to foot. Think of the Frio Kid playing Santy!"

XXI

A Little Local Colour

I mentioned to Rivington that I was in search of characteristic New York scenes and incidents—something typical, I told him, without necessarily having to spell the first syllable with an "i."

"Oh, for your writing business," said Rivington; "you couldn't have applied to a better shop. What I don't know about little old New York wouldn't make a sonnet to a sunbonnet. I'll put you right in the middle of so much local colour that you won't know whether you are a magazine cover or in the erysipelas ward. When do you want to begin?"

Rivington is a young-man-about-town and a New Yorker by birth, preference and incommutability.

I told him that I would be glad to accept his escort and guardianship so that I might take notes of Manhattan's grand, gloomy and peculiar idiosyncrasies, and that the time of so doing would be at his own convenience.

"We'll begin this very evening," said Rivington, himself interested, like a good fellow. "Dine with me at seven, and then I'll steer you up against metropolitan phases so thick you'll have to have a kinetoscope to record 'em."

So I dined with Rivington pleasantly at his club, in Forty-eleventh street, and then we set forth in pursuit of the elusive tincture of affairs.

As we came out of the club there stood two men on the sidewalk near the steps in earnest conversation.

"And by what process of ratiocination," said one of them, "do you arrive at the conclusion that the division of society into producing and non-possessing classes predicates failure when compared with competitive systems that are monopolizing in tendency and result inimically to industrial evolution?"

"Oh, come off your perch!" said the other man, who wore glasses. "Your premises won't come out in the wash. You wind-jammers who apply bandy-legged theories to concrete categorical syllogisms send logical conclusions skallybootin' into the infinitesimal ragbag. You can't pull my leg with an old sophism with whiskers on it. You quote Marx and Hyndman and Kautsky—what are they?—shines! Tolstoi?—his garret is full of rats. I put it to you over the home-plate that the idea of a cooperative commonwealth and an abolishment of competitive systems simply takes the rag off the bush and gives me hyperesthesia of the roopteetoop! The skookum house for yours!"

I stopped a few yards away and took out my little notebook.

"Oh, come ahead," said Rivington, somewhat nervously; "you don't want to listen to that."

"Why, man," I whispered, "this is just what I do want to hear. These slang types are among your city's most distinguishing features. Is this the Bowery variety? I really must hear more of it."

"If I follow you," said the man who had spoken first, "you do not believe it possible to reorganize society on the basis of common interest?"

"Shinny on your own side!" said the man with glasses. "You never heard any such music from my foghorn. What I said was that I did not believe it practicable just now. The guys with wads are not in the frame of mind to slack up on the mazuma, and the man with the portable tin banqueting canister isn't exactly ready to join the Bible class. You can bet your variegated socks that the situation is all spifflicated up from the Battery to breakfast! What the country needs is for some bully old bloke like Cobden or some wise guy like old Ben Franklin to sashay up to the front and biff the nigger's head with the baseball. Do you catch my smoke? What?"

Rivington pulled me by the arm impatiently.

"Please come on," he said. "Let's go see something. This isn't what you want."

"Indeed, it is," I said resisting. "This tough talk is the very stuff that counts. There is a picturesqueness about the speech of the lower order of people that is quite unique. Did you say that this is the Bowery variety of slang?"

"Oh, well," said Rivington, giving it up, "I'll tell you straight. That's one of our college professors talking. He ran down for a day or two at the club. It's a sort of fad with him lately to use slang in his conversation. He thinks it improves language. The man he is talking to is one of New York's famous social economists. Now will you come on. You can't use that, you know."

"No," I agreed; "I can't use that. Would you call that typical of New York?"

"Of course not," said Rivington, with a sigh of relief. "I'm glad you see the difference. But if you want to hear the real old tough Bowery slang I'll take you down where you'll get your fill of it."

"I would like it," I said; "that is, if it's the real thing. I've often read it in books, but I never heard it. Do you think it will be dangerous to go unprotected among those characters?"

"Oh, no," said Rivington; "not at this time of night. To tell the truth, I haven't been along the Bowery in a long time, but I know it as well as I do Broadway. We'll look up some of the typical Bowery boys and get them to talk. It'll be worth your while. They talk a peculiar dialect that you won't hear anywhere else on earth."

Rivington and I went east in a Forty-second street car and then south on the Third avenue line.

At Houston street we got off and walked.

"We are now on the famous Bowery," said Rivington; "the Bowery celebrated in song and story."

We passed block after block of "gents'" furnishing stores—the windows full of shirts with prices attached and cuffs inside. In other windows were neckties and no shirts. People walked up and down the sidewalks.

"In some ways," said I, "this reminds me of Kokomono, Ind., during the peach-crating season."

Rivington was nettled.

"Step into one of these saloons or vaudeville shows," said he, "with a large roll of money, and see how quickly the Bowery will sustain its reputation."

"You make impossible conditions," said I, coldly.

By and by Rivington stopped and said we were in the heart of the Bowery. There was a policeman on the corner whom Rivington knew.

"Hallo, Donahue!" said my guide. "How goes it? My friend and I are down this way looking up a bit of local colour. He's anxious to meet one of the Bowery types. Can't you put us on to something genuine in that line—something that's got the colour, you know?"

Policeman Donahue turned himself about ponderously, his florid face full of good-nature. He pointed with his club down the street.

"Sure!" he said huskily. "Here comes a lad now that was born on the Bowery and knows every inch of it. If he's ever been above Bleecker street he's kept it to himself."

A man about twenty-eight or twenty-nine, with a smooth face, was sauntering toward us with his hands in his coat pockets. Policeman Donahue stopped him with a courteous wave of his club.

"Evening, Kerry," he said. "Here's a couple of gents, friends of mine, that want to hear you spiel something about the Bowery. Can you reel 'em off a few yards?"

"Certainly, Donahue," said the young man, pleasantly. "Good evening, gentlemen," he said to us, with a pleasant smile. Donahue walked off on his beat.

"This is the goods," whispered Rivington, nudging me with his elbow. "Look at his jaw!"

"Say, cull," said Rivington, pushing back his hat, "wot's doin'? Me and my friend's taking a look down de old line—see? De copper tipped us off dat you was wise to de bowery. Is dat right?"

I could not help admiring Rivington's power of adapting himself to his surroundings.

"Donahue was right," said the young man, frankly; "I was brought up on the Bowery. I have been news-boy, teamster, pugilist, member of an organized band of 'toughs,' bartender, and a 'sport' in various meanings of the word. The experience certainly warrants the supposition that I have at least a passing acquaintance with a few phases of Bowery life. I will be pleased to place whatever knowledge and experience I have at the service of my friend Donahue's friends."

Rivington seemed ill at ease.

"I say," he said—somewhat entreatingly, "I thought—you're not stringing us, are you? It isn't just the kind of talk we expected. You haven't even said 'Hully gee!' once. Do you really belong on the Bowery?"

"I am afraid," said the Bowery boy, smilingly, "that at some time you have been enticed into one of the dives of literature and had the counterfeit coin of the Bowery passed upon you. The 'argot' to which you doubtless refer was the invention of certain of your literary 'discoverers' who invaded the unknown wilds below Third avenue and put strange sounds into the mouths of the inhabitants. Safe in their homes far to the north and west, the credulous readers who were beguiled by this new 'dialect' perused and believed. Like Marco Polo and Mungo Park— pioneers indeed, but ambitious souls who could not draw the line of demarcation between discovery and invention—the literary bones of these explorers are dotting the trackless wastes of the subway. While it is true that after the publication of the mythical language attributed to the dwellers along the Bowery certain of its pat phrases and apt metaphors were adopted and, to a limited extent, used in this locality, it was because our people are prompt in assimilating whatever is to their commercial advantage. To the tourists who visited our newly discovered clime, and who expected a realization of their literary guide books, they supplied the demands of the market.

"But perhaps I am wandering from the question. In what way can I assist you, gentlemen? I beg you will believe that the hospitality of the street is extended to all. There are, I regret to say, many catchpenny places of entertainment, but I cannot conceive that they would entice you."

I felt Rivington lean somewhat heavily against me. "Say!" he remarked, with uncertain utterance; "come and have a drink with us."

"Thank you, but I never drink. I find that alcohol, even in the smallest quantities, alters the perspective. And I must preserve my perspective, for I am studying the Bowery. I have lived in it nearly thirty years, and I am just beginning to understand its heartbeats. It is like a great river fed by a hundred alien streams. Each influx brings strange seeds on its flood, strange silt and weeds, and now and then a flower of rare promise. To construe this river requires a man who can build dykes against the overflow, who is a naturalist, a geologist, a humanitarian, a diver and a strong swimmer. I love my Bowery. It was my cradle and is my inspiration. I have published one book. The critics have been kind. I put my heart in it. I am writing another, into which I hope to put both heart and brain. Consider me your guide, gentlemen. Is there anything I can take you to see, any place to which I can conduct you?"

I was afraid to look at Rivington except with one eye.

"Thanks," said Rivington. "We were looking up. . . that is. . . my friend. . . confound it; it's against all precedent, you know. . . awfully obliged. . . just the same."

"In case," said our friend, "you would like to meet some of our Bowery young men I would be pleased to have you visit the quarters of our East Side Kappa Delta Phi Society, only two blocks east of here."

"Awfully sorry," said Rivington, "but my friend's got me on the jump to-night. He's a terror when he's out after local colour. Now, there's nothing I would like better than to drop in at the Kappa Delta Phi, but—some other time!"

We said our farewells and boarded a home-bound car. We had a rabbit on upper Broadway, and then I parted with Rivington on a street corner.

"Well, anyhow," said he, braced and recovered, "it couldn't have happened anywhere but in little old New York."

Which to say the least, was typical of Rivington.

XXII

GEORGIA'S RULING

I f you should chance to visit the General Land Office, step into the draughtsmen's room and ask to be shown the map of Salado County. A leisurely German—possibly old Kampfer himself—will bring it to you. It will be four feet square, on heavy drawing-cloth. The lettering and the figures will be beautifully clear and distinct. The title will be in splendid, undecipherable German text, ornamented with classic Teutonic designs—very likely Ceres or Pomona leaning against the initial letters with cornucopias venting grapes and wieners. You must tell him that this is not the map you wish to see; that he will kindly bring you its official predecessor. He will then say, "Ach, so!" and bring out a map half the size of the first, dim, old, tattered, and faded.

By looking carefully near its northwest corner you will presently come upon the worn contours of Chiquito River, and, maybe, if your eyes are good, discern the silent witness to this story.

THE COMMISSIONER OF THE LAND Office was of the old style; his antique courtesy was too formal for his day. He dressed in fine black, and there was a suggestion of Roman drapery in his long coat-skirts. His collars were "undetached" (blame haberdashery for the word); his tie was a narrow, funereal strip, tied in the same knot as were his shoe-strings. His gray hair was a trifle too long behind, but he kept it smooth and orderly. His face was clean-shaven, like the old statesmen's. Most people thought it a stern face, but when its official expression was off, a few had seen altogether a different countenance. Especially tender and gentle it had appeared to those who were about him during the last illness of his only child.

The Commissioner had been a widower for years, and his life, outside his official duties, had been so devoted to little Georgia that people spoke of it as a touching and admirable thing. He was a reserved man, and dignified almost to austerity, but the child had come below it all and rested upon his very heart, so that she scarcely missed the mother's love that had been taken away. There was a wonderful companionship between them, for she had many of his own ways, being thoughtful and serious beyond her years.

One day, while she was lying with the fever burning brightly in her checks, she said suddenly:

"Papa, I wish I could do something good for a whole lot of children!"

"What would you like to do, dear?" asked the Commissioner. "Give them a party?"

"Oh, I don't mean those kind. I mean poor children who haven't homes, and aren't loved and cared for as I am. I tell you what, papa!"

"What, my own child?"

"If I shouldn't get well, I'll leave them you—not *give* you, but just lend you, for you must come to mamma and me when you die too. If you can find time, wouldn't you do something to help them, if I ask you, papa?"

"Hush, hush dear, dear child," said the Commissioner, holding her hot little hand against his cheek; "you'll get well real soon, and you and I will see what we can do for them together."

But in whatsoever paths of benevolence, thus vaguely premeditated, the Commissioner might tread, he was not to have the company of his beloved. That night the little frail body grew suddenly too tired to struggle further, and Georgia's exit was made from the great stage when she had scarcely begun to speak her little piece before the footlights. But there must be a stage manager who understands. She had given the cue to the one who was to speak after her.

A week after she was laid away, the Commissioner reappeared at the office, a little more courteous, a little paler and sterner, with the black frock-coat hanging a little more loosely from his tall figure.

His desk was piled with work that had accumulated during the four heartbreaking weeks of his absence. His chief clerk had done what he could, but there were questions of law, of fine judicial decisions to be made concerning the issue of patents, the marketing and leasing of school lands, the classification into grazing, agricultural, watered, and timbered, of new tracts to be opened to settlers.

The Commissioner went to work silently and obstinately, putting back his grief as far as possible, forcing his mind to attack the complicated and important business of his office. On the second day after his return he called the porter, pointed to a leather-covered chair that stood near his own, and ordered it removed to a lumber-room at the top of the building. In that chair Georgia would always sit when she came to the office for him of afternoons.

As time passed, the Commissioner seemed to grow more silent, solitary, and reserved. A new phase of mind developed in him. He could not endure the presence of a child. Often when a clattering youngster belonging to one of the clerks would come chattering into the big business-room adjoining his little apartment, the Commissioner would steal softly and close the door. He would always cross the street to avoid meeting the school-children when they came dancing along in happy groups upon the sidewalk, and his firm mouth would close into a mere line.

It was nearly three months after the rains had washed the last dead flower-petals from the mound above little Georgia when the "land-shark" firm of Hamlin and Avery filed papers upon what they considered the "fattest" vacancy of the year.

It should not be supposed that all who were termed "land-sharks" deserved the name. Many of them were reputable men of good business character. Some of them could walk into the most august councils of the State and say: "Gentlemen, we would like to have this, and that, and matters go thus." But, next to a three years' drought and the boll-worm, the Actual Settler hated the Land-shark. The land-shark haunted the Land Office, where all the land records were kept, and hunted "vacancies"—that is, tracts of unappropriated public domain, generally invisible upon the official maps, but actually existing "upon the ground." The law entitled any one possessing certain State scrip to file by virtue of same upon any land not previously legally appropriated. Most of the scrip was now in the hands of the land-sharks. Thus, at the cost of a few hundred dollars, they often secured lands worth as many thousands. Naturally, the search for "vacancies" was lively.

But often—very often—the land they thus secured, though legally "unappropriated," would be occupied by happy and contented settlers, who had laboured for years to build up their homes, only to discover that their titles were worthless, and to receive peremptory notice to quit. Thus came about the bitter and not unjustifiable hatred felt by the toiling settlers toward the shrewd and seldom merciful speculators who so often turned them forth destitute and homeless from their fruitless labours. The history of the state teems with their antagonism. Mr. Land-shark seldom showed his face on "locations" from which he should have to eject the unfortunate victims of a monstrously tangled land system, but let his emissaries do the work. There was lead in every cabin, moulded into balls for him; many of his brothers had enriched the grass with their blood. The fault of it all lay far back.

When the state was young, she felt the need of attracting newcomers, and of rewarding those pioneers already within her borders. Year after year she issued land scrip—Headrights, Bounties, Veteran Donations, Confederates; and to railroads, irrigation companies, colonies, and tillers of the soil galore. All required of the grantee was that he or it should have the scrip properly surveyed upon the public domain by the county or district surveyor, and the land thus appropriated became the property of him or it, or his or its heirs and assigns, forever.

In those days—and here is where the trouble began—the state's domain was practically inexhaustible, and the old surveyors, with princely—yea, even Western American—liberality, gave good measure and over-flowing. Often the jovial man of metes and bounds would dispense altogether with the tripod and chain. Mounted on a pony that could cover something near a "vara" at a step, with a pocket compass to direct his course, he would trot out a survey by counting the beat of his pony's hoofs, mark his corners, and write out his field notes with the complacency produced by an act of duty well performed. Sometimes—and who could blame the surveyor?—when the pony was "feeling his oats," he might step a little higher and farther, and in that case the beneficiary of the scrip might get a thousand or two more acres in his survey than the scrip called for. But look at the boundless leagues the state had to spare! However, no one ever had to complain of the pony under-stepping. Nearly every old survey in the state contained an excess of land.

In later years, when the state became more populous, and land values increased, this careless work entailed incalculable trouble, endless litigation, a period of riotous land-grabbing, and no little bloodshed. The land-sharks voraciously attacked these excesses in the old surveys, and filed upon such portions with new scrip as unappropriated public domain. Wherever the identifications of the old tracts were vague, and the corners were not to be clearly established, the Land Office would recognize the newer locations as valid, and issue title to the locators. Here was the greatest hardship to be found. These old surveys, taken from the pick of the land, were already nearly all occupied by unsuspecting and peaceful settlers, and thus their titles were demolished, and the choice was placed before them either to buy their land over at a double price or to vacate it, with their families and personal belongings, immediately. Land locators sprang up by hundreds. The country was held up and searched for "vacancies" at the point of a compass. Hundreds of thousands of dollars' worth of splendid acres were wrested from their innocent purchasers and holders. There began a vast hegira of evicted settlers in tattered wagons; going nowhere, cursing injustice, stunned, purposeless, homeless, hopeless. Their children began to look up to them for bread, and cry.

IT WAS IN CONSEQUENCE OF these conditions that Hamilton and Avery had filed upon a strip of land about a mile wide and three miles long, comprising about two thousand acres, it being the excess over complement of the Elias Denny three-league survey on Chiquito River, in one of the middle-western counties. This two-thousand-acre body of land was asserted by them to be vacant land, and improperly considered a part of the Denny survey. They based this assertion and their claim upon the land upon the demonstrated facts that the beginning corner of the Denny survey was plainly identified; that its field notes called to run west 5,760 varas, and then called for Chiquito River; thence it ran south, with the meanders—and so on—and that the Chiquito River was, on the ground, fully a mile farther west from the point reached by course and distance. To sum up: there were two thousand acres of vacant land between the Denny survey proper and Chiquito River.

One sweltering day in July the Commissioner called for the papers in connection with this new location. They were brought, and heaped, a foot deep, upon his desk—field notes, statements, sketches, affidavits, connecting lines—documents of every description that shrewdness and money could call to the aid of Hamlin and Avery.

The firm was pressing the Commissioner to issue a patent upon their location. They possesed inside information concerning a new railroad that would probably pass somewhere near this land.

The General Land Office was very still while the Commissioner was delving into the heart of the mass of evidence. The pigeons could be heard on the roof of the old, castle-like building, cooing and fretting. The clerks were droning everywhere, scarcely pretending to earn their salaries. Each little sound echoed hollow and loud from the bare, stone-flagged floors, the plastered walls, and the iron-joisted ceiling. The impalpable, perpetual limestone dust that never settled, whitened a long streamer of sunlight that pierced the tattered window-awning.

It seemed that Hamlin and Avery had builded well. The Denny survey was carelessly made, even for a careless period. Its beginning corner was identical with that of a well-defined old Spanish grant, but its other calls were sinfully vague. The field notes contained no other object that survived—no tree, no natural object save Chiquito River, and it was a mile wrong there. According to precedent, the Office would be justified in giving it its complement by course and distance, and considering the remainder vacant instead of a mere excess.

The Actual Settler was besieging the office with wild protests *in re*. Having the nose of a pointer and the eye of a hawk for the land-shark, he had observed his myrmidons running the lines upon his ground. Making inquiries, he learned that the spoiler had attacked his home, and he left the plough in the furrow and took his pen in hand.

One of the protests the Commissioner read twice. It was from a woman, a widow, the granddaughter of Elias Denny himself. She told how her grandfather had sold most of the survey years before at a trivial price—land that was now a principality in extent and value. Her mother had also sold a part, and she herself had succeeded to this western portion, along Chiquito River. Much of it she had been forced to part with in order to live, and now she owned only about three hundred acres, on which she had her home. Her letter wound up rather pathetically:

"I've got eight children, the oldest fifteen years. I work all day and half the night to till what little land I can and keep us in clothes and books. I teach my children too. My neighbours is all poor and has big families. The drought kills the crops every two or three years and then we has hard times to get enough to eat. There is ten families on this land what the land-sharks is trying to rob us of, and all of them got titles from me. I sold to them cheap, and they aint paid out yet, but part of them is, and if their land should be took from them I would die. My grandfather was an honest man, and he helped to build up this state, and he taught his children to be honest, and how could I make it up to them who bought from me? Mr. Commissioner, if you let them land-sharks take the roof from over my children and the little from them as they has to live on, whoever again calls this state great or its government just will have a lie in their mouths."

The Commissioner laid this letter aside with a sigh. Many, many such letters he had received. He had never been hurt by them, nor had he ever felt that they appealed to him personally. He was but the state's servant, and must follow its laws. And yet, somehow, this reflection did not always eliminate a certain responsible feeling that hung upon him. Of all the state's officers he was supremest in his department, not even excepting the Governor. Broad, general land laws he followed, it was true, but he had a wide latitude in particular ramifications. Rather than law, what he followed was Rulings: Office Rulings and precedents. In the complicated and new questions that were being engendered by the state's development the Commissioner's ruling was rarely appealed from. Even the courts sustained it when its equity was apparent.

The Commissioner stepped to the door and spoke to a clerk in the other room—spoke as he always did, as if he were addressing a prince of the blood:

"Mr. Weldon, will you be kind enough to ask Mr. Ashe, the state school-land appraiser, to please come to my office as soon as convenient?"

Ashe came quickly from the big table where he was arranging his reports.

"Mr. Ashe," said the Commissioner, "you worked along the Chiquito River, in Salado County, during your last trip, I believe. Do you remember anything of the Elias Denny three-league survey?"

"Yes, sir, I do," the blunt, breezy, surveyor answered. "I crossed it on my way to Block H, on the north side of it. The road runs with the Chiquito River, along the valley. The Denny survey fronts three miles on the Chiquito."

"It is claimed," continued the commissioner, "that it fails to reach the river by as much as a mile."

The appraiser shrugged his shoulder. He was by birth and instinct an Actual Settler, and the natural foe of the land-shark.

"It has always been considered to extend to the river," he said, dryly.

"But that is not the point I desired to discuss," said the Commissioner. "What kind of country is this valley portion of (let us say, then) the Denny tract?"

The spirit of the Actual Settler beamed in Ashe's face.

"Beautiful," he said, with enthusiasm. "Valley as level as this floor, with just a little swell on, like the sea, and rich as cream. Just enough brakes to shelter the cattle in winter. Black loamy soil for six feet, and then clay. Holds water. A dozen nice little houses on it, with windmills and gardens. People pretty poor, I guess—too far from market—but comfortable. Never saw so many kids in my life."

"They raise flocks?" inquired the Commissioner.

"Ho, ho! I mean two-legged kids," laughed the surveyor; "two-legged, and bare-legged, and tow-headed."

"Children! oh, children!" mused the Commissioner, as though a new view had opened to him; "they raise children!

"It's a lonesome country, Commissioner," said the surveyor. "Can you blame 'em?"

"I suppose," continued the Commissioner, slowly, as one carefully pursues deductions from a new, stupendous theory, "not all of them are tow-headed. It would not be unreasonable, Mr. Ashe, I conjecture, to believe that a portion of them have brown, or even black, hair."

"Brown and black, sure," said Ashe; "also red."

"No doubt," said the Commissioner. "Well, I thank you for your courtesy in informing me, Mr. Ashe. I will not detain you any longer from your duties."

Later, in the afternoon, came Hamlin and Avery, big, handsome, genial, sauntering men, clothed in white duck and low-cut shoes. They permeated the whole office with an aura of debonair prosperity. They passed among the clerks and left a wake of abbreviated given names and fat brown cigars.

These were the aristocracy of the land-sharks, who went in for big things. Full of serene confidence in themselves, there was no corporation, no syndicate, no railroad company or attorney general too big for them to tackle. The peculiar smoke of their rare, fat brown cigars was to be perceived in the sanctum of every department of state, in every committee-room of the Legislature, in every bank parlour and every private caucus-room in the state Capital. Always pleasant, never in a hurry, in seeming to possess unlimited leisure, people wondered when they gave their attention to the many audacious enterprises in which they were known to be engaged.

By and by the two dropped carelessly into the Commissioner's room and reclined lazily in the big, leather-upholstered arm-chairs. They drawled a good-natured complaint of the weather, and Hamlin told the Commissioner an excellent story he had amassed that morning from the Secretary of State.

But the Commissioner knew why they were there. He had half promised to render a decision that day upon their location.

The chief clerk now brought in a batch of duplicate certificates for the Commissioner to sign. As he traced his sprawling signature, "Hollis Summerfield, Comr. Genl. Land Office," on each one, the chief clerk stood, deftly removing them and applying the blotter.

"I notice," said the chief clerk, "you've been going through that Salado County location. Kampfer is making a new map of Salado, and I believe is platting in that section of the county now."

"I will see it," said the Commissioner. A few moments later he went to the draughtsmen's room.

As he entered he saw five or six of the draughtsmen grouped about Kampfer's desk, gargling away at each other in pectoral German, and gazing at something thereupon. At the Commissioner's approach they scattered to their several places. Kampfer, a wizened little German, with long, frizzled ringlets and a watery eye, began to stammer forth some sort of an apology, the Commissioner thought, for the congregation of his fellows about his desk.

"Never mind," said the Commissioner, "I wish to see the map you are making"; and, passing around the old German, seated himself upon the high draughtsman's stool. Kampfer continued to break English in trying to explain.

"Herr Gommissioner, I assure you blenty sat I haf not it bremeditated—sat it wass—sat it itself make. Look you! from se field notes wass it blatted—blease to observe se calls: South, 10 degrees west 1,050 varas; south, 10 degrees east 300 varas; south, 100; south, 9 west, 200; south, 40 degrees west 400—and so on. Herr Gommissioner, nefer would I have—"

The Commissioner raised one white hand, silently, Kampfer dropped his pipe and fled.

With a hand at each side of his face, and his elbows resting upon the desk, the Commissioner sat staring at the map which was spread and fastened there—staring at the sweet and living profile of little Georgia drawn thereupon—at her face, pensive, delicate, and infantile, outlined in a perfect likeness.

When his mind at length came to inquire into the reason of it, he saw that it must have been, as Kampfer had said, unpremeditated. The old draughtsman had been platting in the Elias Denny survey, and Georgia's likeness, striking though it was, was formed by nothing more than the meanders of Chiquito River. Indeed, Kampfer's blotter, whereon his preliminary work was done, showed the laborious tracings of the calls and the countless pricks of the compasses. Then, over his faint pencilling, Kampfer had drawn in India ink with a full, firm pen the similitude of Chiquito River, and forth had blossomed mysteriously the dainty, pathetic profile of the child.

The Commissioner sat for half an hour with his face in his hands, gazing downward, and none dared approach him. Then he arose and walked out. In the business office he paused long enough to ask that the Denny file be brought to his desk.

He found Hamlin and Avery still reclining in their chairs, apparently oblivious of business. They were lazily discussing summer opera, it being, their habit—perhaps their pride also—to appear supernaturally indifferent whenever they stood with large interests imperilled. And they stood to win more on this stake than most people knew. They possessed inside information to the effect that a new railroad would, within a year, split this very Chiquito River valley and send land values ballooning all along its route. A dollar under thirty thousand profit on this location, if it should hold good, would be a loss to their expectations. So, while they chatted lightly and waited for the Commissioner to open the subject, there was a quick, sidelong sparkle in their eyes, evincing a desire to read their title clear to those fair acres on the Chiquito.

A clerk brought in the file. The Commissioner seated himself and wrote upon it in red ink. Then he rose to his feet and stood for a while looking straight out of the window. The Land Office capped the summit of a bold hill. The eyes of the Commissioner passed over the roofs of many houses set in a packing of deep green, the whole checkered by strips of blinding white streets. The horizon, where his gaze was focussed, swelled to a fair wooded eminence flecked with faint dots of shining white. There was the cemetery, where lay many who were forgotten, and a few who had not lived in vain. And one lay there, occupying very small space, whose childish heart had been large enough to desire, while near its last beats, good to others. The Commissioner's lips moved slightly as he whispered to himself: "It was her last will and testament, and I have neglected it so long!"

The big brown cigars of Hamlin and Avery were fireless, but they still gripped them between their teeth and waited, while they marvelled at the absent expression upon the Commissioner's face.

By and by he spoke suddenly and promptly.

"Gentlemen, I have just indorsed the Elias Denny survey for patenting. This office will not regard your location upon a part of it as legal." He paused a moment, and then, extending his hand as those dear old-time ones used to do in debate, he enunciated the spirit of that Ruling that subsequently drove the land-sharks to the wall, and placed the seal of peace and security over the doors of ten thousand homes.

"And, furthermore," he continued, with a clear, soft light upon his face, "it may interest you to know that from this time on this office will consider that when a survey of land made by virtue of a certificate granted by this state to the men who wrested it from the wilderness and the savage—made in good faith, settled in good faith, and left in good faith to their children or innocent purchasers—when such a survey, although overrunning its complement, shall call for any natural object visible to the eye of man, to that object it shall hold, and be good and valid. And the children of this state shall lie down to sleep at night, and rumours of disturbers of title shall not disquiet them. For," concluded the Commissioner, "of such is the Kingdom of Heaven."

In the silence that followed, a laugh floated up from the patent-room below. The man who carried down the Denny file was exhibiting it among the clerks.

"Look here," he said, delightedly, "the old man has forgotten his name. He's written 'Patent to original grantee,' and signed it 'Georgia Summerfield, Comr.'"

The speech of the Commissioner rebounded lightly from the impregnable Hamlin and Avery. They smiled, rose gracefully, spoke of the baseball team, and argued feelingly that quite a perceptible breeze had arisen from the east. They lit fresh fat brown cigars, and drifted courteously away. But later they made another tiger-spring for their quarry in the courts. But the courts, according to reports in the papers, "coolly roasted them" (a remarkable performance, suggestive of liquid-air didoes), and sustained the Commissioner's Ruling.

And this Ruling itself grew to be a Precedent, and the Actual Settler framed it, and taught his children to spell from it, and there was sound sleep o' nights from the pines to the sage-brush, and from the chaparral to the great brown river of the north.

But I think, and I am sure the Commissioner never thought otherwise, that whether Kampfer was a snuffy old instrument of destiny, or whether the meanders of the Chiquito accidentally platted themselves into that memorable sweet profile or not, there was brought about "something good for a whole lot of children," and the result ought to be called "Georgia's Ruling."

XXIII

Blind Man's Holiday

Alas for the man and for the artist with the shifting point of perspective! Life shall be a confusion of ways to the one; the landscape shall rise up and confound the other. Take the case of Lorison. At one time he appeared to himself to be the feeblest of fools; at another he conceived that he followed ideals so fine that the world was not yet ready to accept them. During one mood he cursed his folly; possessed by the other, he bore himself with a serene grandeur akin to greatness: in neither did he attain the perspective.

Generations before, the name had been "Larsen." His race had bequeathed him its fine-strung, melancholy temperament, its saving balance of thrift and industry.

From his point of perspective he saw himself an outcast from society, forever to be a shady skulker along the ragged edge of respectability; a denizen *des trois-quartz de monde*, that pathetic spheroid lying between the *haut* and the *demi*, whose inhabitants envy each of their neighbours, and are scorned by both. He was self-condemned to this opinion, as he was self-exiled, through it, to this quaint Southern city a thousand miles from his former home. Here he had dwelt for longer than a year, knowing but few, keeping in a subjective world of shadows which was invaded at times by the perplexing bulks of jarring realities. Then he fell in love with a girl whom he met in a cheap restaurant, and his story begins.

The Rue Chartres, in New Orleans, is a street of ghosts. It lies in the quarter where the Frenchman, in his prime, set up his translated pride and glory; where, also, the arrogant don had swaggered, and dreamed of gold and grants and ladies' gloves. Every flagstone has its grooves worn by footsteps going royally to the wooing and the fighting. Every house has a princely heartbreak; each doorway its untold tale of gallant promise and slow decay.

By night the Rue Chartres is now but a murky fissure, from which the groping wayfarer sees, flung against the sky, the tangled filigree of Moorish iron balconies. The old houses of monsieur stand yet, indomitable against the century, but their essence is gone. The street is one of ghosts to whosoever can see them.

A faint heartbeat of the street's ancient glory still survives in a corner occupied by the Café Carabine d'Or. Once men gathered there to plot against kings, and to warn presidents. They do so yet, but they are not the same kind of men. A brass button will scatter these; those would have set their faces against an army. Above the door hangs the sign board, upon which has been depicted a vast animal of unfamiliar species. In the act of firing upon this monster is represented an unobtrusive human levelling an obtrusive gun, once the colour of bright gold. Now the legend above the picture is faded beyond conjecture; the gun's relation to the title is a matter of faith; the menaced animal, wearied of the long aim of the hunter, has resolved itself into a shapeless blot.

The place is known as "Antonio's," as the name, white upon the red-lit transparency, and gilt upon the windows, attests. There is a promise in "Antonio"; a justifiable expectancy of savoury things in oil and pepper and wine, and perhaps an angel's whisper of garlic. But the rest of the name is "O'Riley." Antonio O'Riley!

The Carabine d'Or is an ignominious ghost of the Rue Chartres. The café where Bienville and Conti dined, where a prince has broken bread, is become a "family ristaurant."

Its customers are working men and women, almost to a unit. Occasionally you will see chorus girls from the cheaper theatres, and men who follow avocations subject to quick vicissitudes; but at Antonio's—name rich in Bohemian promise, but tame in fulfillment—manners debonair and gay are toned down to the "family" standard. Should you light a cigarette, mine host will touch you on the "arrum" and remind you that the proprieties are menaced. "Antonio" entices and beguiles from fiery legend without, but "O'Riley" teaches decorum within.

It was at this restaurant that Lorison first saw the girl. A flashy fellow with a predatory eye had followed her in, and had advanced to take the other chair at the little table where she stopped, but Lorison slipped into the seat before him. Their acquaintance began, and grew, and now for two months they had sat at the same table each evening, not meeting by appointment, but as if by a series of fortuitous and happy accidents. After dining, they would take a walk together in one of the little city parks, or among the panoramic markets where exhibits a continuous vaudeville of sights and sounds. Always at eight o'clock their steps led them to a certain street corner, where she prettily but firmly bade him good night and left him. "I do not live far from here," she frequently said, "and you must let me go the rest of the way alone."

But now Lorison had discovered that he wanted to go the rest of the way with her, or happiness would depart, leaving, him on a very lonely corner of life. And at the same time that he made the discovery, the secret of his banishment from the society of the good laid its finger in his face and told him it must not be.

Man is too thoroughly an egoist not to be also an egotist; if he love, the object shall know it. During a lifetime he may conceal it through stress of expediency and honour, but it shall bubble from his dying lips, though it disrupt a neighbourhood. It is known, however, that most men do not wait so long to disclose their passion. In the case of Lorison, his particular ethics positively forbade him to declare his sentiments, but he must needs dally with the subject, and woo by innuendo at least.

On this night, after the usual meal at the Carabine d'Or, he strolled with his companion down the dim old street toward the river.

The Rue Chartres perishes in the old Place d'Armes. The ancient Cabildo, where Spanish justice fell like hail, faces it, and the Cathedral, another provincial ghost, overlooks it. Its centre is a little, iron-railed park of flowers and immaculate gravelled walks, where citizens take the air of evenings. Pedestalled high above it, the general sits his cavorting steed, with his face turned stonily down the river toward English Turn, whence come no more Britons to bombard his cotton bales.

Often the two sat in this square, but to-night Lorison guided her past the stone-stepped gate, and still riverward. As they walked, he smiled to himself to think that all he knew of her—except that be loved her—was her name, Norah Greenway, and that she lived with her brother. They had talked about everything except themselves. Perhaps her reticence had been caused by his.

They came, at length, upon the levee, and sat upon a great, prostrate beam. The air was pungent with the dust of commerce. The great river slipped yellowly past. Across it Algiers lay, a longitudinous black bulk against a vibrant electric haze sprinkled with exact stars.

The girl was young and of the piquant order. A certain bright melancholy pervaded her; she possessed an untarnished, pale prettiness doomed to please. Her voice, when she spoke, dwarfed her theme. It was the voice capable of investing little subjects with a large interest. She sat at ease, bestowing her skirts with the little womanly touch, serene as if the begrimed pier were a summer garden. Lorison poked the rotting boards with his cane.

He began by telling her that he was in love with some one to whom he durst not speak of it. "And why not?" she asked, accepting swiftly his fatuous presentation of a third person of straw. "My place in the world," he answered, "is none to ask a woman to share. I am an outcast from honest people; I am wrongly accused of one crime, and am, I believe, guilty of another."

Thence he plunged into the story of his abdication from society. The story, pruned of his moral philosophy, deserves no more than the slightest touch. It is no new tale, that of the gambler's declension. During one night's sitting he lost, and then had imperilled a certain amount of his employer's money, which, by accident, he carried with him. He continued to lose, to the last wager, and then began to gain, leaving the game winner to a somewhat formidable sum. The same night his employer's safe was robbed. A search was had; the winnings of Lorison were found in his room, their total forming an accusative nearness to the sum purloined. He was taken, tried and, through incomplete evidence, released, smutched with the sinister *devoirs* of a disagreeing jury.

"It is not in the unjust accusation," he said to the girl, "that my burden lies, but in the knowledge that from the moment I staked the first dollar of the firm's money I was a criminal—no matter whether I lost or won. You see why it is impossible for me to speak of love to her."

"It is a sad thing," said Norah, after a little pause, "to think what very good people there are in the world."

"Good?" said Lorison.

"I was thinking of this superior person whom you say you love. She must be a very poor sort of creature."

"I do not understand."

"Nearly," she continued, "as poor a sort of creature as yourself."

"You do not understand," said Lorison, removing his hat and sweeping back his fine, light hair. "Suppose she loved me in return, and were willing to marry me. Think, if you can, what would follow. Never a day would pass but she would be reminded of her sacrifice. I would read a condescension in her smile, a pity even in her affection, that would madden me. No. The thing would stand between us forever. Only equals should mate. I could never ask her to come down upon my lower plane."

An arc light faintly shone upon Lorison's face. An illumination from within also pervaded it. The girl saw the rapt, ascetic look; it was the face either of Sir Galahad or Sir Fool.

"Quite starlike," she said, "is this unapproachable angel. Really too high to be grasped."

"By me, yes."

She faced him suddenly. "My dear friend, would you prefer your star fallen?" Lorison made a wide gesture.

"You push me to the bald fact," he declared; "you are not in sympathy with my argument. But I will answer you so. If I could reach my particular star, to drag it down, I would not do it; but if it were fallen, I would pick it up, and thank Heaven for the privilege."

They were silent for some minutes. Norah shivered, and thrust her hands deep into the pockets of her jacket. Lorison uttered a remorseful exclamation.

"I'm not cold," she said. "I was just thinking. I ought to tell you something. You have selected a strange confidante. But you cannot expect a chance acquaintance, picked up in a doubtful restaurant, to be an angel."

"Norah!" cried Lorison.

"Let me go on. You have told me about yourself. We have been such good friends. I must tell you now what I never wanted you to know. I am—worse than you are. I was on the stage. . . I sang in the chorus. . . I was pretty bad, I guess. . . I stole diamonds from the prima donna. . . they arrested me. . . I gave most of them up, and they let me go. . . I drank wine every night. . . a great deal. . . I was very wicked, but—"

Lorison knelt quickly by her side and took her hands.

"Dear Norah!" he said, exultantly. "It is you, it is you I love! You never guessed it, did you? 'Tis you I meant all the time. Now I can speak. Let me make you forget the past. We have both suffered; let us shut out the world, and live for each other. Norah, do you hear me say I love you?"

"In spite of—"

"Rather say because of it. You have come out of your past noble and good. Your heart is an angel's. Give it to me."

"A little while ago you feared the future too much to even speak."

"But for you; not for myself. Can you love me?"

She cast herself, wildly sobbing, upon his breast.

"Better than life—than truth itself—than everything."

"And my own past," said Lorison, with a note of solicitude—"can you forgive and—"

"I answered you that," she whispered, "when I told you I loved you." She leaned away, and looked thoughtfully at him. "If I had not told you about myself, would you have—would you—"

"No," he interrupted; "I would never have let you know I loved you. I would never have asked you this—Norah, will you be my wife?"

She wept again.

"Oh, believe me; I am good now—I am no longer wicked! I will be the best wife in the world. Don't think I am—bad any more. If you do I shall die, I shall die!"

While he was consoling, her, she brightened up, eager and impetuous. "Will you marry me to-night?" she said. "Will you prove it that way. I have a reason for wishing it to be to-night. Will you?"

Of one of two things was this exceeding frankness the outcome: either of importunate brazenness or of utter innocence. The lover's perspective contained only the one.

"The sooner," said Lorison, "the happier I shall be."

"What is there to do?" she asked. "What do you have to get? Come! You should know."

Her energy stirred the dreamer to action.

"A city directory first," he cried, gayly, "to find where the man lives who gives licenses to happiness. We will go together and rout him out. Cabs, cars, policemen, telephones and ministers shall aid us."

"Father Rogan shall marry us," said the girl, with ardour. "I will take you to him."

A N HOUR LATER THE TWO stood at the open doorway of an immense, gloomy brick building in a narrow and lonely street. The license was tight in Norah's hand.

"Wait here a moment," she said, "till I find Father Rogan."

She plunged into the black hallway, and the lover was left standing, as it were, on one leg, outside. His impatience was not greatly taxed. Gazing curiously into what seemed the hallway to Erebus, he was presently reassured by a stream of light that bisected the darkness, far down the passage. Then he heard her call, and fluttered lampward, like the moth. She beckoned him through a doorway into the room whence emanated the light. The room was bare of nearly everything except books, which had subjugated all its space. Here and there little spots of territory had been reconquered. An elderly, bald man, with a superlatively calm, remote eye, stood by a table with a book in his hand, his finger still marking a page. His dress was sombre and appertained to a religious order. His eye denoted an acquaintance with the perspective.

"Father Rogan," said Norah, "this is *he*."

"The two of ye," said Father Rogan, "want to get married?"

They did not deny it. He married them. The ceremony was quickly done. One who could have witnessed it, and felt its scope, might have trembled at the terrible inadequacy of it to rise to the dignity of its endless chain of results.

Afterward the priest spake briefly, as if by rote, of certain other civil and legal addenda that either might or should, at a later time, cap the ceremony. Lorison tendered a fee, which was declined, and before the door closed after the departing couple Father Rogan's book popped open again where his finger marked it.

In the dark hall Norah whirled and clung to her companion, tearful.

"Will you never, never be sorry?"

At last she was reassured.

At the first light they reached upon the street, she asked the time, just as she had each night. Lorison looked at his watch. Half-past eight.

Lorison thought it was from habit that she guided their steps toward the corner where they always parted. But, arrived there, she hesitated, and then released his arm. A drug store stood on the corner; its bright, soft light shone upon them.

"Please leave me here as usual to-night," said Norah, sweetly. "I must—I would rather you would. You will not object? At six to-morrow evening I will meet you at Antonio's. I want to sit with you there once more. And then—I will go where you say." She gave him a bewildering, bright smile, and walked swiftly away.

Surely it needed all the strength of her charm to carry off this astounding behaviour. It was no discredit to Lorison's strength of mind that his head began to whirl. Pocketing his hands, he rambled vacuously over to the druggist's windows, and began assiduously to spell over the names of the patent medicines therein displayed.

As soon as be had recovered his wits, he proceeded along the street in an aimless fashion. After drifting for two or three squares, he flowed into a somewhat more pretentious thoroughfare, a way much frequented by him in his solitary ramblings. For here was a row of shops devoted to traffic in goods of the widest range of choice—handiworks of art, skill and fancy, products of nature and labour from every zone.

Here, for a time, he loitered among the conspicuous windows, where was set, emphasized by congested floods of light, the cunningest spoil of the interiors. There were few passers, and of this Lorison was glad. He was not of the world. For a long time he had touched his fellow man only at the gear of a levelled cog-wheel—at right angles, and upon a different axis. He had dropped into a distinctly new orbit. The stroke of ill fortune had acted upon him, in effect, as a blow delivered upon the apex of a certain ingenious toy, the musical top, which, when thus buffeted while spinning, gives forth, with scarcely retarded motion, a complete change of key and chord.

Strolling along the pacific avenue, he experienced singular, supernatural calm, accompanied by an unusual a activity of brain. Reflecting upon recent affairs, he assured himself of his happiness in having won for a bride the one he had so greatly desired, yet he wondered mildly at his dearth of active emotion. Her strange behaviour in abandoning him without valid excuse on his bridal eve aroused in him only a vague and curious speculation. Again, he found himself contemplating, with complaisant serenity, the incidents of her somewhat lively career. His perspective seemed to have been queerly shifted.

As he stood before a window near a corner, his ears were assailed by a waxing clamour and commotion. He stood close to the window to allow passage to the cause of the hubbub—a procession of human beings, which rounded the corner and headed in his direction. He perceived a salient hue of blue and a glitter of brass about a central figure of dazzling white and silver, and a ragged wake of black, bobbing figures.

Two ponderous policemen were conducting between them a woman dressed as if for the stage, in a short, white, satiny skirt reaching to the knees, pink stockings, and a sort of sleeveless bodice bright with relucent, armour-like scales. Upon her curly, light hair was perched, at a rollicking angle, a shining tin helmet. The costume was to be instantly recognized as one of those amazing conceptions to which competition has harried the inventors of the spectacular ballet. One of the officers bore a long cloak upon his arm, which, doubtless, had been intended to veil the I candid attractions of their effulgent prisoner, but, for some reason, it had not been called into use, to the vociferous delight of the tail of the procession.

Compelled by a sudden and vigorous movement of the woman, the parade halted before the window by which Lorison stood. He saw that she was young, and, at the first glance, was deceived by a sophistical prettiness of her face, which waned before a more judicious scrutiny. Her look was bold and reckless, and upon her countenance, where yet the contours of youth survived, were the finger-marks of old age's credentialed courier, Late Hours.

The young woman fixed her unshrinking gaze upon Lorison, and called to him in the voice of the wronged heroine in straits:

"Say! You look like a good fellow; come and put up the bail, won't you? I've done nothing to get pinched for. It's all a mistake. See how they're treating me! You won't be sorry, if you'll help me out of this. Think of your sister or your girl being dragged along the streets this way! I say, come along now, like a good fellow."

It may be that Lorison, in spite of the unconvincing bathos of this appeal, showed a sympathetic face, for one of the officers left the woman's side, and went over to him.

"It's all right, Sir," he said, in a husky, confidential tone; "she's the right party. We took her after the first act at the Green Light Theatre, on a wire from the chief of police of Chicago. It's only a square or two to the station. Her rig's pretty bad, but she refused to change clothes—or, rather," added the officer, with a smile, "to put on some. I thought I'd explain matters to you so you wouldn't think she was being imposed upon."

"What is the charge?" asked Lorison.

"Grand larceny. Diamonds. Her husband is a jeweller in Chicago. She cleaned his show case of the sparklers, and skipped with a comic-opera troupe."

The policeman, perceiving that the interest of the entire group of spectators was centred upon himself and Lorison—their conference being regarded as a possible new complication—was fain to prolong the situation—which reflected his own importance—by a little afterpiece of philosophical comment.

"A gentleman like you, Sir," he went on affably, "would never notice it, but it comes in my line to observe what an immense amount of trouble is made by that combination—I mean the stage, diamonds and light-headed women who aren't satisfied with good homes. I tell you, Sir, a man these days and nights wants to know what his women folks are up to."

The policeman smiled a good night, and returned to the side of his charge, who had been intently watching Lorison's face during the conversation, no doubt for some indication of his intention to render succour. Now, at the failure of the sign, and at the movement made to continue the ignominious progress, she abandoned hope, and addressed him thus, pointedly:

"You damn chalk-faced quitter! You was thinking of giving me a hand, but you let the cop talk you out of it the first word. You're a dandy to tie to. Say, if you ever get a girl, she'll have a picnic. Won't she work you to the queen's taste! Oh, my!" She concluded with a taunting, shrill laugh that rasped Lorison like a saw. The policemen urged her forward; the delighted train of gaping followers closed up the rear; and the captive Amazon, accepting her fate, extended the scope of her maledictions so that none in hearing might seem to be slighted.

Then there came upon Lorison an overwhelming revulsion of his perspective. It may be that he had been ripe for it, that the abnormal condition of mind in which he had for so long existed was already about to revert to its balance; however, it is certain that the events of the last few minutes had furnished the channel, if not the impetus, for the change.

The initial determining influence had been so small a thing as the fact and manner of his having been approached by the officer. That agent had, by the style of his accost, restored the loiterer to his former place in society. In an instant he had been transformed from a somewhat rancid prowler along the fishy side streets of gentility into an honest gentleman, with whom even so lordly a guardian of the peace might agreeably exchange the compliments.

This, then, first broke the spell, and set thrilling in him a resurrected longing for the fellowship of his kind, and the rewards of the virtuous. To what end, he vehemently asked himself, was this fanciful self-accusation, this empty renunciation, this moral squeamishness through which he had been led to abandon what was his heritage in life, and not beyond his deserts? Technically, he was uncondemned; his sole guilty spot was in thought rather than deed, and cognizance of it unshared by others. For what good, moral or sentimental, did he slink, retreating like the hedgehog from his own shadow, to and fro in this musty Bohemia that lacked even the picturesque?

But the thing that struck home and set him raging was the part played by the Amazonian prisoner. To the counterpart of that astounding belligerent—identical at least, in the way of experience—to one, by her own confession, thus far fallen, had he, not three hours since, been united in marriage. How desirable and natural it had seemed to him then, and how monstrous it seemed now! How the words of diamond thief number two yet burned in his ears: "If you ever get a girl, she'll have a picnic." What did that mean but that women instinctively knew him for one they could hoodwink? Still again, there reverberated the policeman's sapient contribution to his agony: "A man these days and nights wants to know what his women folks are up to." Oh, yes, he had been a fool; he had looked at things from the wrong standpoint.

But the wildest note in all the clamour was struck by pain's forefinger, jealousy. Now, at least, he felt that keenest sting—a mounting love unworthily bestowed. Whatever she might be, he loved her; he bore in his own breast his doom. A grating, comic flavour to his predicament struck him suddenly, and he laughed creakingly as he swung down the echoing pavement. An impetuous desire to act, to battle with his fate, seized him. He stopped upon his heel, and smote his palms together triumphantly. His wife was—where? But there was a tangible link; an outlet more or less navigable, through which his derelict ship of matrimony might yet be safely towed—the priest!

Like all imaginative men with pliable natures, Lorison was, when thoroughly stirred, apt to become tempestuous. With a high and stubborn indignation upon him, be retraced his steps to the intersecting street by which he had come. Down this he hurried to the corner where he had parted with—an astringent grimace tinctured the thought—his wife. Thence still back he harked, following through an unfamiliar district his stimulated recollections of the way they had come from that preposterous wedding. Many times he went abroad, and nosed his way back to the trail, furious.

At last, when he reached the dark, calamitous building in which his madness had culminated, and found the black hallway, he dashed down it, perceiving no light or sound. But he raised his voice, hailing loudly; reckless of everything but that he should find the old mischief-maker with the eyes that looked too far away to see the disaster he had wrought. The door opened, and in the stream of light Father Rogan stood, his book in hand, with his finger marking the place.

"Ah!" cried Lorison. "You are the man I want. I had a wife of you a few hours ago. I would not trouble you, but I neglected to note how it was done. Will you oblige me with the information whether the business is beyond remedy?"

"Come inside," said the priest; "there are other lodgers in the house, who might prefer sleep to even a gratified curiosity."

Lorison entered the room and took the chair offered him. The priest's eyes looked a courteous interrogation.

"I must apologize again," said the young man, "for so soon intruding upon you with my marital infelicities, but, as my wife has neglected to furnish me with her address, I am deprived of the legitimate recourse of a family row."

"I am quite a plain man," said Father Rogan, pleasantly; "but I do not see how I am to ask you questions."

"Pardon my indirectness," said Lorison; "I will ask one. In this room to-night you pronounced me to be a husband. You afterward spoke of additional rites or performances that either should or could be effected. I paid little attention to your words then, but I am hungry to hear them repeated now. As matters stand, am I married past all help?"

"You are as legally and as firmly bound," said the priest, "as though it had been done in a cathedral, in the presence of thousands. The additional observances I referred to are not necessary to the strictest legality of the act, but were advised as a precaution for the future—for convenience of proof in such contingencies as wills, inheritances and the like."

Lorison laughed harshly.

"Many thanks," he said. "Then there is no mistake, and I am the happy benedict. I suppose I should go stand upon the bridal corner, and when my wife gets through walking the streets she will look me up."

Father Rogan regarded him calmly.

"My son," he said, "when a man and woman come to me to be married I always marry them. I do this for the sake of other people whom they might go away and marry if they did not marry each other. As you see, I do not seek your confidence; but your case seems to me to be one not altogether devoid of interest. Very few marriages that have come to my notice have brought such well-expressed regret within so short a time. I will hazard one question: were you not under the impression that you loved the lady you married, at the time you did so?"

"Loved her!" cried Lorison, wildly. "Never so well as now, though she told me she deceived and sinned and stole. Never more than now, when, perhaps, she is laughing at the fool she cajoled and left, with scarcely a word, to return to God only knows what particular line of her former folly."

Father Rogan answered nothing. During the silence that succeeded, he sat with a quiet expectation beaming in his full, lambent eye.

"If you would listen—" began Lorison. The priest held up his hand.

"As I hoped," he said. "I thought you would trust me. Wait but a moment." He brought a long clay pipe, filled and lighted it.

"Now, my son," he said.

Lorison poured a twelve month's accumulated confidence into Father Rogan's ear. He told all; not sparing himself or omitting the facts of his past, the events of the night, or his disturbing conjectures and fears.

"The main point," said the priest, when he had concluded, "seems to me to be this—are you reasonably sure that you love this woman whom you have married?"

"Why," exclaimed Lorison, rising impulsively to his feet—"why should I deny it? But look at me—am fish, flesh or fowl? That is the main point to me, I assure you."

"I understand you," said the priest, also rising, and laying down his pipe. "The situation is one that has taxed the endurance of much older men than you—in fact, especially much older men than you. I will try to relieve you from it, and this night. You shall see for yourself into exactly what predicament you have fallen, and how you shall, possibly, be extricated. There is no evidence so credible as that of the eyesight."

Father Rogan moved about the room, and donned a soft black hat. Buttoning his coat to his throat, he laid his hand on the doorknob. "Let us walk," he said.

The two went out upon the street. The priest turned his face down it, and Lorison walked with him through a squalid district, where the houses loomed, awry and desolate-looking, high above them. Presently they turned into a less dismal side street, where the houses were smaller, and, though hinting of the most meagre comfort, lacked the concentrated wretchedness of the more populous byways.

At a segregated, two-story house Father Rogan halted, and mounted the steps with the confidence of a familiar visitor. He ushered Lorison into a narrow hallway, faintly lighted by a cobwebbed hanging lamp. Almost immediately a door to the right opened and a dingy Irishwoman protruded her head.

"Good evening to ye, Mistress Geehan," said the priest, unconsciously, it seemed, falling into a delicately flavoured brogue. "And is it yourself can tell me if Norah has gone out again, the night, maybe?"

"Oh, it's yer blissid riverence! Sure and I can tell ye the same. The purty darlin' wint out, as usual, but a bit later. And she says: 'Mother

Geehan,' says she, 'it's me last noight out, praise the saints, this noight is!' And, oh, yer riverence, the swate, beautiful drame of a dress she had this toime! White satin and silk and ribbons, and lace about the neck and arrums—'twas a sin, yer reverence, the gold was spint upon it."

The priest heard Lorison catch his breath painfully, and a faint smile flickered across his own clean-cut mouth.

"Well, then, Mistress Geehan," said he, "I'll just step upstairs and see the bit boy for a minute, and I'll take this gentleman up with me."

"He's awake, thin," said the woman. "I've just come down from sitting wid him the last hour, tilling him fine shtories of ould County Tyrone. 'Tis a greedy gossoon, it is, yer riverence, for me shtories."

"Small the doubt," said Father Rogan. "There's no rocking would put him to slape the quicker, I'm thinking."

Amid the woman's shrill protest against the retort, the two men ascended the steep stairway. The priest pushed open the door of a room near its top.

"Is that you already, sister?" drawled a sweet, childish voice from the darkness.

"It's only ould Father Denny come to see ye, darlin'; and a foine gentleman I've brought to make ye a gr-r-and call. And ye resaves us fast aslape in bed! Shame on yez manners!"

"Oh, Father Denny, is that you? I'm glad. And will you light the lamp, please? It's on the table by the door. And quit talking like Mother Geehan, Father Denny."

The priest lit the lamp, and Lorison saw a tiny, towsled-haired boy, with a thin, delicate face, sitting up in a small bed in a corner. Quickly, also, his rapid glance considered the room and its contents. It was furnished with more than comfort, and its adornments plainly indicated a woman's discerning taste. An open door beyond revealed the blackness of an adjoining room's interior.

The boy clutched both of Father Rogan's hands. "I'm so glad you came," he said; "but why did you come in the night? Did sister send you?"

"Off wid ye! Am I to be sint about, at me age, as was Terence McShane, of Ballymahone? I come on me own r-r-responsibility."

Lorison had also advanced to the boy's bedside. He was fond of children; and the wee fellow, laying himself down to sleep alone in that dark room, stirred his heart.

"Aren't you afraid, little man?" he asked, stooping down beside him.

"Sometimes," answered the boy, with a shy smile, "when the rats make too much noise. But nearly every night, when sister goes out, Mother Geehan stays a while with me, and tells me funny stories. I'm not often afraid, sir."

"This brave little gentleman," said Father Rogan, "is a scholar of mine. Every day from half-past six to half-past eight—when sister comes for him—he stops in my study, and we find out what's in the inside of books. He knows multiplication, division and fractions; and he's troubling me to begin wid the chronicles of Ciaran of Clonmacnoise, Corurac McCullenan and Cuan O'Lochain, the gr-r-reat Irish histhorians." The boy was evidently accustomed to the priest's Celtic pleasantries. A little, appreciative grin was all the attention the insinuation of pedantry received.

Lorison, to have saved his life, could not have put to the child one of those vital questions that were wildly beating about, unanswered, in his own brain. The little fellow was very like Norah; he had the same shining hair and candid eyes.

"Oh, Father Denny," cried the boy, suddenly, "I forgot to tell you! Sister is not going away at night any more! She told me so when she kissed me good night as she was leaving. And she said she was so happy, and then she cried. Wasn't that queer? But I'm glad; aren't you?"

"Yes, lad. And now, ye omadhaun, go to sleep, and say good night; we must be going."

"Which shall I do first, Father Denny?"

"Faith, he's caught me again! Wait till I get the sassenach into the annals of Tageruach, the hagiographer; I'll give him enough of the Irish idiom to make him more respectful."

The light was out, and the small, brave voice bidding them good night from the dark room. They groped downstairs, and tore away from the garrulity of Mother Geehan.

Again the priest steered them through the dim ways, but this time in another direction. His conductor was serenely silent, and Lorison followed his example to the extent of seldom speaking. Serene he could not be. His heart beat suffocatingly in his breast. The following of this blind, menacing trail was pregnant with he knew not what humiliating revelation to be delivered at its end.

They came into a more pretentious street, where trade, it could be surmised, flourished by day. And again the priest paused; this time before a lofty building, whose great doors and windows in the lowest floor were carefully shuttered and barred. Its higher apertures were dark, save in the third story, the windows of which were brilliantly lighted. Lorison's ear caught a distant, regular, pleasing thrumming, as of music above. They stood at an angle of the building. Up, along the side nearest them, mounted an iron stairway. At its top was an upright, illuminated parallelogram. Father Rogan had stopped, and stood, musing.

"I will say this much," he remarked, thoughtfully: "I believe you to be a better man than you think yourself to be, and a better man than I thought some hours ago. But do not take this," he added, with a smile, "as much praise. I promised you a possible deliverance from an unhappy perplexity. I will have to modify that promise. I can only remove the mystery that enhanced that perplexity. Your deliverance depends upon yourself. Come."

He led his companion up the stairway. Halfway up, Lorison caught him by the sleeve. "Remember," he gasped, "I love that woman."

"You desired to know.

"I—Go on."

The priest reached the landing at the top of the stairway. Lorison, behind him, saw that the illuminated space was the glass upper half of a door opening into the lighted room. The rhythmic music increased as they neared it; the stairs shook with the mellow vibrations.

Lorison stopped breathing when he set foot upon the highest step, for the priest stood aside, and motioned him to look through the glass of the door.

His eye, accustomed to the darkness, met first a blinding glare, and then he made out the faces and forms of many people, amid an extravagant display of splendid robings—billowy laces, brilliant-hued finery, ribbons, silks and misty drapery. And then he caught the meaning of that jarring hum, and he saw the tired, pale, happy face of his wife, bending, as were a score of others, over her sewing machine— toiling, toiling. Here was the folly she pursued, and the end of his quest.

But not his deliverance, though even then remorse struck him. His shamed soul fluttered once more before it retired to make room for the other and better one. For, to temper his thrill of joy, the shine of the satin and the glimmer of ornaments recalled the disturbing figure of the bespangled Amazon, and the base duplicate histories lit by the glare of footlights and stolen diamonds. It is past the wisdom of him who only sets the scenes, either to praise or blame the man. But this time his love overcame his scruples. He took a quick step, and reached out his hand for the doorknob. Father Rogan was quicker to arrest it and draw him back.

"You use my trust in you queerly," said the priest sternly. "What are you about to do?"

"I am going to my wife," said Lorison. "Let me pass."

"Listen," said the priest, holding him firmly by the arm. "I am about to put you in possession of a piece of knowledge of which, thus far, you have scarcely proved deserving. I do not think you ever will; but I will not dwell upon that. You see in that room the woman you married, working for a frugal living for herself, and a generous comfort for an idolized brother. This building belongs to the chief costumer of the city. For months the advance orders for the coming Mardi Gras festivals have kept the work going day and night. I myself secured employment here for Norah. She toils here each night from nine o'clock until daylight, and, besides, carries home with her some of the finer costumes, requiring more delicate needlework, and works there part of the day. Somehow, you two have remained strangely ignorant of each other's lives. Are you convinced now that your wife is not walking the streets?"

"Let me go to her," cried Lorison, again struggling, "and beg her forgiveness!"

"Sir," said the priest, "do you owe me nothing? Be quiet. It seems so often that Heaven lets fall its choicest gifts into hands that must be taught to hold them. Listen again. You forgot that repentant sin must not compromise, but look up, for redemption, to the purest and best. You went to her with the fine-spun sophistry that peace could be found in a mutual guilt; and she, fearful of losing what her heart so craved, thought it worth the price to buy it with a desperate, pure, beautiful lie. I have known her since the day she was born; she is as innocent and unsullied in life and deed as a holy saint. In that lowly street where she dwells she first saw the light, and she has lived there ever since, spending her days in generous self-sacrifice for others. Och, ye spalpeen!" continued Father Rogan, raising his finger in kindly anger at Lorison. "What for, I wonder, could she be after making a fool of hersilf, and shamin' her swate soul with lies, for the like of you!"

"Sir," said Lorison, trembling, "say what you please of me. Doubt it as you must, I will yet prove my gratitude to you, and my devotion to her. But let me speak to her once now, let me kneel for just one moment at her feet, and—"

"Tut, tut!" said the priest. "How many acts of a love drama do you think an old bookworm like me capable of witnessing? Besides, what kind of figures do we cut, spying upon the mysteries of midnight millinery! Go to meet your wife to-morrow, as she ordered you, and obey her thereafter, and maybe some time I shall get forgiveness for the part I have played in this night's work. Off wid yez down the shtairs, now! 'Tis late, and an ould man like me should be takin' his rest."

XXIV

MADAME BO-PEEP, OF THE RANCHES

"A unt Ellen," said Octavia, cheerfully, as she threw her black kid gloves carefully at the dignified Persian cat on the window-seat, "I'm a pauper."

"You are so extreme in your statements, Octavia, dear," said Aunt Ellen, mildly, looking up from her paper. "If you find yourself temporarily in need of some small change for bonbons, you will find my purse in the drawer of the writing desk."

Octavia Beaupree removed her hat and seated herself on a footstool near her aunt's chair, clasping her hands about her knees. Her slim and flexible figure, clad in a modish mourning costume, accommodated itself easily and gracefully to the trying position. Her bright and youthful face, with its pair of sparkling, life-enamoured eyes, tried to compose itself to the seriousness that the occasion seemed to demand.

"You good auntie, it isn't a case of bonbons; it is abject, staring, unpicturesque poverty, with ready-made clothes, gasolined gloves, and probably one o'clock dinners all waiting with the traditional wolf at the door. I've just come from my lawyer, auntie, and, 'Please, ma'am, I ain't got nothink 't all. Flowers, lady? Buttonhole, gentleman? Pencils, sir, three for five, to help a poor widow?' Do I do it nicely, auntie, or, as a bread-winner accomplishment, were my lessons in elocution entirely wasted?"

"Do be serious, my dear," said Aunt Ellen, letting her paper fall to the floor, "long enough to tell me what you mean. Colonel Beaupree's estate—"

"Colonel Beaupree's estate," interrupted Octavia, emphasizing her words with appropriate dramatic gestures, "is of Spanish castellar architecture. Colonel Beaupree's resources are—wind. Colonel Beaupree's stocks are—water. Colonel Beaupree's income is—all in. The statement lacks the legal technicalities to which I have been listening for an hour, but that is what it means when translated."

"Octavia!" Aunt Ellen was now visibly possessed by consternation. "I can hardly believe it. And it was the impression that he was worth a million. And the De Peysters themselves introduced him!"

Octavia rippled out a laugh, and then became properly grave.

"*De mortuis nil*, auntie—not even the rest of it. The dear old colonel—what a gold brick he was, after all! I paid for my bargain fairly—I'm all here, am I not?—items: eyes, fingers, toes, youth, old family, unquestionable position in society as called for in the contract—no wild-cat stock here." Octavia picked up the morning paper from the floor. "But I'm not going to 'squeal'—isn't that what they call it when you rail at Fortune because you've, lost the game?" She turned the pages of the paper calmly. "'Stock market'—no use for that. 'Society's doings'—that's done. Here is my page—the wish column. A Van Dresser could not be said to 'want' for anything, of course. 'Chamber-maids, cooks, canvassers, stenographers—'"

"Dear," said Aunt Ellen, with a little tremor in her voice, "please do not talk in that way. Even if your affairs are in so unfortunate a condition, there is my three thousand—"

Octavia sprang up lithely, and deposited a smart kiss on the delicate cheek of the prim little elderly maid.

"Blessed auntie, your three thousand is just sufficient to insure your Hyson to be free from willow leaves and keep the Persian in sterilized cream. I know I'd be welcome, but I prefer to strike bottom like Beelzebub rather than hang around like the Peri listening to the music from the side entrance. I'm going to earn my own living. There's nothing else to do. I'm a—Oh, oh, oh!—I had forgotten. There's one thing saved from the wreck. It's a corral—no, a ranch in—let me see—Texas: an asset, dear old Mr. Bannister called it. How pleased he was to show me something he could describe as unencumbered! I've a description of it among those stupid papers he made me bring away with me from his office. I'll try to find it."

Octavia found her shopping-bag, and drew from it a long envelope filled with typewritten documents.

"A ranch in Texas," sighed Aunt Ellen. "It sounds to me more like a liability than an asset. Those are the places where the centipedes are found, and cowboys, and fandangos."

"'The Rancho de las Sombras,'" read Octavia from a sheet of violently purple typewriting, "'is situated one hundred and ten miles southeast of San Antonio, and thirty-eight miles from its nearest railroad station, Nopal, on the I. and G. N. Ranch, consists of 7,680 acres of well-watered land, with title conferred by State patents, and twenty-two sections, or 14,080 acres, partly under yearly running lease and partly bought under

State's twenty-year-purchase act. Eight thousand graded merino sheep, with the necessary equipment of horses, vehicles and general ranch paraphernalia. Ranch-house built of brick, with six rooms comfortably furnished according to the requirements of the climate. All within a strong barbed-wire fence.

"'The present ranch manager seems to be competent and reliable, and is rapidly placing upon a paying basis a business that, in other hands, had been allowed to suffer from neglect and misconduct.

"'This property was secured by Colonel Beaupree in a deal with a Western irrigation syndicate, and the title to it seems to be perfect. With careful management and the natural increase of land values, it ought to be made the foundation for a comfortable fortune for its owner.'"

When Octavia ceased reading, Aunt Ellen uttered something as near a sniff as her breeding permitted.

"The prospectus," she said, with uncompromising metropolitan suspicion, "doesn't mention the centipedes, or the Indians. And you never did like mutton, Octavia. I don't see what advantage you can derive from this—desert."

But Octavia was in a trance. Her eyes were steadily regarding something quite beyond their focus. Her lips were parted, and her face was lighted by the kindling furor of the explorer, the ardent, stirring disquiet of the adventurer. Suddenly she clasped her hands together exultantly.

"The problem solves itself, auntie," she cried. "I'm going to that ranch. I'm going to live on it. I'm going to learn to like mutton, and even concede the good qualities of centipedes—at a respectful distance. It's just what I need. It's a new life that comes when my old one is just ending. It's a release, auntie; it isn't a narrowing. Think of the gallops over those leagues of prairies, with the wind tugging at the roots of your hair, the coming close to the earth and learning over again the stories of the growing grass and the little wild flowers without names! Glorious is what it will be. Shall I be a shepherdess with a Watteau hat, and a crook to keep the bad wolves from the lambs, or a typical Western ranch girl, with short hair, like the pictures of her in the Sunday papers? I think the latter. And they'll have my picture, too, with the wild-cats I've slain, single-handed, hanging from my saddle horn. 'From the Four Hundred to the Flocks' is the way they'll headline it, and they'll print photographs of the old Van Dresser mansion and the church where I was married. They won't have my picture, but they'll get an artist to draw it. I'll be wild and woolly, and I'll grow my own wool."

"Octavia!" Aunt Ellen condensed into the one word all the protests she was unable to utter.

"Don't say a word, auntie. I'm going. I'll see the sky at night fit down on the world like a big butter-dish cover, and I'll make friends again with the stars that I haven't had a chat with since I was a wee child. I wish to go. I'm tired of all this. I'm glad I haven't any money. I could bless Colonel Beaupree for that ranch, and forgive him for all his bubbles. What if the life will be rough and lonely! I—I deserve it. I shut my heart to everything except that miserable ambition. I—oh, I wish to go away, and forget—forget!"

Octavia swerved suddenly to her knees, laid her flushed face in her aunt's lap, and shook with turbulent sobs.

Aunt Ellen bent over her, and smoothed the coppery-brown hair.

"I didn't know," she said, gently; "I didn't know—that. Who was it, dear?"

When Mrs. Octavia Beaupree, née Van Dresser, stepped from the train at Nopal, her manner lost, for the moment, some of that easy certitude which had always marked her movements. The town was of recent establishment, and seemed to have been hastily constructed of undressed lumber and flapping canvas. The element that had congregated about the station, though not offensively demonstrative, was clearly composed of citizens accustomed to and prepared for rude alarms.

Octavia stood on the platform, against the telegraph office, and attempted to choose by intuition from the swaggering, straggling string, of loungers the manager of the Rancho de las Sombras, who had been instructed by Mr. Bannister to meet her there. That tall, serious, looking, elderly man in the blue flannel shirt and white tie she thought must be he. But, no; he passed by, removing his gaze from the lady as hers rested on him, according to the Southern custom. The manager, she thought, with some impatience at being kept waiting, should have no difficulty in selecting her. Young women wearing the most recent thing in ash-coloured travelling suits were not so plentiful in Nopal!

Thus keeping a speculative watch on all persons of possible managerial aspect, Octavia, with a catching breath and a start of surprise, suddenly became aware of Teddy Westlake hurrying along the platform in the direction of the train—of Teddy Westlake or his sun-browned ghost in cheviot, boots and leather-girdled hat—Theodore Westlake, Jr., amateur polo (almost) champion, all-round butterfly and cumberer of the soil; but a broader, surer, more emphasized and determined Teddy than the one she had known a year ago when last she saw him.

He perceived Octavia at almost the same time, deflected his course, and steered for her in his old, straightforward way. Something like awe came upon her as the strangeness of his metamorphosis was brought into closer range; the rich, red-brown of his complexion brought out so vividly his straw-coloured mustache and steel-gray eyes. He seemed more grown-up, and, somehow, farther away. But, when he spoke, the old, boyish Teddy came back again. They had been friends from childhood.

"Why, 'Tave!" he exclaimed, unable to reduce his perplexity to coherence. "How—what—when—where?"

"Train," said Octavia; "necessity; ten minutes ago; home. Your complexion's gone, Teddy. Now, how—what—when—where?"

"I'm working down here," said Teddy. He cast side glances about the station as one does who tries to combine politeness with duty.

"You didn't notice on the train," he asked, "an old lady with gray curls and a poodle, who occupied two seats with her bundles and quarrelled with the conductor, did you?"

"I think not," answered Octavia, reflecting. "And you haven't, by any chance, noticed a big, gray-mustached man in a blue shirt and six-shooters, with little flakes of merino wool sticking in his hair, have you?"

"Lots of 'em," said Teddy, with symptoms of mental delirium under the strain. "Do you happen to know any such individual?"

"No; the description is imaginary. Is your interest in the old lady whom you describe a personal one?"

"Never saw her in my life. She's painted entirely from fancy. She owns the little piece of property where I earn my bread and butter—the Rancho de las Sombras. I drove up to meet her according to arrangement with her lawyer."

Octavia leaned against the wall of the telegraph office. Was this possible? And didn't he know?

"Are you the manager of that ranch?" she asked weakly.

"I am," said Teddy, with pride.

"I am Mrs. Beaupree," said Octavia faintly; "but my hair never would curl, and I was polite to the conductor."

For a moment that strange, grown-up look came back, and removed Teddy miles away from her.

"I hope you'll excuse me," he said, rather awkwardly. "You see, I've been down here in the chaparral a year. I hadn't heard. Give me your checks, please, and I'll have your traps loaded into the wagon. José will follow with them. We travel ahead in the buckboard."

Seated by Teddy in a feather-weight buckboard, behind a pair of wild, cream-coloured Spanish ponies, Octavia abandoned all thought for the exhilaration of the present. They swept out of the little town and down the level road toward the south. Soon the road dwindled and disappeared, and they struck across a world carpeted with an endless reach of curly mesquite grass. The wheels made no sound. The tireless ponies bounded ahead at an unbroken gallop. The temperate wind, made fragrant by thousands of acres of blue and yellow wild flowers, roared gloriously in their ears. The motion was aërial, ecstatic, with a thrilling sense of perpetuity in its effect. Octavia sat silent, possessed by a feeling of elemental, sensual bliss. Teddy seemed to be wrestling with some internal problem.

"I'm going to call you madama," he announced as the result of his labours. "That is what the Mexicans will call you—they're nearly all Mexicans on the ranch, you know. That seems to me about the proper thing."

"Very well, Mr. Westlake," said Octavia, primly.

"Oh, now," said Teddy, in some consternation, "that's carrying the thing too far, isn't it?"

"Don't worry me with your beastly etiquette. I'm just beginning to live. Don't remind me of anything artificial. If only this air could be bottled! This much alone is worth coming for. Oh, look I there goes a deer!"

"Jack-rabbit," said Teddy, without turning his head.

"Could I—might I drive?" suggested Octavia, panting, with rose-tinted cheeks and the eye of an eager child.

"On one condition. Could I—might I smoke?"

"Forever!" cried Octavia, taking the lines with solemn joy. "How shall I know which way to drive?"

"Keep her sou' by sou'east, and all sail set. You see that black speck on the horizon under that lowermost Gulf cloud? That's a group of live-oaks and a landmark. Steer halfway between that and the little hill to the left. I'll recite you the whole code of driving rules for the Texas prairies: keep the reins from under the horses' feet, and swear at 'em frequent."

"I'm too happy to swear, Ted. Oh, why do people buy yachts or travel in palace-cars, when a buckboard and a pair of plugs and a spring morning like this can satisfy all desire?"

"Now, I'll ask you," protested Teddy, who was futilely striking match after match on the dashboard, "not to call those denizens of the air plugs. They can kick out a hundred miles between daylight and dark." At last he succeeded in snatching a light for his cigar from the flame held in the hollow of his hands.

"Room!" said Octavia, intensely. "That's what produces the effect. I know now what I've wanted—scope—range—room!"

"Smoking-room," said Teddy, unsentimentally. "I love to smoke in a buckboard. The wind blows the smoke into you and out again. It saves exertion."

The two fell so naturally into their old-time goodfellowship that it was only by degrees that a sense of the strangeness of the new relations between them came to be felt.

"Madama," said Teddy, wonderingly, "however did you get it into your bead to cut the crowd and come down here? Is it a fad now among the upper classes to trot off to sheep ranches instead of to Newport?"

"I was broke, Teddy," said Octavia, sweetly, with her interest centred upon steering safely between a Spanish dagger plant and a clump of chaparral; "I haven't a thing in the world but this ranch—not even any other home to go to."

"Come, now," said Teddy, anxiously but incredulously, "you don't mean it?"

"When my husband," said Octavia, with a shy slurring of the word, "died three months ago I thought I had a reasonable amount of the world's goods. His lawyer exploded that theory in a sixty-minute fully illustrated lecture. I took to the sheep as a last resort. Do you happen to know of any fashionable caprice among the gilded youth of Manhattan that induces them to abandon polo and club windows to become managers of sheep ranches?"

"It's easily explained in my case," responded Teddy, promptly. "I had to go to work. I couldn't have earned my board in New York, so I chummed a while with old Sandford, one of the syndicate that owned the ranch before Colonel Beaupree bought it, and got a place down here. I wasn't manager at first. I jogged around on ponies and studied the business in detail, until I got all the points in my head. I saw where it was losing and what the remedies were, and then Sandford put me in charge. I get a hundred dollars a month, and I earn it."

"Poor Teddy!" said Octavia, with a smile.

"You needn't. I like it. I save half my wages, and I'm as hard as a water plug. It beats polo."

"Will it furnish bread and tea and jam for another outcast from civilization?"

"The spring shearing," said the manager, "just cleaned up a deficit in last year's business. Wastefulness and inattention have been the rule heretofore. The autumn clip will leave a small profit over all expenses. Next year there will be jam."

When, about four o'clock in the afternoon, the ponies rounded a gentle, brush-covered hill, and then swooped, like a double cream-coloured cyclone, upon the Rancho de las Sombras, Octavia gave a little cry of delight. A lordly grove of magnificent live-oaks cast an area of grateful, cool shade, whence the ranch had drawn its name, "de las Sombras"—of the shadows. The house, of red brick, one story, ran low and long beneath the trees. Through its middle, dividing its six rooms in half, extended a broad, arched passageway, picturesque with flowering cactus and hanging red earthern jars. A "gallery," low and broad, encircled the building. Vines climbed about it, and the adjacent ground was, for a space, covered with transplanted grass and shrubs. A little lake, long and narrow, glimmered in the sun at the rear. Further away stood the shacks of the Mexican workers, the corrals, wool sheds and shearing pens. To the right lay the low hills, splattered with dark patches of chaparral; to the left the unbounded green prairie blending against the blue heavens.

"It's a home, Teddy," said Octavia, breathlessly; "that's what it is—it's a home."

"Not so bad for a sheep ranch," admitted Teddy, with excusable pride. "I've been tinkering on it at odd times."

A Mexican youth sprang from somewhere in the grass, and took charge of the creams. The mistress and the manager entered the house.

"Here's Mrs. MacIntyre," said Teddy, as a placid, neat, elderly lady came out upon the gallery to meet them. "Mrs. Mac, here's the boss. Very likely she will be wanting a hunk of ham and a dish of beans after her drive."

Mrs. MacIntyre, the housekeeper, as much a fixture on the place as the lake or the live-oaks, received the imputation of the ranch's resources of refreshment with mild indignation, and was about to give it utterance when Octavia spoke.

"Oh, Mrs. MacIntyre, don't apologize for Teddy. Yes, I call him Teddy. So does every one whom he hasn't duped into taking him seriously. You see, we used to cut paper dolls and play jackstraws together ages ago. No one minds what he says."

"No," said Teddy, "no one minds what he says, just so he doesn't do it again."

Octavia cast one of those subtle, sidelong glances toward him from beneath her lowered eyelids—a glance that Teddy used to describe as an upper-cut. But there was nothing in his ingenuous, weather-tanned face to warrant a suspicion that he was making an allusion—nothing. Beyond a doubt, thought Octavia, he had forgotten.

"Mr. Westlake likes his fun," said Mrs. MacIntyre, as she conducted Octavia to her rooms. "But," she added, loyally, "people around here usually pay attention to what he says when he talks in earnest. I don't know what would have become of this place without him."

Two rooms at the east end of the house had been arranged for the occupancy of the ranch's mistress. When she entered them a slight dismay seized her at their bare appearance and the scantiness of their furniture; but she quickly reflected that the climate was a semi-tropical one, and was moved to appreciation of the well-conceived efforts to conform to it. The sashes had already been removed from the big windows, and white curtains waved in the Gulf breeze that streamed through the wide jalousies. The bare floor was amply strewn with cool rugs; the chairs were inviting, deep, dreamy willows; the walls were papered with a light, cheerful olive. One whole side of her sitting room was covered with books on smooth, unpainted pine shelves. She flew to these at once. Before her was a well-selected library. She caught glimpses of titles of volumes of fiction and travel not yet seasoned from the dampness of the press.

Presently, recollecting that she was now in a wilderness given over to mutton, centipedes and privations, the incongruity of these luxuries struck her, and, with intuitive feminine suspicion, she began turning to the fly-leaves of volume after volume. Upon each one was inscribed in fluent characters the name of Theodore Westlake, Jr.

Octavia, fatigued by her long journey, retired early that night. Lying upon her white, cool bed, she rested deliciously, but sleep coquetted long with her. She listened to faint noises whose strangeness kept her faculties on the alert—the fractious yelping of the coyotes, the ceaseless, low symphony of the wind, the distant booming of the frogs about the lake, the lamentation of a concertina in the Mexicans' quarters. There were many conflicting feelings in her heart—thankfulness and rebellion, peace and disquietude, loneliness and a sense of protecting care, happiness and an old, haunting pain.

She did what any other woman would have done—sought relief in a wholesome tide of unreasonable tears, and her last words, murmured to herself before slumber, capitulating, came softly to woo her, were "He has forgotten."

The manager of the Rancho de las Sombras was no dilettante. He was a "hustler." He was generally up, mounted, and away of mornings before the rest of the household were awake, making the rounds of the flocks and camps. This was the duty of the major-domo, a stately old Mexican with a princely air and manner, but Teddy seemed to have a great deal of confidence in his own eyesight. Except in the busy seasons, he nearly always returned to the ranch to breakfast at eight o'clock, with Octavia and Mrs. Maclntyre, at the little table set in the central hallway, bringing with him a tonic and breezy cheerfulness full of the health and flavour of the prairies.

A few days after Octavia's arrival he made her get out one of her riding skirts, and curtail it to a shortness demanded by the chaparral brakes.

With some misgivings she donned this and the pair of buckskin leggings he prescribed in addition, and, mounted upon a dancing pony, rode with him to view her possessions. He showed her everything— the flocks of ewes, muttons and grazing lambs, the dipping vats, the shearing pens, the uncouth merino rams in their little pasture, the water-tanks prepared against the summer drought—giving account of his stewardship with a boyish enthusiasm that never flagged.

Where was the old Teddy that she knew so well? This side of him was the same, and it was a side that pleased her; but this was all she ever saw of him now. Where was his sentimentality—those old, varying moods of impetuous love-making, of fanciful, quixotic devotion, of heart-breaking gloom, of alternating, absurd tenderness and haughty dignity? His nature had been a sensitive one, his temperament bordering closely on the artistic. She knew that, besides being a follower of fashion and its fads and sports, he had cultivated tastes of a finer nature. He had written things, he had tampered with colours, he was something of a student in certain branches of art, and once she had been admitted to all his aspirations and thoughts. But now—and she could not avoid the conclusion—Teddy had barricaded against her every side of himself except one—the side that showed the manager of the Rancho de las Sombras and a jolly chum who had forgiven and forgotten. Queerly enough the words of Mr. Bannister's description of her property came into her mind—"all inclosed within a strong barbed-wire fence."

"Teddy's fenced, too," said Octavia to herself.

It was not difficult for her to reason out the cause of his fortifications. It had originated one night at the Hammersmiths' ball. It occurred at a time soon after she had decided to accept Colonel Beaupree and his million, which was no more than her looks and the entrée she held to the inner circles were worth. Teddy had proposed with all his impetuosity and fire, and she looked him straight in the eyes, an said, coldly and finally: "Never let me hear any such silly nonsense from you again." "You won't," said Teddy, with an expression around his mouth, and—now Teddy was inclosed within a strong barbed-wire fence.

It was on this first ride of inspection that Teddy was seized by the inspiration that suggested the name of Mother Goose's heroine, and he at once bestowed it upon Octavia. The idea, supported by both a similarity of names and identity of occupations, seemed to strike him as a peculiarly happy one, and he never tired of using it. The Mexicans on the ranch also took up the name, adding another syllable to accommodate their lingual incapacity for the final "p," gravely referring to her as "La Madama Bo-Peepy." Eventually it spread, and "Madame Bo-Peep's ranch" was as often mentioned as the "Rancho de las Sombras."

Came the long, hot season from May to September, when work is scarce on the ranches. Octavia passed the days in a kind of lotus-eater's dream. Books, hammocks, correspondence with a few intimate friends, a renewed interest in her old water-colour box and easel—these disposed of the sultry hours of daylight. The evenings were always sure to bring enjoyment. Best of all were the rapturous horseback rides with Teddy, when the moon gave light over the wind-swept leagues, chaperoned by the wheeling night-hawk and the startled owl. Often the Mexicans would come up from their shacks with their guitars and sing the weirdest of heart-breaking songs. There were long, cosy chats on the breezy gallery, and an interminable warfare of wits between Teddy and Mrs. MacIntyre, whose abundant Scotch shrewdness often more than overmatched the lighter humour in which she was lacking.

And the nights came, one after another, and were filed away by weeks and months—nights soft and languorous and fragrant, that should have driven Strephon to Chloe over wires however barbed, that might have drawn Cupid himself to hunt, lasso in hand, among those amorous pastures—but Teddy kept his fences up.

One July night Madame Bo-Peep and her ranch manager were sitting on the east gallery. Teddy had been exhausting the science of prognostication as to the probabilities of a price of twenty-four cents for the autumn clip, and had then subsided into an anesthetic cloud of Havana smoke. Only as incompetent a judge as a woman would have failed to note long ago that at least a third of his salary must have gone up in the fumes of those imported Regalias.

"Teddy," said Octavia, suddenly, and rather sharply, "what are you working down here on a ranch for?"

"One hundred per," said Teddy, glibly, "and found."

"I've a good mind to discharge you."

"Can't do it," said Teddy, with a grin.

"Why not?" demanded Octavia, with argumentative heat.

"Under contract. Terms of sale respect all unexpired contracts. Mine runs until 12 P.M., December thirty-first. You might get up at midnight on that date and fire me. If you try it sooner I'll be in a position to bring legal proceedings."

Octavia seemed to be considering the prospects of litigation.

"But," continued Teddy cheerfully, "I've been thinking of resigning anyway."

Octavia's rocking-chair ceased its motion. There were centipedes in this country, she felt sure; and Indians, and vast, lonely, desolate, empty wastes; all within strong barbed-wire fence. There was a Van Dresser pride, but there was also a Van Dresser heart. She must know for certain whether or not he had forgotten.

"Ah, well, Teddy," she said, with a fine assumption of polite interest, "it's lonely down here; you're longing to get back to the old life—to polo and lobsters and theatres and balls."

"Never cared much for balls," said Teddy virtuously.

"You're getting old, Teddy. Your memory is failing. Nobody ever knew you to miss a dance, unless it occurred on the same night with another one which you attended. And you showed such shocking bad taste, too, in dancing too often with the same partner. Let me see, what was that Forbes girl's name—the one with wall eyes—Mabel, wasn't it?"

"No; Adéle. Mabel was the one with the bony elbows. That wasn't wall in Adéle's eyes. It was soul. We used to talk sonnets together, and Verlaine. Just then I was trying to run a pipe from the Pierian spring."

"You were on the floor with her," said Octavia, undeflected, "five times at the Hammersmiths'."

"Hammersmiths' what?" questioned Teddy, vacuously.

"Ball—ball," said Octavia, viciously. "What were we talking of?"

"Eyes, I thought," said Teddy, after some reflection; "and elbows."

"Those Hammersmiths," went on Octavia, in her sweetest society prattle, after subduing an intense desire to yank a handful of sunburnt, sandy hair from the head lying back contentedly against the canvas of the steamer chair, "had too much money. Mines, wasn't it? It was something that paid something to the ton. You couldn't get a glass of plain water in their house. Everything at that ball was dreadfully overdone."

"It was," said Teddy.

"Such a crowd there was!" Octavia continued, conscious that she was talking the rapid drivel of a school-girl describing her first dance. "The balconies were as warm as the rooms. I—lost—something at that ball." The last sentence was uttered in a tone calculated to remove the barbs from miles of wire.

"So did I," confessed Teddy, in a lower voice.

"A glove," said Octavia, falling back as the enemy approached her ditches.

"Caste," said Teddy, halting his firing line without loss. "I hobnobbed, half the evening with one of Hammersmith's miners, a fellow who kept his hands in his pockets, and talked like an archangel about reduction plants and drifts and levels and sluice-boxes."

"A pearl-gray glove, nearly new," sighed Octavia, mournfully.

"A bang-up chap, that McArdle," maintained Teddy approvingly. "A man who hated olives and elevators; a man who handled mountains as croquettes, and built tunnels in the air; a man who never uttered a word of silly nonsense in his life. Did you sign those lease-renewal applications yet, madama? They've got to be on file in the land office by the thirty-first."

Teddy turned his head lazily. Octavia's chair was vacant.

A CERTAIN CENTIPEDE, CRAWLING ALONG the lines marked out by fate, expounded the situation. It was early one morning while Octavia and Mrs. MacIntyre were trimming the honeysuckle on the west gallery. Teddy had risen and departed hastily before daylight in response to word that a flock of ewes had been scattered from their bedding ground during the night by a thunder-storm.

The centipede, driven by destiny, showed himself on the floor of the gallery, and then, the screeches of the two women giving him his cue, he scuttled with all his yellow legs through the open door into the furthermost west room, which was Teddy's. Arming themselves with domestic utensils selected with regard to their length, Octavia and Mrs. MacIntyre, with much clutching of skirts and skirmishing for the position of rear guard in the attacking force, followed.

Once outside, the centipede seemed to have disappeared, and his prospective murderers began a thorough but cautious search for their victim.

Even in the midst of such a dangerous and absorbing adventure Octavia was conscious of an awed curiosity on finding herself in Teddy's sanctum. In that room he sat alone, silently communing with those secret thoughts that he now shared with no one, dreamed there whatever dreams he now called on no one to interpret.

It was the room of a Spartan or a soldier. In one corner stood a wide, canvas-covered cot; in another, a small bookcase; in another, a grim stand of Winchesters and shotguns. An immense table, strewn with letters, papers and documents and surmounted by a set of pigeon-holes, occupied one side.

The centipede showed genius in concealing himself in such bare quarters. Mrs. MacIntyre was poking a broom-handle behind the bookcase. Octavia approached Teddy's cot. The room was just as the manager had left it in his hurry. The Mexican maid had not yet given it her attention. There was his big pillow with the imprint of his head still in the centre. She thought the horrid beast might have climbed the cot and hidden itself to bite Teddy. Centipedes were thus cruel and vindictive toward managers.

She cautiously overturned the pillow, and then parted her lips to give the signal for reinforcements at sight of a long, slender, dark object lying there. But, repressing it in time, she caught up a glove, a pearl-gray glove, flattened—it might be conceived—by many, many months of nightly pressure beneath the pillow of the man who had forgotten the Hammersmiths' ball. Teddy must have left so hurriedly that morning that he had, for once, forgotten to transfer it to its resting-place by day.

Even managers, who are notoriously wily and cunning, are sometimes caught up with.

Octavia slid the gray glove into the bosom of her summery morning gown. It was hers. Men who put themselves within a strong barbed-wire fence, and remember Hammersmith balls only by the talk of miners about sluice-boxes, should not be allowed to possess such articles.

After all, what a paradise this prairie country was! How it blossomed like the rose when you found things that were thought to be lost! How delicious was that morning breeze coming in the windows, fresh and sweet with the breath of the yellow ratama blooms! Might one not stand, for a minute, with shining, far-gazing eyes, and dream that mistakes might be corrected?

Why was Mrs. MacIntyre poking about so absurdly with a broom?

"I've found it," said Mrs. MacIntyre, banging the door. "Here it is."

"Did you lose something? asked Octavia, with sweetly polite non-interest.

"The little devil!" said Mrs. MacIntyre, driven to violence. "Ye've no forgotten him alretty?"

Between them they slew the centipede. Thus was he rewarded for his agency toward the recovery of things lost at the Hammersmiths' ball.

It seems that Teddy, in due course, remembered the glove, and when he returned to the house at sunset made a secret but exhaustive search for it. Not until evening, upon the moonlit eastern gallery, did he find it. It was upon the hand that he had thought lost to him forever, and so he was moved to repeat certain nonsense that he had been commanded never, never to utter again. Teddy's fences were down.

This time there was no ambition to stand in the way, and the wooing was as natural and successful as should be between ardent shepherd and gentle shepherdess.

The prairies changed to a garden. The Rancho de las Sombras became the Ranch of Light.

A few days later Octavia received a letter from Mr. Bannister, in reply to one she had written to him asking some questions about her business. A portion of the letter ran as follows:

"I am at a loss to account for your references to the sheep ranch. Two months after your departure to take up your residence upon it, it was discovered that Colonel Beaupree's title was worthless. A deed came to light showing that he disposed of the property before his death. The matter was reported to your manager, Mr. Westlake, who at once repurchased the property. It is entirely beyond my powers of conjecture to imagine how you have remained in ignorance of this fact. I beg that you that will at once confer with that gentleman, who will, at least, corroborate my statement."

Octavia sought Teddy, with battle in her eye.

"What are you working on this ranch for?" she asked once more.

"One hundred—" he began to repeat, but saw in her face that she knew. She held Mr. Bannister's letter in her hand. He knew that the game was up.

"It's my ranch," said Teddy, like a schoolboy detected in evil. "It's a mighty poor manager that isn't able to absorb the boss's business if you give him time."

"Why were you working down here?" pursued Octavia still struggling after the key to the riddle of Teddy.

"To tell the truth, 'Tave," said Teddy, with quiet candour, "it wasn't for the salary. That about kept me in cigars and sunburn lotions. I was sent south by my doctor. 'Twas that right lung that was going to the bad on account of over-exercise and strain at polo and gymnastics. I needed climate and ozone and rest and things of that sort."

In an instant Octavia was close against the vicinity of the affected organ. Mr. Bannister's letter fluttered to the floor.

"It's—it's well now, isn't it, Teddy?"

"Sound as a mesquite chunk. I deceived you in one thing. I paid fifty thousand for your ranch as soon as I found you had no title. I had just about that much income accumulated at my banker's while I've been herding sheep down here, so it was almost like picking the thing up on a bargain-counter for a penny. There's another little surplus of unearned increment piling up there, 'Tave. I've been thinking of a wedding trip in a yacht with white ribbons tied to the mast, through the Mediterranean, and then up among the Hebrides and down Norway to the Zuyder Zee."

"And I was thinking," said Octavia, softly, "of a wedding gallop with my manager among the flocks of sheep and back to a wedding breakfast with Mrs. MacIntyre on the gallery, with, maybe, a sprig of orange blossom fastened to the red jar above the table."

Teddy laughed, and began to chant:

> *"Little Bo-Peep has lost her sheep,*
> *And doesn't know where to find 'em.*
> *Let 'em alone, and they'll come home,*
> *And—"*

Octavia drew his head down, and whispered in his ear, But that is one of the tales they brought behind them.

A Note About the Author

O. Henry (1862–1910) was an American short story writer. Born and raised in North Carolina, O. Henry—whose real name was William Sydney Porter—moved to Texas in 1882 in search of work. He met and married Athol Estes in Austin, where he became well known as a musician and socialite. In 1888, Athol gave birth to a son who died soon after, and in 1889 a daughter named Margaret was born. Porter began working as a teller and bookkeeper at the First National Bank of Austin in 1890 and was fired four years later and accused of embezzlement. Afterward, he began publishing a satirical weekly called *The Rolling Stone*, but in 1895 he was arrested in Houston following an audit of his former employer. While waiting to stand trial, Henry fled to Honduras, where he lived for six months before returning to Texas to surrender himself upon hearing of Athol's declining health. She died in July of 1897 from tuberculosis, and Porter served three years at the Ohio Penitentiary before moving to Pittsburgh to care for his daughter. While in prison, he began publishing stories under the pseudonym "O. Henry," finding some success and launching a career that would blossom upon his release with such short stories as "The Gift of the Magi" (1905) and "The Ransom of Red Chief" (1907). He is recognized as one of America's leading writers of short fiction, and the annual O. Henry Award—which has been won by such writers as William Faulkner, John Updike, and Eudora Welty—remains one of America's most prestigious literary prizes.

A Note from the Publisher

Spanning many genres, from non-fiction essays to literature classics to children's books and lyric poetry, Mint Edition books showcase the master works of our time in a modern new package. The text is freshly typeset, is clean and easy to read, and features a new note about the author in each volume. Many books also include exclusive new introductory material. Every book boasts a striking new cover, which makes it as appropriate for collecting as it is for gift giving. Mint Edition books are only printed when a reader orders them, so natural resources are not wasted. We're proud that our books are never manufactured in excess and exist only in the exact quantity they need to be read and enjoyed. To learn more and view our library, go to minteditionbooks.com

bookfinity & ◥ MINT EDITIONS

Enjoy more of your favorite classics with Bookfinity,
a new search and discovery experience for readers.
With Bookfinity, you can discover more vintage
literature for your collection, find your Reader Type,
track books you've read or want to read,
and add reviews to your favorite books.
Visit www.bookfinity.com, and click on
Take the Quiz to get started.

Don't forget to follow us
@bookfinityofficial and @mint_editions